*Also by Lynn Freed*

HOME GROUND

# Lynn Freed

POSEIDON PRESS

# *The Bungalow*

## A NOVEL

New York  London  Toronto  Sydney  Tokyo  Singapore

**POSEIDON PRESS**
Simon & Schuster Building
Rockefeller Center
1230 Avenue of the Americas
New York, New York 10020

Designed by Deirdre C. Amthor

Manufactured in the United States of America

1   3   5   7   9   10   8   6   4   2

Library of Congress Cataloging-in-Publication Data

Freed, Lynn.
The bungalow : a novel / Lynn Freed.
p.        cm.
I. Title.
PR9369.3.F68B86        1993
823—dc20                                    92-24814
CIP
ISBN: 0-671-75587-0

# Acknowledgments

I have received generous support from the National Endowment for the Arts, the John Simon Guggenheim Foundation, the Rockefeller Foundation, the Corporation of Yaddo, and the MacDowell Colony. I cannot adequately thank Ileene Smith, whose counsel and patience have seen me through, and Lois Wallace, without whom I would be lost. To them and many others I owe this book.

For Ma and Dad

# Réplique

She married him in cold blood. Stunningly ugly she was.

I open my notebook, uncap my pen, jot down the words and blow the ink dry. Then I look out to sea. It is silver in the afternoon sun, blinding, churned into white horses by a hot, steady wind.

The hotel verandah on which I sit is sheltered by a whitewashed wall at either end, a yellow-and-white striped awning above. Out on the lawn, yellow-and-white striped umbrellas snap and billow in the wind. The new owners have built a freshwater pool at the edge of the cliff, leaving the old pool, far below, to return to the sea. Next door, a block of condominiums rises through twenty-four stories, to a penthouse on the twenty-fifth. By comparison, the lighthouse on the beach looks quaint now, sentimental perhaps.

"Two teas, madam." The waiter stands poised while I clear my things off the table.

I point out my daughter to him, ask him to go and tell her to come up. She is down at the pool, lying still as death on a deck chair, her pink English face lifted raw to the African sun. Four or five boys wrestle noisily in the water, splashing her without seeing her. Compared to local fifteen-year-old girls, she is plump, child-like in her ponytail and cotton swimsuit. When the waiter arrives, she sits up, smiles, shielding her eyes with an arm. She has her father's smile, my eyes, his skin. An alien, he would have said, a bloody alien. Meaning that, for all her schoolgirl enthusiasm, she doesn't belong in this place.

Perhaps if I had actually seen his body after the murder—brains and blood, the nostrils slit to ribbons, one eye out of its socket (I invent these things; all I know is "stabbed")—perhaps then I would have felt the loss more violently. If I had even *thought* he might die, perhaps I would have tried to notice things about him more carefully, things to remember for the future (although I know, I *know* this never works). Even so, I *could* have tried to look beyond what people told me, what I thought I saw for myself. As it is, all I remember now is his absence. The bungalow without him in it. The peacocks gone. Dust on the binoculars. Cobwebs in his boots.

I watch her climb the steps, her towel around her neck. She has his wide shoulders and sinewy arms, but not the careful deliberation of movement, the float of the head. Considering these absences again, now, in this place, I suffer the loss of myself as I was then, and turn away, pinching the bridge of my nose between two fingers.

She flaps her towel across the chair and sits down. "What's wrong, Mummy?"

"Stainless steel," I say, reaching for the teapot. "Africa's endless love affair with stainless steel."

She looks politely, and then lifts her cup. "But what?" she insists.

"I'd rather you went alone this evening. Would you mind very much? I'll walk you to the bungalow gate."

She smiles. She's generous with me when I behave like a child. "I knew you'd ask," she says. "Of *course* I don't mind." She breaks open a scone and butters it, spreads it with apricot jam, then cream. She hums as she does this.

Normally, I'd warn her off too much butter, too much cream. But this time I just smile and say, "Nice?" She's at home with tea and scones, like a worker opening his lunch tin in the field. Aphorisms and incongruities do not amuse her. She's after facts, always has been. Since we arrived in this place, she too has been carrying a notebook. In it, she jots things down—plants, trees, the dates of this and that. When she looks up from the page to check the spelling of a Zulu word, an Indian name, with her high English voice rising politely at the end of the question, I want to snatch away the paper and tear it up.

"What I can't work out," she says, swallowing her vowels with the scone, "is exactly what a black person in this country could have hoped to achieve by murdering a white one. Especially then."

I sigh and look back out to sea. " 'Achievement' is hardly in it," I say. I have learned to play this English game of pouncing on a word, winding around it, away from the larger issues.

She grins. "Point taken!"

But I don't enjoy playing, nor can I bear her hearty delight, her sails spread like some batty player in an English detective fiction. "I think you should wash your hair," I say, "and do it up. Maya is coming for supper and bringing her daughter."

She nods absentmindedly, pouring another cup for herself. "But I mean—I've always thought that what you wrote in *Absence of Others* is what happened. In the main, that is."

"Fiction is orderly; life's a mess."

She bows her head, scolded. Despite her matter-of-factness, she holds the love story to her chest like a pillow or a bear. Until now, the murder has given it shape. It has enhanced her life. This much I know.

I know, too, that there are things I have selfishly hidden from her, things about him that are more hers than mine. Even the place, the place itself, which was, in a way, as much as I knew of him, as far as I wanted to know him, I suppose. I open my mouth to speak, but self-pity has me by the throat. It is the kind of self-pity that includes her. It is for us.

"Mum?" Her hand settles onto my shoulder, unsure of its welcome.

I grasp it in both of mine, kiss it violently, hold its palm to my cheek. Two old women with white hair and white shoes smile at us from the next table. Hester slides her hand from my grasp, buries it between her thighs, and looks away.

I clear my throat. "There are things I could tell you, Hester," I say softly. "But it's hard to remember beyond what I've remembered already. To tell it again would be to reinvent it. Do you understand what I'm saying?"

# 1

It was 1975. For eleven years I had been coming and going like so many others who had left to live overseas. Peered out of the plane window at the sun roaring up over the African plains, and felt my heart heave with joy. Filled my weeks at home with dinners and lunches and teas and shopping. And then wept when it was time to leave again.

Sitting around the swimming pools of women who had stayed behind, observing their nannies and drivers and hairdos and varnished nails, I had liked to think myself above hairdressers and manicures. With a husband who washed the dishes, with foreign degrees and foreign stories to tell—I had felt, among these women, delightfully unconventional. They, too, had seemed to think so. They had told me how much younger I seemed than they. How thrilling my life was in comparison to theirs. And even if they'd believed this only for the assurance that they too could seem younger and be thrilled by living in the real world—so what? If I gave them hope, they, in turn, made me feel very fortunate to have left.

So too did my parents. I loved my parents the way some mothers love their children—without ambition, and full of lies. With other people I was different. Fretful, critical, proud. If there were a meaning to these differences, I hadn't yet tried to find it. All I knew was that only by leaving had I been able to give them the happiness of my coming back. Seeing them behind the airport barrier, their arms around each other for once, I felt, as I had felt since first I left—that I was the only person who could make sense for them of their old age.

This time, however, things were different.

"It was *you* he kept asking and asking for," my mother said again, "even when he wasn't compos mentis." She stopped just short of running her fingers through her nest of teased, dyed hair. She couldn't commit the luxury of the gesture on a Saturday, when it had just been done. So she rubbed her eyes instead, and then looked up through their folds and pouches and added, "Lying there with all those ghastly tubes and things. Gasping for breath."

We sat in the shade of the verandah, with lunch laid out on the table as usual—cold meats, fried fish, a few salads, and some puddings, all under small net umbrellas to keep off the flies.

It is a commonplace among expatriates that one might miss the death of a parent—the phone lines down, a plane immobilised on a runway, a connection missed, and then the distance to cover. Still, even though my father hadn't died—hadn't, apparently, even had a heart attack, just a fright—still I accepted the blame for my absence from my mother. I even welcomed the novelty of it.

"Is he talking to you today?" I asked.

Instantly, her eyes watered over. She shook her head vigorously, reaching into her bag for a hanky and then clearing her nose with two fierce blows. The performance had always made my father wince. Me too.

"Believe me," she said, tucking the hanky into her sleeve. "Believe me, he can be a cruel man if he wants to be."

I believed her, always had. I'd seen him use the cold front of his good behaviour to punish her for her excesses of temperament. For ruining his life.

"I only cut him out of the will because I was worried *sick* he'd use the money on another woman. Go waltzing off around the world with that tart Jill Stafford. How was I to know he'd go and have a heart attack when he found out?"

She'd been asking me this question for the week since I'd come home. A few years before, wondering about my own life, I'd asked my father whether he'd ever regretted marrying. It was one of the dozens of questions I'd wanted to ask, ten thousand miles away. But then, each time I'd come back, such intimacies had seemed impossible, face to face. This question, however, I'd blurted out after one of their fights. And he'd answered instantly. "After Catherine was born," he'd said, lacing up a shoe and then stamping down that foot. "There was never any peace after that."

14

## The Bungalow

"There was always madness in his family," my mother went on. "Just think of Josephine, or old Uncle Tertius. He wasn't quite right either, you know, although they went to the ends of the earth to deny it."

We faced each other, the forty-odd years and one man between us like an intrigue of history. Age and smoking had dulled the whites and blacks of her eyes. A bright wing of rouge radiated along each high cheekbone, right into the roots of her hair. Pinkish make-up ran in the furrows of her brow and in the loops of her cheeks, lipstick in the creases around her mouth. In her vexation or her grief, she'd smudged away the pencilled half of one eyebrow, leaving tufts of grey.

Once she had been magnificent. A dark temptress who had turned a man's life. She had paused at the top of the stairs on a Saturday evening, dressed up for the Majestic, with her head held high, and its bundle of black hair gleaming. I remembered my father waiting below, scanning the front page of the evening paper. And me—unnoticed by either—wishing he would turn, just this once, to watch her descend.

I rose and went over to hug her from behind, laid one cheek against her forehead, breathing in the familiar hair spray and smoke, and the new, sweet smell of her old age.

"Ma," I said, "I'll talk to him. I'll snap him out of it."

"Ha!" she cried. "*He's* got what he wants now, one way or another, hasn't he? He's got me to change the will back. You'd do better, my girl, to give some thought to your own future."

• • •

The maisonette my parents rented was part of a huge old house that had been divided up, garden too, by the Maynard-Smythes, who lived on the other side. High on the ridge, with stone walls, leaded windows, large rooms and elegant fittings, the place was so much like our old house that my parents seemed to consider it their own. Old Maynard-Smythe had a head on his shoulders, my mother liked to say. He hadn't sold out for a song, like my father, after Sharpeville. Oh no, he'd hung on, stuck it out. And now look at what he had—a small gold mine!

In their half of the gold mine, my parents stalked each other like game. If she went to sit in the study, so did he. If he went to his Rotary lunch, or down to the shops to find a particular brand of golf sock, she waited at the hall window, holding the magnifier to her watch. Coming through the door, he went straight through to the liquor cabinet to check the level of the gin. Without their work—their theatre sold, new young talent from Jo'burg taking over the local productions—the marriage was lost for a focus. And so, they waited for their visits to me. She waited for her cataracts to ripen, she drank and waited. Or they waited for me to come home.

. . .

I watched her sleeping off a large lunch and two martinis. Her head had flopped over the back of the chair, her mouth hanging open. In the shadow of the verandah, with her hair shifted skew off her face and her cheeks sucked in between her jaws, she looked dead.

"Ma!" I whispered.

A snore rattled out into the afternoon. She jerked awake, and stared. "What's the matter?" she drawled.

"Nothing. It's four o'clock. I ordered tea."

She sighed and shook her head and coughed and reached for her cigarettes. "After thirty," she announced, "it's not so easy to fall pregnant."

"In America," I said, "it's quite normal to wait."

"Don't give me that normal!" she snapped, lighting a cigarette and then sending out smoke to mix with the leafy smells of a garden going to pot. "You've always used one country to get away with murder in the other."

The words struck me with a surprising blow. How had I, in all my years of coming to conclusions, failed to see the matter quite so bluntly? And how had she, in whom thought and utterance occurred so simultaneously, managed to keep this observation to herself?

"What I simply cannot work out," she went on—lifting the cosy to touch the pot as Grace placed the tray before her—"is why a *marvellous* girl like you wants to settle for a life without children."

I accepted my tea and considered the dozens of ways I had tried to reassure her that I wanted no such thing. That I had settled for nothing yet, not even a country. But sitting there with her, listening to her familiar phrases of misgiving, I suddenly felt my presence there as I had so often felt it overseas. Illegitimate. A whim, a luxury.

"There's more to it," she said. "That much I know. Is something the matter? Have you had yourself examined?"

"Ma, I've told you. There's nothing more to it."

But my mother felt entitled by her old age, and by her reputation for unrelenting frankness, to believe whatever she chose to believe. And to ask the same question as often as she wished. If an answer didn't suit, she simply asked again. "There's more to it," she insisted, pulling on a cigarette. "It's selfish. It's perverse."

I knew she meant "perverted." She'd always used the one word for the other, and usually it was funny. But now there was something perverted in the scene itself—tea set, tray cloth, tray, and teaspoons, the crescent of her lipstick on the teacup. And the lounge beyond, closed off and airless in its golds and emeralds— things that had remained unchanged through all the changes, and had somehow never belonged there in the first place.

I looked at my watch. "I'm going to have a bath," I said. "Edwina said they haven't got hot water, or electricity, or a phone on the farm." All day, lie upon lie had been fluttering up through my throat and out into the air. They seemed to give me hope. "If there's no one there to follow me home, I'll stay over—"

"Believe me," she said, twin streams of smoke spewing from her nostrils, "whatever a man says, he wants to see his name carried on. Even your father. I've always felt, you know, that his big regret was not having had a son."

# 2

Driving off to the party in my father's old Rover, I suddenly felt free and full of hope. I plunged a cassette into the tape deck and rolled down the window. "Very superstitious" roared out into the dusk, against the wishes of the government. " 'Writing's on the wall,' " I shouted at the top of my voice as I sailed down slope after slope. I was going into the company of strangers. No hairdos, no drivers, no manicures. " 'When you believe in things that you don't understand, then you suffer,' " I wailed.

I quietened down when I came upon the chaos at Berea junction. I'd completely forgotten my sister Catherine's warning always to take the long way across the ridge. And I'd forgotten this madness of workers set free for a long weekend—thousands of them swarming to the depot and station. It was like a war won—the shouting and whistling, the whoops, the red-eyed antics of those already drunk on kaffir beer.

I had never had a talent for history, couldn't place things properly or remember the causes and effects of great events. But there were scenes that I remembered—a Russian peasant standing in a field, bewildered by the sound of faroff gunfire. The Czar and Czarina listening too, and taking tea on the verandah. And then I, the audience, knowing what came next.

I knew now, of course, what was coming next. What had always been coming next. And next. And next. And never came. But, sitting there, immobilised in that familiar scene, I heard nothing but the din, saw nothing but the people and their familiar faces, their plastic baskets, and homemade cigarettes, and old felt hats, and boxes tied up with string. And then the Indian newspaper boys darting between the cars. *"Daily Witness!"* *"Daily Witness!"* "Bomb scare in Port Shepstone!"

A township bus edged into my lane, and I rolled up the window to close out the fumes. I leaned across the seat and rolled the other one up too. As I sat up again, something just out of focus and separated from the general confusion outside, made me look up. A crowd of young black faces were laughing down at me. Some banged at the glass of the fixed bus window. A few fists stabbed the air in the black freedom salute.

I had never known how to turn away from the hostility of a crowd. Never as a girl at school. Never even as an adult. To open my windows again would prove nothing. Nothing I could do would alter the assurance these people had that their presence, squashed into a bus, had terrified a white woman into rolling up her windows.

. . .

By the time I reached the shabby Victorian house of Bruce Carter, chairman of the English Department, night had come on suddenly, and, with it, the wind from the sea. Flying ants, brought out by the late-afternoon rain, clouded around the street lamps. I sat for a while in the dark, listening to the ticking of the engine as it cooled, hoping that Edwina had got to the party before me.

I hadn't seen Edwina since I'd left for America eight years before. Somehow, with that departure, I'd chosen a life that didn't include her, not even on my visits home. But this time I wanted her back. I wanted to meet different people, *real* people. The sort of people I thought Edwina would know.

"Mostly the 'varsity set, I'm afraid," she'd said. "But Hugh will be there—ever see him anymore? And Krishnah Chowdree, just out of detention, thanks to Hugh. Krishnah's something of a local hero. Written a book, you know. Banned here, but published overseas."

Overseas. The magic of it. Going overseas. Just back from overseas. I climbed down from the street into the dim glow of the Carters' front porch light, wishing for some reflective surface in which to see myself.

I'd taken care to dress simply. But even simply dressed, I felt all wrong. I caught a glimpse of myself in the glass of the front door and wished I'd worn a bra. And tied my hair back into a knot. Left off the eye make-up. Dark-skinned, black-eyed, with my black hair falling to my shoulders and my nipples standing out in fright, I felt like a gypsy here. A Jewish gypsy who had come, by some dark trick, on an invitation.

The door pulled wide, and I was staring all at once into the beady lapis of Hugh's eyes.

"Aha!" he said. He didn't move to let me in, but stood there, smiling with an edge of teeth, his bad hand plunged, as usual, into the pocket of his slacks. Facing him like that again—his sunburnt face and neck and arms, his starched white shirt, his thatch of tawny hair gone grey and lifting, just the top layer of it, in the wind—I felt, suddenly, as if I'd never been away.

"Edwina just phoned to say she couldn't come," he said, touching my elbow lightly. "Asked me to look out for you."

Behind him people moved about in candlelight. Candles, glued onto saucers, flared and trembled in the wind.

"Shut the bloody door!" someone shouted.

Hugh retrieved his hand and closed the door. "Stand fast," he said, "I'll rustle up some wine."

I stood fast, slightly sickened by the smell of scented wax, and by the stale and damp of servants' stew, and beer, and floor polish. People turned here and there to observe me. A roar of men came from the far verandah. They stood out there in short shorts and sandals, drinking beer straight out of bottles.

The hall in which I stood was bare, except for a table, a few globe chairs, and a battered upright piano against the opposite wall. The piano keys—chipped and discoloured—grinned across the room like rotten teeth. Through an archway, I could see the lounge. A mahogany lounge suite with caned backs and sides and rigid sprung cushions had been pushed against the walls. Two giant pillows covered in a lurid multicoloured velvet served as extra seats. And a balding floral carpet had been cut to fit the room. Except for one wall of books, double-stacked and orderly, the house seemed to contain a chaos of unloved things, things salvaged, perhaps, from the distress of others leaving. It was as if the people here were themselves perched and nested like migratory birds. Ready for flight in a change of season.

"Here," said Hugh, handing me a plastic tumbler of yellow wine. He led me to one of the cane-backed chairs and squatted next to me. "Eight years, is it?" he said, fingering a packet of cigarettes out of his shirt pocket.

I watched him tap one cigarette out and hang it between his lips with his good hand; then light it deftly with the other. No movement wasted. Everything he did and said rehearsed into the blood. Now as ever.

"I often thought of phoning you," I said. Actually, I'd heard on my first visit home that he'd taken up with a Belgian anthropologist, a woman of natural beauty, immense sophistication, and extreme intelligence. And, after that, I'd given up thinking of him at all.

"Still married?" he asked, sending a smoke ring out into the air.

"Barely. And you?"

He laughed silently. "I am still as you found me. But you seem— what shall I say?—" He ran the back of his crooked finger along the arch of my foot and looked up into my face. "How are you placed for tonight?"

I nodded. That afternoon, I had finally wrestled my new diaphragm into position with just such a question in mind. It was for just such an invitation that I had marched into Planned Parenthood a few weeks before to acquire it. And then buried it, closed into its clam shell, deep in the hollow of a boot. Every now and then, I'd taken it out, just to hold it, like a talisman, between the palms of my hands. Or I'd hinged open its shell and lifted it out, sniffed the latex, held it up to the light, a perfect circle.

"Seem what?" I asked. "What do I seem?"

He settled onto the floor, resting his elbow on his knee, his chin in his hand. "Sobered," he said.

"Ah! *You've* got her, Stillington!" A huge horse of a woman with yellowish eyes and yellow-grey hair came to stand before us. "Greetings!" she said to me. "Ruth Frank? I'm Cynthia Carter. Sorry Edwina can't make it. Come," she said, holding out a hand to pull me up. "I want you to meet the crowd."

I followed her to a vinyl beanbag nesting a woman in a tie-dyed smock. "Ruth, this is Bunny, John Conradie's new wife. You know John, don't you? The history prof? No? Well, anyway, here's Bunny."

Bunny Conradie smiled up at me with the complacency of a young and pregnant second wife. "What a *super* dress!" she said, extending an armful of African wire bangles. "Cynthia, be a sweetie! Get me a glass of plonk!"

"Oh God!" I cried. "I forgot the wine in the car!"

Cynthia grabbed me by the arm. "For*get* about the wine! Bruce!" she yelled. "Bring Bunny a cup of plonk!"

Bunny cosied into a ball and ran a hand over her belly. "I hear you live in the States," she said.

I nodded. I knew what was coming next.

"What do you do there?" she asked.

Both women waited in silence. So did others around them, pretending not to listen.

"Nothing," I said.

I saw them eye each other then, and felt myself back in school, pinched between enemies in prayers. Everything I said, even "nothing," carried with it the taboo of easy come and easy go. But how could I explain to them that there was nothing easy about it? These people were much worse off than I. In debt to their building societies and fathers-in-law, with too few degrees from the wrong sorts of institutions, what hope did they have of ever getting out?

"But Edwina said you'd been lecturing in English," Cynthia insisted. "Jane Austen?" She cocked her head on one side, and gave me a wry smile.

"Oh no!" I laughed. "I never taught Jane Austen."

Cynthia gave up and turned away to look around the room. "Have you met our Krishnah?" she asked. "He's the guest of honour."

I pretended to look around too. But I wished with all my heart I hadn't come.

"He's published a book," Bunny said. "Overseas. Isn't that super?"

"Super," I agreed.

"You could always write a book about us," said Bunny. "It's all the rage these days."

Something about this woman, settled into a life she thought all other women wanted, provoked me. "I think," I said, "that you have nothing to fear from me."

Cynthia tipped her ash into a vast, untamed spider plant hanging above Bunny's head. "Well, that's a relief anyhow," she said.

"What was it like going to live in America?" Bunny asked, patting the cushion next to her for me to sit down. "It must've been a hell of a shock after here."

I smiled, sorry now to have been so sharp. But I didn't sit down. There was no telling the truth to this sort of person. And, anyway, what was the truth? A shock? That's all? Even so, how would I explain it? Where would I begin?

"John's dying to get out," she said. "I'm the one who's not keen. What do you think?"

I shook my head. "But, I wouldn't know where to begin," I said.

• • •

*That first summer in New York City, I found that my clothes were all wrong. The flimsy shorts and strappy sundresses that had served quite well at home couldn't be worn there without subjecting me to the wild antics and suggestions of men. Or to the ravings of some mad person at large on the streets. But when I tried on a wraparound skirt and a blouse that covered my arms to the elbows, I seemed to vanish in the department-store mirror. On the way home, searching for my reflection in plate-glass windows, I decided I'd be better off indoors.*

*Anyway, there was little to go out for. The sun was of no use in such a place. Worse than useless, it was a torment. Without a breeze, without a beach, and hot at the wrong time of the year, there was no festival in the season. Every patch and stretch of grass was circumscribed. Each tree placed and fenced. And everywhere there was the stench of traffic and rubbish and dogs.*

*Sometimes, Clive brought home mangoes, and, once, a bag of lichees from the Chinese store. These gifts I accepted gratefully. But the mangoes had been picked too soon. They were sour and green. The lichees were old and watery. I threw them down the chute. And broke down completely when my sheets were missing one night from the dryer. It wasn't as if I didn't understand theft. I had grown up with it. But when I thought of my mother choosing them for colour and thread count, with wool blankets to match, the crime took on a significance beyond what I could explain to Clive.*

*Time, that first summer, was different too. There were no ceremonies to mark things off. I had lunch standing in front of the refrigerator, tea in a mug at any time of the day. In our two rooms, with the traffic roaring fourteen stories down, and the air conditioner buzzing, I found myself warping hour into day, day into week, waiting for Clive to come home.*

*And what of Clive? From the start, an insufficiency of desire had passed between us like a curse. I had suffered it first—accepted it, hidden it away as Clive rose and fell above me. But then, as soon as we were married, it settled onto him. Night after night he gave up, defeated. "It's the Jewish thing," he said. "The wife-mother thing." And I, considering his mother, who was vulgar and fat and ugly and shrill, found myself worrying not only about myself, but about all the other women—not wives, or mothers, or Jewish—who could take my place. They infected my dreams. Vicious, scratching dreams, with Clive smiling and a strange woman smiling, and myself screaming voiceless at them both. And then, at the end, free of him, free to leave, I would wake in fright—my hair and body steaming—to the airbrakes of a truck shuddering to a halt on the street below.*

*What we had in our one room, and then in our two rooms, and then in our four rooms with a view of the river, and bicycles in the basement, and dinner parties on a Saturday night, was a marriage. The real world, to which I had thought I had come, was quite absent. Or, if there in some unexpected form, empty of comfort. Lonely beyond any loneliness I had ever known.*

. . .

Someone touched me on the shoulder from behind. "Here," he said. "Let's have your opinion on this."

The group behind me widened to let me in.

"We're onto one of our favourite subjects," he explained. "Blacks at the university. Academic standards."

"Ha! Ha!" barked a man with a little fox face. "What standards?" He turned to me. "I was just telling them, there's an

African chap I'm tutoring who spells 'England' with two *i*'s—not capitalised, mind you—i-n-g-l-i-n-d!" He looked around for applause. "Doesn't that just take the biscuit?"

They all laughed. I laughed too. It wasn't funny, though, never had been.

"Well, what're we supposed to do to prepare them?" someone demanded. "Where are we supposed to start?"

"At birth!" cried a young black man in glasses. "The future of our country lies in the hope of our children."

"With all due respect, Enos old boy, I might as well try teaching them to walk on water. What hope? It's too late."

"Precisely!" said the black man, curling his lips back from his teeth. "What about our lost generations? What will be done about them?"

I dreaded being pulled into this sort of thing. I had nothing useful to say about lost generations or uneducated youth. In this company, the country itself felt like an American public service announcement. It seemed like a cause, an idea, attached to nothing.

The fox-faced man turned to me. "They're expecting us, you see, to solve the blunders of history."

"*Blunders!*" shrieked someone behind me. "*Blunders!*"

I turned and the group turned with me. A small beaky Indian in blue jeans and sandals faced us. He cocked his head and sneered. "You people and your blunders!" he spat out.

"In the States," I offered quickly, "they solve things with euphemisms. You must have heard of 'affirmative action'?"

"You should hear *our* euphemisms!" a grey-haired woman insisted. "Did you ever hear of 'Plurals'?"

"Oh yes!" I laughed. "I heard that long ago!"

Fox-face fixed me with a glare. People shuffled and coughed. I understood too late that there were things they didn't want me to know. They wanted no worldly wisdom from me. What they needed was an outside audience. A foreign witness to a unique failure. If I refused the role, they'd shun me. They were turning away right now, discussing matters of administration, leaving me to Bruce Carter.

"Hello, Ruth," he said. "Let me introduce you to Krishnah. Krish"—he tapped the Indian on the arm—"this is Ruth Frank. She lives in America."

Krishnah turned and the crowd turned with him.

"I'm very glad to meet you," I said. "I've heard so much about you."

"Of course you have," he replied. "Everybody has heard about me. I'm quite notorious, you see." He had a high-pitched singsong voice that hit me in the bone.

"Me too, in a way," I said, hoping, against the caution rising in my chest, to find a friend.

"And for what are you notorious, may I ask?" He clamped his teeth shut in a frightening grimace, the lower set locked firmly over the upper.

I felt the heat rise from my chest to my neck, from neck to cheeks to ears. I glanced around for Hugh. I thought I heard him, but he wasn't there. "Well, not quite notorious," I said. "More like peculiar, I suppose."

"Oh, 'peculiar' is it?" Krishnah chanted. "And what is it about you that is 'peculiar,' may I ask?"

"Coming back here, I suppose. My American friends seem to think I'm quite mad." I tried a laugh.

He frowned at me in silence, as if trying to understand.

"Leaving safety, perhaps—" I suggested.

"Safety?" he echoed quickly. "Please be so good as to tell me if I am to understand that we are facing an act of heroism on your part in returning to this country?"

Someone whispered in the crowd. There was a snort.

A vise closed around my chest, almost stopping my breathing. "Heroism isn't in it," I said softly.

"Oh, but you were very heroic indeed," Krishnah shouted, "to leave the safety of America, and come out here to—excuse me?— where is it that you are staying?"

I paused. "With my parents."

"With your *parents!*" he cried. "Oh, my word, but that is very heroic indeed! To leave the safety of America to come back and stay with one's *parents!*"

"I think you're missing her point, Krish," Bruce said.

"Ah! Missing her point, am I? Did I not hear that America is a very safe place? Did I not hear that a certain person left America to return to this very unsafe place, and is presently staying with her *parents?* And should I not know how very brave that is, living as I do with my own parents in their house?" He appealed to the crowd, raising his palms to the ceiling.

"I was trying to explain the attitude of others towards me," I said, loosened slightly from the vise by Bruce's kindness. "I am quite aware of the fact that I am not in peril here. I mean that I'm not involved in the struggle."

" 'Not involved,' " he echoed. " 'Not involved in the struggle.' "

And then the game was clear. The pitch and singsong and echoing of his performance freed me from apology and worked me into the sort of anger set free on a spouse, or against the rudeness of strangers in places like New York. "Is there a point to your echoing every phrase I use?" I demanded, my voice rising with my temper.

People looked from him to me and me to him. I watched him closely, ready for a pounce.

But he simply bowed his head and closed his eyes. He held us for some seconds in the silence. "Forgive me," he said at last. "I am really out of touch, you see. When you are as cut off as I have been, you learn to repeat and repeat things so that you don't go mad. It's a habit I have now. Sometimes I forget that there is a very peaceful world going on out there, a very safe place."

I saw the trap, but seeing didn't stop me, like the fat girl in school, from trying to make friends with the bully. "In fact," I assured him, "America is anything but safe, as you probably know. I was simply trying to give you the truth. Surely you would prefer that?"

He jerked upright, eyes wide. "Sssooo!" he hissed. "You are giving me the gift of *truth*, is it?"

He paused. I didn't answer.

"But surely, Krish," Bruce said, "you must acknowledge the validity of a non-position? Especially for an outsider?"

Krishnah ignored him, jerking his head this way, that way, like a bird. "The question is," he said at last, "What is the *effect* of truth, isn't that so? It is a case of *morality*, wouldn't you say? You can't just go around saying, 'I'm telling the truth and I'm O.K.,' can you? Like one of those books on psychology that all you Americans love to read. Isn't it?"

The audience looked at me. Bunny cupped a hand around her mouth and whispered something to Cynthia.

"Rubbish!" I lied. "No one I know reads those books."

"What do they read, then? Their glorious Constitution? All those white-haired, white male landowners writing down one truth after another? My word!" he shouted at the crowd. "Perhaps those Americans would find my own book altogether too hot to handle? Perhaps they think I should go back where I came from, like their own black people? Or take a job in the Botanic Gardens like my own founding fathers? What do you think?"

The group laughed. People moved off. Someone brought Krishnah a glass of Oros and water and some biscuits on a plate. It was a victory parade, and he the local favourite.

"Hey, Krishnah! Lay off, old boy." Hugh edged himself in next to me and rested an arm around my shoulders, arresting me where I was. "Krishnah was at Balliol," he explained, "where he learned very bad manners."

"Pudding's on, people," Cynthia announced from the doorway. "It's help yourselves."

As the crowd moved off, Hugh kept his hand on my shoulder. "Ready?" he asked.

"You leave first," I said. "I'll follow in ten minutes."

. . .

I drove fast through the cane, switched on the radio, switched it off again. Perhaps Hugh's bungalow would restore me. Carry me beyond the ordinary claims of my own small history. Going to the Carters' party had been a mistake. It had, somehow, claimed me back after all these years, and in all the old ways. And yet, claimed, I'd felt abandoned. Poor in belonging. Miserably strange. So what if I were free to come and go? From what? I asked myself. To what? I wanted to know.

As I swung hard onto the coastal road, a dark head flashed

across the beam of my headlight. I leapt onto the brake. The bottle of wine I'd forgotten shattered against the dashboard. The car bucked and skidded and then cut out with a shudder.

"Shit!" I whispered, rolling down the window. "Are you there?" I called into the dark. "Are you O.K.?"

No sound came back. The car smelled sour with wine and dust. I climbed out. My sandals sank into warm mud. Like snow, the mud seemed to have muffled all normal night sounds. And there was no moon to see by. I could hear the roar of the surf, nothing else. Holding on to the car with one hand, I crept slowly towards the front wheels. The beams shone straight out, above the dark surface of the road, lighting up, now, in the distance, the white-painted tree trunks of the hotel driveway.

"Oh, thank *God!*" I whispered at the sight.

A warm wind blew off the sea. After a while I heard the bush rustling. I heard an African singing or shouting somewhere in the distance, a car hooting. I was almost sure there had been no thud. I hadn't heard it, hadn't felt it as I'd felt the dog I'd hit on the Merritt Parkway. That had stayed with me for months—the dead sound, the dead feel of it.

"Is anyone hurt?" I asked into the darkness. "Please answer me."

Nothing came back.

"Please," I said more loudly, making my way back to the car door, "if you need help, don't be afraid."

By the time I arrived at Hugh's bungalow, I was almost sure I hadn't hit anyone. Still, the solitary scene, its violence, victim or no victim, made my hand shake as I reached up for the knocker.

# 3

The first time Hugh Stillington had brought me out to the bungalow, I hadn't been ready for his world. I'd sat on the verandah thinking of things to say as he'd dismissed the servants in a perfect Zulu and then poured me a sherry from an old cut-glass decanter.

"Do you imagine you'll be comfortable in America?" he'd asked over his shoulder. With five generations of sugar behind him and a reputation for righteous reform, he was miles from the vulgarity of my own world and its contempt for anything local.

He had found me in 1967, flushed with play, at Edwina's engagement party. Three years at Oxford had not only sharpened my wit and tongue, but had changed the way I looked. I'd learned a new style of dress there quite different from the one I'd suffered under my mother's co-ordinating eye and taste for embellishment. I'd grown my hair too, tied it back into a knot to balance the length of my nose; cut down on make-up, thrown out my costume jewelry and synthetic fibres.

Hugh Stillington, Edwina had announced, was a lost cause—an eccentric, who carried on at his Africans about crop rotation and eating fish when he should have been running for Parliament. He'd given up, she said, given in to the old-fashioned seduction of land and people. Which was all very well for him—his sons had been in England for fifteen years. Bloody aliens! Hugh had roared. Comfortable, like their mother, in cold, damp, noisy places. He wouldn't have them back.

It was one thing, however, to flirt with Hugh at Edwina's in the company of her friends. Quite another to sit on the verandah of his bungalow, watching bats swoop and squeak across the dark of the sky, wondering whether he was the sort of man who would be touched by my virginity. I knew that the women in his set had no such *burdens, especially at the age of twenty-one. And that virginity was nothing to be proud of. Still, I was proud. And he was over forty. He had the massive blueness and blondness of another breed. And he had a crippled hand. I watched him wrap its three fingers around the stem of a sherry glass, wishing I had something more to offer him.*

*"Have you ever been to America?" I asked.*

*"Ah yes. Twice."*

*I considered the ease of such an answer. Twice. Even Edwina, who came and went to Europe whenever she liked, had never been to America.*

*"Mind you, I've never ventured much further than New York and Washington. Other than the museums, I can see little virtue in the place." He lifted the decanter to the light of the moon, his shirt sleeve sloughed into the crook of his arm. Except for his skin, which wore the ruddy badge of sun and alcohol, he seemed more sober than the rest of his class and breed. There was a fierceness in the squared angles of his nose and brow and chin, in the way his lips turned up into a smile without really smiling.*

*"When do you leave?" he asked.*

*"March."*

*He settled back into a chair, holding his glass between his hands. "Why?"*

*"Actually," I said, "it's rather mad. I'm going to do post-graduate work in New York. I have a scholarship. There's someone there—"*

*"Ah!"*

*I laughed. "I hardly know him, actually. It's really quite mad when you come to think of it." I heard myself repeating words, and my voice and accent taking on the swoop and wheeze of the women I thought he must be used to. My mother had told me that the Stillington fortune had dwindled to nothing, and that it served them right. Old Nigel Stillington virtually ran the Royal Country Club, she said, and still wasn't lifting a finger, despite his so-called liberal views, to open up the membership to the better sort of Jew like my father.*

*" 'Actually,' 'actually'—" Hugh sat forward, resting his elbows on his knees. "Actually, Miss Frank, I would guess that your journey isn't nearly mad enough."*

*"Why?"*

31

# Lynn Freed

"Why? Because, you choose to be here, with me. Come," he said, standing up. "I want to take you inside."

I took his hand, taking the blame in silence. But I hated the idea of having chosen to be there with him. It took away the romance of being given no choice at all. And exposed my choice of America for what it was. Cheap. How could he understand that if I were flying off at the suggestion of a man I hardly knew, it was because that seemed to be the only choice worth making? I was only beginning to understand myself that I had no talent for choosing. Or for knowing my own mind and heart. What was there to know? Despite my apparent boldness of thought, my head had always hesitated between safety and daring. Except for its primitive leaps of hope, my heart lay still and waiting.

Everyone else had accepted without question that I was going to America to get some more degrees, a clever girl like me. I had almost come to believe it myself. The fact that my parents couldn't afford an overseas education for me, that I would have to use up my scholarship money for the plane ticket alone was still an unspoken secret among us. The whole plan seemed to fit well with Clive's green card, with the way he kept apart from other Jewish men ready to take a wife. Just as I stood apart from the sort of Jewish women who majored in psych and socio at the local university and announced their engagements just before graduation.

The style I had acquired at twenty-one—which consisted of little more than a skittish intolerance for group enthusiasms—seemed consistent with wanting Clive Brasch for a husband. Wanting him without even knowing him, without loving him. What did I know about love anyway? Love, I'd assumed, would bend to my decisions. And so, I'd decided, I loved Clive already. Loved him for his slight stoop and slim hips and skewed, off-centre smile. Loved him as I lay naked in the dark with Hugh Stillington a month before departure. It was a matter of pride. Something Hugh would never have understood.

· · ·

"Lose your way?" Hugh asked, opening the door.

I shook my head. If I told him about the incident on the road, he'd rush out into the night like a warrior. The police would be called in. The diaphragm jelly would lose its potency.

I followed him into the lounge. It was lit only by a pale moon off the sea, but still I could make out the hulk of the couch, the chairs opposite, the round brass tray on the coffee table, two glasses on it. In the gloom, the place seemed bigger, the walls and ceiling lost in darkness. And Hugh older. His eyes had vanished in their sockets, deep shadows cut across his cheeks.

"I'm going to brain that bloody Krishnah tomorrow," he said, pouring the Cognac. "Shall I brain him for you?"

I stood in the dark, trying to think up a clever answer. But, something in the kindness of the question itself, or in the playful cadence of his voice, had closed my throat with tears. I turned away.

"Good God!" he said, coming over. He pulled a handkerchief from his pocket and handed it to me. "He can be like a dog at meat, that little bugger," he said. "When he's faced with someone like you, he sees red. I'll certainly have a word with him tomorrow."

"Someone like me?"

"We hate in others what we most fear in ourselves."

"But *what?*"

"What you Americans might term 'selling out.' He had a chance to leave and didn't take it. Now, I fear, he's facing the smallness, the meanness of his life here. So, he's taking risks. For *nothing*, for *no* earthly reason!"

I shook my head, and blew my nose, and then announced, "I may have run into someone on the coastal road."

"What?"

"I'm almost sure I did. I stopped the car, and looked around and called, but there was no one there."

"Hmm." He stalked to the French doors, stood there, his hands clasped behind him. A pair of binoculars hung from a hook near the door. Their lenses caught the moonlight. "Don't stop next time," he said, coming back. He picked up my glass and handed it to me. "Here, I think you should have this."

I swallowed the Cognac in two gulps, feeling its magic immediately. It sharpened the smell of him, the smell of the place itself. Sweat and Cognac and smoke, salt, damp, rot, sweet coir matting.

Outside, the wind was picking up. "There'll be a storm tomorrow," he said. He came to stand before me. "God," he murmured, "God, what a gorgeous woman you've become!"

I laughed, I shivered. If I were in need of reasons to be taking a lover, I could easily find them in phrases like this. But is wasn't just his praise I wanted, the please and thank-you of a gift. Like any conqueror, I wanted more, much more. I wanted to lay waste his will, to attach his world. I wanted him to touch me with his crippled hand. He brushed it lightly down my back, its nail across my skin like a pinpoint. I laid my head against his chest, listening to the thudding of his heart, feeling for a moment, with his lips on my hair, his arms closed tight around me, that I had come into safe harbour.

. . .

The next morning, I walked out onto the verandah to watch the sun rise over the sea. It was pale, diffused by a storm building up on the horizon. A strong wind blew. Waves, coming in fierce and high with a late spring tide, crashed onto the beach over a hundred feet below. The river, too, ran strong for the time of year. Its waters traced a cloud of brown almost a mile into the green of the sea.

The beach itself looked as desolate as ever. Because of the curve and height of the cliff, it was mostly in shadow, even in the morning. Without shark nets, there had never been a question of swimming. But now the waves seemed to have tumbled the old breaker of rocks, to have stolen half the beach. What was left was strewn with rubbish, laced by tidemarks of black oil.

"Some cup of tea, madam?"

I drew Hugh's toweling gown more tightly around me. "I'm coming in," I said. "It's cold."

But inside was also cold. The bungalow took the wind ungraciously, rattling and sighing like an old sow. The num-num hedge, grown wild with neglect, brushed back and forth against the bedroom wall. The boy had run off for no reason, the maid complained, as she brought in the tray. And monkeys were stealing the bananas again. What could she do?

I smiled, watching the dark tea arc beautifully from the spout into the cup.

Nothing had changed out here. With its bottle-green wicker

and worn rush matting, its flowered linen slipcovers and teak and brass and bits of dinner and silver services that had survived a succession of unsupervised servants, Hugh's bungalow still seemed as it had seemed before—beyond the reach of normal life and rules.

The place had been built before the turn of the century by Hugh's great-grandfather, the provincial administrator, for his Indian mistress—cut deep into the bush far north of town before there was a bridge or a proper road to reach it by. Even now, with the new northern route slicing up to Zululand, there were a good ten kilometers to drive through the cane after the turnoff, before reaching the old Umgeni Beach Hotel. And then the narrow, unpaved strip that meandered along the cliff to the bungalow gate.

Except for the lip of the land from bluff to bluff on which the hotel and the bungalow stood, the area all around was zoned for Indians. Their pink and green houses dotted the hills. Their corrugated iron shacks reappeared year after year, flood after flood, along the river banks. And the stylish cottages with names like "Villa Esperanza" and "Buena Vista" and pools and views and thatch and imported tile—holiday places built by rich upcountry people in more recent times—were gathered further south, into separate municipalities, around the better beaches.

Rain began to drum down on the corrugated iron roof. Wind drove it across the verandah, green as glass. I took my tea to the window to wait for it to stop. And, when it did, went out again onto the steaming verandah to watch two ships moving through the light. Even as I stood there wanting to go home, thinking up more lies to loosen myself from the tight collar of my parents' concern—even as I did—I knew I'd had no moment like this anywhere before. Not ever this keen sense of being in the right place.

# 4

My father chose Friday night at Catherine's for his debut into normal life. He'd been practising for days. First, a stroll from his bedroom to his dressing room and back again, leaning heavily on my arm. Then, a day or so later, ordering all the doors and windows shut, he'd made it into the upstairs hall, and, from there, downstairs. And then, that afternoon, out onto the verandah, where he asked me to join him after lunch while my mother slept inside.

He never gave things away at the beginning. At first, he clasped his hands around one knee and said, once again, how glad he was that there were weeks to go before I had to leave.

I nodded, staring out at the false calm of the sea, wondering more than ever how I could bear to go away again.

"Ruth," he said then, "may I presume upon your private life?"

I looked up, my heart suddenly wild with dread.

"You see, certain matters cannot remain undiscussed. You can trust me. I think you know that."

I trusted him as I had always trusted him—to play by the rules of English schoolboy decency and fair play.

"What I would like you to consider are two things. Your financial situation. And mine. As you know, I have never worshipped Mammon. Unfortunately, you couldn't count on me were you ever to be on your own."

My tears, stopped in my throat at the thought of leaving, spilled out suddenly for myself.

He sat quite still, waiting for me to calm down. "I hope I'm wrong," he said, "but I have the impression that your marriage isn't entirely a happy one."

One way or another, he'd been asking me this question for years. But even now, treading so lightly on danger, I couldn't say what it was I wanted, what I wouldn't give up.

"Perhaps it was a little rash to give up lecturing?" he suggested. "How easy would it be to take it up again?"

Someone knocked.

"Yes, Grace?"

"Master, I must bring the tea?"

"Presently. We'll wait for the Madam to wake up. Come," he said to me. "Let's stroll down to the bottom of the garden. I'm going to try to make it on my own."

He stepped carefully through the grass and down each slope, me following, to the stand of lichee trees planted along the hedge. There he stood looking out to sea, his hands settled into the pockets of his shorts.

"Look at them lined up and waiting to come in," he said. "You'd think, one of these days, it would occur to them to build a bigger harbour."

I looked at the freighters sitting lightly on the sea, and thought, with little joy, of Clive counting the weeks till my return.

And then, noticing my face as he might notice a picture skew on the wall, he pulled out a clean white hanky—ironed into a perfect square—and held me by the chin, and dabbed my cheeks.

"You know," he said, kissing me on the forehead, "I can never bear it when you have to leave."

And then he turned away, and walked slowly back up the hill.

. . .

Catherine had told me she was having a bigger crowd than usual for Friday night. In addition to both sides of the family, there was to be some Rhodesian immigrant Jeffrey had hired at the request of the rabbi; the new American consul, who was a Jew, and his family; Julian Black—remember him?—back from America for his father's funeral; the Kaplans, because their house was being fumigated for white ants; *and*, if I could imagine, the Chief, who was coming into town for one of his prayer breakfasts the next day.

Word had got out long ago that Chief Sibusi stayed with Jeffrey

Lynn Freed

and Catherine whenever he came to town. And that the dogs, who couldn't tell one black man from another, had to be locked onto the upstairs verandah for the duration of the visit.

Since I'd left, Jeffrey had become quite a figure in the community. Apart from expanding his father's factory in knitted underwear into a vast international empire (if you could read beyond the labels—designed to disguise the country of origin, and provided, at a cost, by neighbouring African countries—you'd recognise his products stretched out to dry along the Ganges, sealed into packets of three on the shelves of Marks & Spencer)—apart from this, and his standing as a leader of the Jewish community, Jeffrey had acquired, together with the friendship of the Chief, a reputation for making himself useful as a go-between on the political front. Although no one knew quite where he stood himself.

I dropped my parents at the front door and then drove around to the back to park. From the dark of the path outside, I watched my father bend to kiss Catherine, and then move like a ghost into the crowd. Catherine herself, fixed into her public smile, stood greeting people as they arrived. The lounge glittered with jewelry and crystal and shades of butterfly silk. Indian waiters from the Majestic, in turbans and red sashes, circulated among the guests with trays of kir.

Having the Majestic cater a Friday night was something of a triumph for Catherine. Jeffrey preferred traditional fare—matzo kleis soup, gefilte fish, kighel, kneydlach, kreplach, kosher wine. But, for once, Catherine had refused. She wasn't used to refusing Jeffrey, nor he to being refused. And so, the novelty had given them both a surprise; it had become a celebration.

"*There* she is!" my mother cried out. She waved at me from the couch, where she had cosied up with a tall dark man and a glass of Scotch. "Come over here, darling. I've just been talking about you."

She was in a fine mood tonight, brought on by several Scotches, and by wearing the new shocking-pink-and-black silk frock she'd bought at Gigi's just before my father's heart attack.

"Darling," she boomed, "do you remember Julian Black? He lives in America, too." She looked from him to me, duchess of geography.

38

I remembered him now, a bat-eared bar-mitzvah boy, much older than I, who had gone off to Oxford on a Rhodes and married a horsy English girl, which had broken his parents' hearts.

I shook my head. "Sorry," I said. "Where do you live?"

"Minneapolis." His voice was deep and throaty, very Oxford. Far from the nasal, effeminate whine practised by local Jewish males.

"See?" said my mother. "Isn't it odd that you two haven't met?"

"No," said Julian, "not odd, really. Minneapolis is over a thousand miles from New York."

But my mother was not to be put off by numbers. If my marriage was in jeopardy, as clearly it was—me waiting like a cat for the phone to ring, the beautifully spoken man who rang and left no name, the days and nights I spent away from home, and then the cock-and-bull stories I attached to them—if my marriage were in danger, so might anybody's be. This tall bloke, for instance. How happy could *he* be, the son of Eli Black married to a shiksa? And what did my mother care, anyway, about his happiness? He was nothing to her, nothing at all unless he abandoned the shiksa and fell in love with me, me with him. It was me she feared for. And for herself, on my account.

"Well, don't you like to go to the theatre?" she demanded of Julian. "To the opera? New York is the *hub*—in America, anyway, wouldn't you say? I'd think a thousand miles wouldn't matter a *jot* if one wanted to see something worthwhile."

I saw Julian's ears redden, the pupils of his eyes shrink to pinholes. "Ma," I said, "Minneapolis has its own theatre—"

"Of course," she snorted, "but what *sort* of theatre, a thousand miles away? When *I* was at the Royal Academy, people thought nothing of coming in from all over England to see the London productions. Bristol, Brighton—they'd come in and make a night of it." She eyed me triumphantly, and then peered down into her glass. "Darling," she said, "would you ask your father to get me another drink, please." She reached over and tapped Julian's glass with a long scarlet fingernail. "Would you like my husband to fetch you something else?" she whispered. "I really can't imagine what Catherine's up to, sending waiters around with pink Champagne. It must be something mod. She isn't saving on liquor, I assure you. In this ménage, Scotch and Cognac flow like water."

Catherine caught me by the arm on my way over to my father. "Listen, old girl," she whispered, "the Chief's arriving any minute. Jeffrey asked me to seat him with you."

I glanced around the room. Last visit, I'd had the Chief for an entire evening—a square-faced black man sweating in a dark wool suit. All night he'd carried on about "the political situation" and "the future of this country." This time I wanted a reprieve. "What about the American consul?" I asked.

"I need him on my right," she said. "Look, old girl, just be grateful you only have to put up with this once in a blue moon."

. . .

After kiddush, I settled into the familiar scene. The Kaplans seated with the Goldmans, my parents with the Kupersteins. Old Mrs. Kuperstein into the brandied prunes already. The whole world, it seemed, came in pairs or their leftovers. Sitting there, I felt like one of each. Or neither. I picked up my place card and examined my name, printed carefully in pencil on the cloudy Venetian glass.

"So, you're back for a visit?" Julian said from my left.

I turned to him, trying to ignore my mother, who was watching us through the fruit-and-flower arrangement down the centre of the table. "My father had a suspected heart attack," I explained. "It took me forty hours to get here."

He nodded, stabbing his fork into a wedge of lemon and then squeezing it over his smoked salmon.

"Is there much of a Jewish community where you live?" my mother called out.

"There must be numbers of South Africans in Minneapolis," I said quickly.

He nodded and rolled his eyes, chewing, swallowing. "More and more," he said. "We avoid them as much as possible."

We. I took a swig of wine and looked over at my mother. But she was satisfied, apparently, that we were talking to each other, and had turned her attention to scraping the capers off her salmon.

Next to me, the Chief was engaged in a discussion with the American consul on the pros and cons of bringing television to the country. Everyone was trying to join in. Further up the table, Nathan Kaplan was shouting, "Believe me! Believe me, Chief!" But the Chief couldn't hear him. Even though Nathan and his brother Meyer—both of whom had recently been caught in a price-fixing racket in tobacco, and then let off on a technicality— even though they were struggling back into position as members of the powerful Jewish industrial elite (the sort of men, like Jeffrey, cultivated by the Chief)—even though *he*, Jeffrey Goldman, claimed loudly to believe in the Kaplan brothers' innocence—still, Nathan was, for the time being anyway, to be kept at a distance from delicate situations. And so Jeffrey had instructed Catherine to exile Nathan to the top of the table, far from the Chief. And there he sat, between his wife and my cousin Paul, himself on the way to a fortune in burglar alarms.

Fortunes were everywhere you looked, these days. With the price of gold sky-high, even my stupid cousins were buying BMWs, putting in pools and tennis courts, taking their wives on trips overseas. Paul, Catherine had told me, had given a party at the Majestic for Marcia's fortieth birthday, where he'd instructed the maître d' to bury a diamond bracelet in her pâté, to place one diamond earring in each pocket of a new fur coat he'd smuggled in.

"I find this country a wasteland," Julian was saying, swilling and nosing his wine. "Not just politically, but intellectually, culturally, aesthetically. I wouldn't mind if I never had to come back."

Usually this sort of speech worked me into closing my eyes and nodding and saying, "I know *exactly* what you mean!" But now I observed this pallid creature on my left—this opera-goer of the Midwest, this symphony seasoner, this reader of the Sunday *New York Times*—and I thought of Hugh, at fifty-two, more at home here than ever.

"Do you feel at home in Minneapolis?" I asked.

"Oh yes! God, yes! Minneapolis is a fantastic city!"

"Excuse me"—the Chief was staring at us through steel-rimmed glasses—"I am very interested in the question of why people choose to leave their homes." He fixed a smile on Julian. "When, may I ask, did you leave this country?"

"Twelve years ago," said Julian.

41

Lynn Freed

"*Twelve years*! In twelve years a great many things have happened."

Julian looked triumphant. "That's why I left," he cried.

I sat back, pleased to be overlooked. The whole table was now in a frenzy of talk on the subject of leaving the country. Tanya Kaplan dug into her bag for photographs of her daughter in Australia. The Rhodesians launched into American immigration policies towards White Rhodesians. My mother couldn't even get in her usual piece about trunk calls and time differences.

"So much of our gold,"said the Chief, "our human gold, has left us. But *this* country is where your real home is."

"Yours, Chief Sibusi," said Julian, "not mine. I have children—"

"No!" said the Chief. "*This* country is your home! We need our doctors. We need our nurses. We need our architects. We need our bricklayers." He looked from me to Julian. "It is my sincere wish that you and other people like you would come back home."

"Pardon me, Chief," Julian said, "when you say 'people like you,' are you referring to Jews?"

But the Chief was not a man to be disconcerted by candour. He buttered a roll and took a bite. "Of course," he said. "Jewish people have always constituted the mainstay of our support in opposing the atrocities committed by this government. We must endeavour to encourage our sons and daughters—"

"My younger daughter has an American passport," my mother announced. "She goes all over the *world* with it, never has a problem."

"But my children are Americans," Julian protested.

"Citizenship is *nothing*!" cried the Chief. Tiny beads of sweat glistened in the pores of his nose. "Look at me? Am I considered a citizen of this country?"

Mrs. Kuperstein looked up, interested. She still couldn't quite work out the Chief's presence on a Friday night, Catherine had told me. "Well, if you ask me—" she began.

But Nathan Kaplan shoved aside the centrepiece and leaned forward. "These people couldn't live all over the world if we cut off their rands from here, could they, Chief?" he shouted.

"I beg your pardon, sir," said Julian, his thick neck reddening from the collar up. "I receive not one cent from this country, and never have."

"Well, you're the exception, hey?" said Nathan, shifting his glance to me.

He was right. Clive did accept small gifts of money from his parents—fifty dollars here, five hundred left behind after one of their visits. My mother sent me money to buy clothes. But, so what? "So what?" I said.

"So, come back and earn it!" Nathan sat back and folded his arms, jerking his head around the table like a snake.

"And you are in a position to issue such injunctions?" Julian demanded.

Jeffrey leapt up and grabbed the dessert wine from the sideboard. "Catherine!" he called. "Where're the puddings?"

But Nathan was through the centrepiece again, his face livid, his eyes bulging. "If it was up to me," he screeched, "my daughters would be on the next boat home, that much I can tell you!"

"Poor daughters!" Julian murmured to me.

I smiled. Suddenly, he didn't seem so bad. In fact, I envied him his single-mindedness. All my life I'd wanted two things at once, two worlds to move between—with me just arrived, just about to leave, and always with somewhere to come home to. But here was a man who felt at home in a place like Minneapolis. Who talked of his wife and himself as "we." And his children as Americans. Clearly, he couldn't wait to go back, just as I couldn't bear to, couldn't bear even to think of going back again, even as I couldn't think of staying on—not in this familiar world anyway, in this sour air, this poisoned, joyless place.

I looked at Catherine reigning over the puddings with a spoon in each hand, her public smile back in place. "Tanya? Fruit salad and ice cream? Apple Charlotte? A bit of each?"

People said Catherine was a cold fish. But they were wrong, dead wrong. There were any number of things and people Catherine hated with a passion. Old people, for instance. She hated the death grip they held over her Friday nights and Jewish holidays. The sound of their chewing, the way they hawked and spat. Their drivers standing around in her kitchen interfering with her servants. She hated her servants too, and ours. The things that went on behind her back and under her nose. Their telegrams from home, their babies dying. She even hated her house, the way it left her open to the world she loathed. Placed high on the ridge, five minutes from our parents and her parents-in-law, with its wide verandahs, vast receiving rooms, wings built on for the children, with children and dogs and parents and anyone at all coming in and out all day, it gave her nowhere to hide.

What she wanted for herself was a private life ten thousand miles away. St. John's Wood, perhaps, a little garden and an English gardener. Duvets in the winter. Mornings at Harrods, Fortnum's, weekends on the Continent with Jeffrey to herself. No relatives, no servants. No engagements, weddings, bar mitzvahs, brises. A child's paradise.

Her two older boys pushed back their chairs and went over to whisper in her ear. They were barefoot, and wore torn T-shirts and shorts. She had told me it was a lot of bloody nonsense, this dressing up for Friday nights the way we ourselves had had to dress—hair washed and curled, stiffened petticoats, our best dresses and our shoes stiff with "It."

Still, she herself dressed up, wore make-up. And tonight, for once, she was wearing her real pearl choker, her pearl-and-diamond earrings. This, I thought, she must have done for the American consul, who might understand how understated they were, and because the Majestic was catering. Usually, she refused to join in with other Jewish women dressed to the nines, women like Tanya Kaplan, with her pale, piggy eyes and short, bleached hair, her sparkling silver talons, and priceless twenty-two-carat custommade diamond-studded collar and matching shackle at the wrist that looked, Catherine and I agreed, like the surface of the moon. Catherine loved to watch Tanya Kaplan eyeing her own plastic bangles, or noticing her children's dirty feet and knees, their local Woolworths shorts.

She loved to have my mother notice, too. My mother, who saw nothing wrong with putting on her own bits and pieces of jewelry if the occasion arose—her diamond watch, the diamond clips she'd inherited from my father's mother, her sister's cast-off pearls—she, too, couldn't work out the point of Catherine's bangles and hoops, however mod they were, however much she'd paid for them at Gigi's. Or why, despite the fact that she'd *asked* Catherine— *begged* her, in fact—to see to it that the children dress properly for Shabbat, *still* they came down to dinner, week after week, looking like poor whites. It was perverted, she said. If Catherine wouldn't consider her own feelings, she could at least consider Dad's.

Perhaps Catherine did consider Dad's feelings, and perhaps she didn't. Whatever the case, every Friday night, when the children came up to kiss him goodbye during pudding, he would look up, smiling nervously, and ask Catherine, "What's this? Where are these rascals going to on Friday night?" The first time, she would pretend not to hear, so that he'd have to ask again. And, finally, she'd sigh, and look up, and say, "Out." Or, "To a party." Then she'd turn back to the puddings with a real smile, a smile that, for a moment, seemed to have malice in it. A frightening smile to see.

"Jeffrey," I said, "have you heard of someone called Krishnah Chowdree?"

"What!" he cried, winking at the Chief, leaning forwards, grinning as if I'd made a joke. "Pop!" he shouted to my father. "Hear that? Better watch out for your younger daughter!"

But my father was concentrating on lining up his pills on the tablecloth in front of him, four in all. And then, with quiet ceremony, swallowing them one by one.

"Chief," said Catherine, "fruit salad and ice cream? Apple Charlotte? A bit of each?"

The Chief raised his hands. "No, no," he said, "just an apple. An apple is all I want, thank you very much. Excuse me," he said, turning to me, "but have you met this Mr. Chowdree?"

"They should have hung him!" Nathan screeched.

Catherine caught my eye. We smiled.

"Hanged," I said to Nathan.

"*Ja!*" Nathan shouted. "After the trouble he stirred up for Jeff and I, we should have hung him personally."

"Hanged," I repeated. "Jeffrey and *me.*"

Tanya nudged him. "She's chaffing you, Naty. She means the *word.*"

"What word?"

A waiter arrived with a silver tray on which were arranged an apple on a plate, a fruit knife and fork, a fingerbowl.

Lynn Freed

"Who's Krishnah Chowdree, for God's sake?" Julian asked me.

"A man I met at a party," I said. "He's just out of detention, wrote a book that they banned here. But he got it published overseas as a matter of fact." Despite myself, I felt important delivering this information. Superior. Daring by association. "Highly educated, articulate, a sort of local Trotsky."

"Trotsky!" Jeffrey cried. "Hear that, Catherine? Your sister goes to parties with troublemakers! Next thing she'll be putting ideas into *your* head!" He grinned, but his eyebrows twitched; the colour was high in his cheeks. Ideas had always discomfited Jeffrey. So had education. As a man who had never made it through the university, he suffered disdain, suspicion, envy, and respect for those who knew things only in theory as he put it.

My father signalled to me through the centrepiece. "Time for us to be on our bicycles, Chopsticks," he said. "Would you go round and fetch the car, please?"

"Just a minute, Pops," Jeffrey said. "Can you hang on five minutes? I want to find out about this Trotsky—"

But I pushed back my chair and stood up. Suddenly, all at once, I was mad to leave, to get back to the maisonette and phone Hugh. I wanted him to come in and fetch me now, immediately. I knew that he would, he had said that he would fetch me day or night, any time I wished. I could phone him at the Estates, at the bungalow, at the club. Until now, I'd been shy to do so. And I'd liked to drive out there myself, to be able to leave whenever I wished. Standing at Catherine's table, however, with the coffee tray rattling down the passage towards the lounge, considering the scene that was to follow—the tin of Nescafé ensconced in its silver container, Catherine poised at the spout of the giant thermos— "Aunty Irma, white? Black?"—and then the dish of sweets handed round, the belches of the old and deaf, their drivers summoned from the kitchen, the dogs roaring into action overhead, the evening over—standing there, leaving Catherine to all of this, I couldn't imagine ever wishing to leave the bungalow again.

The Chief stood up too, and bowed to me, and clasped my hand. "Next time," he said, "I hope to hear you're back for good."

"Why're we leaving before coffee?" my mother demanded. "Roger! Won't it look odd if we leave before coffee?"

46

My father ignored her, signalled me to go for the car.

"Hey!" Mrs. Kuperstein cried out, pointing at the Chief, who was now back at his apple.

Jeffrey rose in his chair. "Catherine!" he called out. "Aunty Irma!"

But it was too late to stop her. Somehow, Mrs. Kuperstein had everyone's attention, mine too. "Funny thing!" she said, still pointing one plump, claw-tipped finger at the Chief. "*My* houseboy likes apples too!"

# 5

I had been hearing them without paying attention for some time. A looping, melancholy shriek, and then another. And now, there they came in a pair, their necks held high, and treading deliberately, like dancers. One peacock stopped, as if on cue, and spread its feathers for us, catching the afternoon sun.

I went to the edge of the verandah and stood in the shade of the Beaumontia. Hugh came up behind me. He wore his usual uniform of leisure—khaki shorts, white shirt, long socks, suede shoes.

"They are the birds of Juno," he said, leaning over the verandah wall and wailing at them in a perfect imitation. The peacocks turned to look at us, and then stalked off in single file into the wild bananas.

The afternoon was brilliant and warm. At this hour, my parents would be sleeping, their heads lolled back, their mouths open, snoring. Clive would be snoring too, with the sun not yet up, sirens whining, and the wind cutting in sharp and chill off the Hudson.

Perhaps my mother was right. Perhaps I *had* lost touch with my common sense. Or perhaps my common sense had been overwhelmed by the narcotic of smells and sounds out here—the salt and damp and rot in everything, the Indian at the local supply store wiping off a mango and holding it out—"See, madam? Stringless! Just take a look, madam!" Or perhaps, after all, I still wore the false immunity of a tourist. Out of touch with normal caution. Uninvolved.

"You're almost obscured in the shadow," Hugh said, smiling or not smiling, I could never tell which.

He ran his hand down my cheek, around the oval of my face,

brushed it lightly down the inside of my arm. I was thinner than usual, and dark from the sun, which emphasized the angles of my face, my nose, the hollows of my eyes. I used no make-up here, and wore my hair braided into a plait down my back.

"Would you consider staying on?" he asked. "Would it be unbearably awkward to arrange?"

I closed my eyes, my head light from the gin and from the heat, from the effect of his touch, and the courtliness of his request. I had three weeks left—seven, if I cooked up some excuse to extend my ticket to its limit.

"I found some splendid stuff in the hall kist the other day," he said.

"What kind of stuff?"

He held out a hand and lead me through the lounge and along the passage to the second bedroom. It was small and close in there, and smelled of camphor and coir matting. The curtains were drawn, their lining perished into threads and hanging down like lace. High in the corners, lizards darted in the shadows. Faded botanical watercolours hung on the walls. A mahogany bed, pushed into a corner, was piled with folded linen, blankets, tablecloths, and ironing.

Hugh lifted something from one of the piles and held it to the light. It was a sort of pantaloon, ballooning from the waist, with the leggings caught in a cuff at the ankles, and mother-of-pearl buttons. The material was flimsy, chiffon perhaps, with gold or silver thread running through it.

I watched him, waiting. If this man drove twenty-five kilometers into town to fetch me in the middle of the night, brought me peacocks, asked me to stay on, dressed me up in the garments of his great-grandfather's mistress, and then made love to me—how close was this to love? I had no measure, nothing to go on except literature, or the contortions of my own stomach and heart. Watching him stroke the cloth, gather it up, and then let it fall again, seeing the fine hairs along his arm, and then the hand itself, the nub of it, the way its three fingers curled so elegantly into the palm—I understood, quite suddenly, that, in fact, I wanted nothing more from him than what I had already.

He settled into the arm chair, observing me undress. I stepped into the pantaloons, found the bolero, struck a pose, and smiled. "Like this?" I asked. But I knew what he wanted to see. In fact, under his steady smiling gaze, I thrilled to the performance itself. Clothes on, clothes off—I went over to sit on his lap, began to unbutton his shirt.

"There's another one I wanted you to try on," he murmured, slipping the bolero off my shoulders, reaching behind me for the tie of the pantaloons.

I lifted his crippled hand, kissed its palm. "Tell me what happened," I whispered.

Suddenly, he grabbed my wrists and slid me off his lap. "Christ!" he said, standing up.

And then I heard it too—a woman's screams, a man shouting.

"Bloody *hell!*" He made for the door, his shirt flapping wide.

By the time I'd dressed and reached the kitchen, the shouting had subsided. A pot of samp and beans hissed and bubbled on the stove. There were voices in the backyard—Hugh's, an African man's, and Regina weeping. I heard Hugh's lighter click and flash, and walked back into the lounge, out onto the verandah.

"Bloody *impossible!*" Hugh said, following close behind. "Bloody *hell!*" He stubbed out his cigarette in a large copper ashtray.

"What happened?" I asked. I'd watched my mother and then Catherine coping with servants fighting, servants sick, servants pregnant. Dishing out aspirin from the locked cupboard, telling them this was the last time, and had they understood? But I lacked the necessary irritation. I'd been away too long.

He looked at me, his face florid with anger. "Never, my dear, try to visit enlightenment upon the tribal prerogatives of others." His fingers drummed away at the chair. "The woman has six or seven children already—she's a grandmother, in fact, worn out, through and through." He looked at me as if that was that.

"So?"

"It was at *her* request, mind you! I should have known better, of course. But she lied. She said she had his blessing. So now I have to cope with deputations of head men coming to me with their complaints. And this benighted husband of hers weaving his way here night after night, drunk as a lord, with concoctions from the sangoma to make the poor woman fertile again. No doubt he was weaving his way here when you nicked him that first night."

I sat up. "*What?*"

He shrugged, reached into his shirt pocket for his cigarette case.

"*What?*" I repeated, high and shrill. "Why didn't you *tell* me?" I demanded, hearing my mother in my voice. "Why didn't you tell me I'd actually *hit* someone?"

His eyebrows shot up. He seemed to smile. "Darling," he said, "he wasn't badly hurt. He's a lucky bugger. And it wasn't your fault. He ran off because the bloody police have caught him here several times already after curfew. And every time, I've bailed him out. Once more, and they'll take away his pass."

He held up his hand, ran a fingertip along the jagged scars, across the stumps. "A monkey mauled me as a child," he said. He lifted the hair off his forehead to show me a pink slash along his scalp. "See here? And here? I was lucky too, wasn't I?"

. . .

One evening, two years earlier, Clive announced that we were not going to be able to have children. He recited the history of his shrunken testicle, three zero sperm counts, no motile sperm.

Zero sperm counts? Motile sperm? I asked him to explain.

"I didn't want to think about it before!" he shouted. He pushed back his chair, his napkin tucked into his belt. "I don't want anyone to hear about this," he said. "No one, not even Catherine, do you understand?"

I nodded. I didn't argue with his right to secrecy. Nor even with his gift of deciding what not to think about. It was my own failure that I felt keenly—the fraud of my good fortune after all.

"What are we going to do?" I asked. What was to become of my life, I wanted to know? Without love, without the baggage of love? Three afternoons a week, I stood in a draughty classroom introducing engineering students to literature. Until today, it had seemed like a temporary arrangement.

"I want to go home," I said.

Clive tapped out two pellets of saccharine and dropped them into *his coffee. He never wanted to go home, not even for a visit. In fact, he objected to the word itself. Home. He wanted me to feel at home with him, in America. He was jealous of my family, and quite rightly so. He understood that I was more theirs than his, just as I was more his than any other man's. My going home felt to him like triumph, with himself the victim. Year after year, me singing and dancing back to see my family.*

*"I think we should go to Mexico," he said. "A week away might do you good."*

. . .

Regina crashed around the antique kitchen. She seemed to resent my presence at the bungalow. When I went in to order tea, she stood her ground in silence, lifting each piece of curried fish with her fingers onto an old, chipped platter.

"Did you make scones?" I asked.

"I'm too old now, madam," she grumbled, picking out the peppercorns and bay leaves and then wetting the edge of the dishcloth to wipe the sauce from the tip of the platter.

The phone rang. I heard Hugh laugh. Outside, her children ran and shouted in the backyard.

"How old are the children?" I asked.

"Some four year, some six year."

I gave up and went back to the lounge.

"That was Edwina," said Hugh. "She and Krishnah are coming for supper."

Thunder began to break for the afternoon storm. The wind picked up.

"Why Krishnah?" I asked.

He leaned towards me in the gloom. One of the peacocks wailed. The doors and windows rattled. "Because Krishnah is a friend, a very good friend. I've known him since he was a boy, you know. In a way, I feel responsible for what he's become—not just the obvious triumphs and tribulations, but the *moral* fibre of the man. He could have left, you know, he could have taken the exit permit and left to join the ragtag and bobtail of exiles in London—when his book came out there, and he wanted to go, that's when they took away his passport—but he stayed. You have to hand him that, you know. Ruth, I want you to like him. Please give him a chance."

I tried out a smile on him, a half smile, as I had tried on the clothes in the spare room.

"You are the colour of night," he said, holding out a hand for me to join him on the couch. "Come here."

But I stayed where I was. I wanted to look at him face to face, to see him as I'd seen him that first time, at Edwina's. I couldn't. Once I had known him here, I could only know him as I knew him now—as a character in a dream, someone who would say, "You are the colour of the night," and then vanish into shadow—while I, observing it all as if through the glass of sleep, was happy, unsurprised, player and audience both.

# 6

"Please explain to me," Edwina said, smiling, "why so many Jews leave the country."

She had changed in eight years, become a beauty in her motherhood. With her light hair pinned up carelessly, a flowered print sundress, local sandals, silver bangles clacking up and down her arm, she had the sort of easy, long-boned elegance that fitted perfectly on the verandah of the bungalow.

"My dear," said Krishnah, throwing a peach pip into the garden, "you have simply to consider history."

Edwina laughed, flickering the tip of her tongue across her upper lip. She made no secret now of the fact that her father had changed his name from Slomovitz to Sloane. For a while, after we left school, she'd thought of changing it back again, of becoming a Jew herself. But she'd come up against the new American rabbi demanding ritual baths for women and years of Talmudic study. So, she'd given up, and taken up causes instead—soup kitchens, family-planning clinics, part-time lecturing at the Indian University. And then she'd met Dickie Gibson, and married him, and gone to live in the hills. Now her own daughters were growing up just as she had, she'd told me—neither fish nor fowl. One was already at Rangston, singing "Away in a Manger" and "All Things Bright and Beautiful."

"Do you think it's self-preservation that makes Jews flee a country like this," she asked, "or just that the roots don't go so deep?"

"You're mouthing the prejudices of your jolly hockey-sticks set!" Krishnah snapped. "How far back do you think your mother's roots stretch? The relief of Ladysmith? The Royal Country Club? Ha! Your father, of course, doesn't qualify 'root-wise,' as you Americans would say, hey?" He looked at me, his lips pursed into an expression of triumph. But the effect was marred by the thrust of his lower jaw, giving him the look of a petulant child.

Edwina laughed. "You silly old tart! What are you getting so hot under the collar about?"

"Ugh!" he waved her away with a hand. "Leave me out of your boring chatter!"

I watched him fold himself away from her, and remembered what Hugh had said about the smallness of Krishnah's life, its meanness. To me, however, Krishnah was small and mean himself. I couldn't forgive him as everyone else seemed to do.

"If you're thinking about Indians," Edwina persisted, "it's different. They've never had a diaspora."

Krishnah grasped the arms of his chair and sat forwards. "Because we've never been exiled! So *what*?"

"Keep your hair on, old boy!" Hugh said. He turned to Edwina. "What do you say about Jews exiled from this country?" he asked. "Ditto the Indians? Where do they all belong? Tel Aviv? Bombay? Johannesburg?"

"They belong *here*, of course!" she cried. "But that's not the *point*—"

I settled back while they argued on, the three of them, about Jews and Indians, exile and diaspora. The lights of ships sparkled on the sea, a warm wind blew, the Beaumontia perfumed the air.

Regina came to stand in the doorway. "Master, telephone for Master."

"Planning to marry Hugh, Miss America?" Krishnah asked, as soon as Hugh was gone. "I think you'd adjust quite nicely to reigning over the relics of the Stillington Estates. Still," he sighed, "we'd better face facts. He'll never marry a Jew."

"Well, he's a stupid fool!" Edwina cried. "Ruth," she said, "ignore him. He's just jealous. He wants Hugh for himself." She smiled at Krishnah, but it was more like a glare, a warning.

Krishnah ran his fingers through his hair. "Just consider what he'd be getting into with a Jewish wife," he said. "The I.U.A., the P.L.O., the whole catastrophe! Anyway, I think he'd make a dreadful husband. He's like Tolstoy, wed to peasant reform."

"Jealous, jealous, jealous!" Edwina sang.

I laughed, but I wanted to leave, and I knew I couldn't; I didn't have the car. "Anyway," I said, "I'm married already."

"So what?" he snapped. "You're in good company. Have a husband in each country. Isn't that the idea?"

I looked over his head, out to sea, trying to hold my smile. Perhaps Hugh was right. What Krishnah hated in me was just this: the choices I seemed to have, even in men. If he'd left, he couldn't have come back. And the choice remained. I understood all this. And yet I also knew my understanding was nothing to him. Less than nothing, it was an irritant, as I was an irritant to him. Whatever I said would only make things worse.

"That was the American consul," Hugh announced from the doorway. "Anyone for tennis tomorrow?"

"*Everyone*'s playing tennis with the American consul these days!" said Krishnah. "It's become so *chic* since people discovered that tennis is the path to green card."

"Want to play?" Hugh asked. "I already accepted for you. At the Estates."

Krishnah frowned, pretending to consider, but I was surprised to see that he was really rather pleased. Edwina watched him too. She stretched a hand over and touched his arm. "Play," she coaxed softly, "it's a good idea."

He looked at her, sulking.

"We'll all come, shall we?" she suggested. "Ruth, let's go and watch!"

"I met the consul the other night," I offered, not wanting to say yes or no. "He's a Jew."

Hugh laughed. "You Jews and your nonsequiturs! It really is quite comic!"

. . .

*Feeling alien among American Jews had made Clive and me less alien to each other. "High Holy Day" was a term we both found hilarious. We also laughed at the price of the tickets, at temples that looked like churches, at organs, and choirs, and responsive reading in English. And, even though I myself had never read Hebrew well enough to follow the services intelligently at home, I liked to think—as I stood silently among American Jews, missing home on* purpose—that what mattered to me was to have things properly done.

One year, Clive announced that the academic community were putting together their own High Holy Day services. They had rented the chapel of a local Catholic university, he said. And it was free. Why didn't we try it out on Yom Kippur?

•  •  •

Indian summer was late that year. At the door of the chapel, a girl in a peasant skirt and blouse handed us a mimeographed booklet. Inside, it was already hot and close. Children ran about, their cries echoing around the rotunda. Some had discovered the kneelers and fought over pulling them out or pushing them in again. Others played under the white sheeting that cloaked the statuary and icons around the walls and in front of the altar. The morning sun shone full through a double-storey stained-glass depiction of Christ on the cross.

"Here," Clive said, nudging me into a pew near the back.

Tik-tik. "One, two—can you hear me?" A bearded man in a ponytail and embroidered shirt stood at the microphone. Behind him, on the steps of the altar, the young woman who had been handing out the booklets picked out a few phrases on an electric guitar.

I nudged Clive and winked. But he was concentrating on the booklet. So I looked too. It was full of incantations and prayers transliterated from Hebrew into English. Shma Yees-ro-ail, Adonai elo-hay-noo, Adonai egh-ud.

"Would the congregation please rise?"

We rose. Children stopped in fright, searching out their parents.

The bearded man introduced himself as a rabbi and a therapist. The girl, he said, had spent several years on a kibbutz. This was not to be a traditional service. Anyone who wished was welcome to join in at any time.

The service began with a folk version of the Kol Nidrei, accompanied by the girl on the guitar. People hummed along. We stood up, sat down, read what was printed in the booklet. By the time the sermon began, it was unbearably hot. People shuffled and flapped their booklets around their faces. I closed my eyes.

A great deal of misunderstanding had arisen between Gentile and

Lynn Freed

*Jew, the therapist explained, because of misunderstanding about the
meaning of Jewish vows. According to the Talmud, he said, these
were* not *the vows made between man and man (by which he was to
be taken to mean also woman and woman, or man and woman); they
were those between man or woman, and God the Almighty—*

*I sat up. Suddenly I felt lucky to be so far away from home, so free.
I was thrilled to be a stranger in such a mad, strange place. I picked
up Clive's hand and kissed it on the palm. "Let's go out for lunch,"
I whispered.*

*"Please turn to page five—"*

*The guitar struck up again, the girl began to sing. But then,
suddenly, there was a thud, a crack, a twang of guitar strings rever-
berating through the loudspeakers. People turned to each other. Some
stood up to look.*

*Clive pulled his hand away. "What's going on?" he asked.*

*"Excuse me! People!" the therapist shouted. He retrieved the mi-
crophone from the floor. "Our singer has fainted," he announced. "Is
there a doctor in the congregation?"*

*"Should I go up?" Clive hovered between staying and going. As a
physiologist, he seemed to miss the real drama of medicine, even a
fainting. "Should I go?" he asked again.*

*"It's probably the heat," I said.*

*But he pointed to the aisles. On both sides of us, men in suits were
storming to the front. "Hey! There goes old Feinsinger!" he cried.
"What's old Feinsinger going up for? He's in OB-GYN! Should I—"*

*"Thank you! Thank you!" the rabbi called out. "We're O.K. now.
Thank you, doctors! Would you all please return to your seats? We
need some air up here! Thank you! Thank you, doctors, for all your
help!"*

• • •

"Krishnah's father ran a newspaper, a good one, that the government kept closing down," Hugh said.

We sat in the dark, on the verandah. The night was loud with
bats and crickets, the crash of surf, an animal whooping in the
bush.

"Extraordinarily intelligent chap, the father," he added, "well
educated, not the usual shrill voice of protest, I assure you. They

58

live just over the hill, very modestly, of course. There's a rich brother in town—the Bombay Bazaar group. But they're estranged—the brothers, I mean."

I heard him without listening, as if I knew the story already.

"As far as I'm concerned," he went on, "the last luxury is intelligence. Come the revolution, I shall be sad to see it used up as fuel for dogma."

Whatever he was talking about, the real subject, I knew, was Krishnah. "I don't know about tomorrow," I said. "I should go back to town, I think."

He lifted my hand and kissed me on the wrist. "Spend another day with me. Let me take you back on Monday morning. Will you allow me that?"

I heard Regina moving around in the kitchen, banging pots, running water. "She can't stand him either, you know," I said. "I've hardly seen her like that with anyone but me."

He returned my hand to my lap. "She's jealous of you, surely that's obvious? And she hates coolies." He spat the word at me, then plucked a cigarette from the pack in his pocket, hung it between his lips. His face flared livid with the flash of his lighter. He must have been a fierce father, I thought, wanting his own way just as I wanted mine.

"That bloody husband of hers is back," he said. "I saw him skulking behind the hedge when Krishnah was leaving. Hopeless, you know, quite hopeless to try to make sense of this country. But," he added, slapping his hands onto his knees, "it's been a 'learning experience,' as you Americans would say."

He stood up and I stood too. He often used America to scold me, everyone did. But it had lost its bite. In fact, I wondered now whether he, too, weren't a bit jealous. As if America were a lover not quite left behind. I thought he was. He frowned at me, drew deeply on his cigarette, then turned away without a word. I followed him into the lounge, watched him cut across to the kitchen, closing the door behind him.

For a while, I stood there in the dark, listening to their voices lilting and sinking into the sighs and clicks of Zulu. Then I slipped off my sandals, unzipped my sundress, and let it fall around my feet. I wore no underwear. Hugh preferred me that way. Or women that way, probably women. I didn't care. The women he had had were not interesting to me, not even his Belgian anthropologist. She was everywhere in the bungalow—a postcard from Bruges marking the place in a book, a madeleine tin in the kitchen. I took no pleasure from the fact that Regina's madeleines were hard and dry. Even if she'd made them moist, golden, perfect—even if Hugh's eyes clouded when he took a bite—it would have made no difference to me. My own jealousy—the demon, the incubus, the doppelganger of my marriage—had abandoned me all at once out here, gone away.

I sank onto the couch and linked my hands behind my head, crooked one knee. Hugh never sulked. When he came out, he'd already have forgotten about Krishnah. He'd stand a moment in the doorway, waiting for his eyes to adjust to the dark. "Ruth?" he'd say softly. And I'd say nothing. Not to provoke him, but because I liked to hear him call my name again, and to watch him plunge his hands into his pockets, stalk into the room, stop and smile when he found me there. I stroked the hair in my armpit. Already it was growing sleek and black. He would stroke it too, nuzzle me like a horse. Perhaps he'd fetch a chair and ask me to stand on it, or to come back out onto the verandah with him. At times like this, his voice would be deep and rich. "Lovely, lovely woman," he'd say. "Ruth, Ruth, Ruth."

The kitchen door opened and closed. "Ruth?" Hugh said, peering into the room. "Darling, are you there?" I could hear him breathing. "Ruth?" he said again. And then he saw me, and I saw a gleam of teeth, felt him thud across the matting towards me.

# 7

We drove along the coastal road in silence. A dense haze obscured the horizon. I rolled down the window and hung my head out into the soft, hot wind.

Hugh tapped my thigh. "If you're feeling the least awkward about this," he shouted, "I want you to know that none of my family will be at the Estates today."

I smiled up at the sky, sat up again. It was lovely, after all, to be driving off with him on a Sunday afternoon. Lovely to see him in his tennis togs and sunglasses, steering deftly with three fingers, his good hand resting on my thigh.

"Krishnah's coming under his own steam," he said. "You and Edwina could sit on the verandah of the clubhouse, or up at the main house, whichever you prefer. Dickie Gibson's coming as the fourth."

"And Mrs. American consul?"

He shook his head. "Can't come."

We turned in through the cane and wound towards the thruway, under it, up into the hills on the other side. The road cut around Indian villages, crisscrossed railway tracks, higher and higher. Finally, we stopped at a pair of large, black, wrought-iron gates, with a gatehouse on one side, and a grizzled black watchman asleep in there.

Hugh tapped the hooter and the watchman jumped, grinned, lumbered for the gates, and pushed them open.

Inside, the driveway meandered between flowering jacarandas, carpet lawns, and flower beds, a lily pond, a stream with weeping willows along its banks, up towards a house at the top of the hill.

"Looks as if we're the first," Hugh said, pulling up the brake.

It was a large, rambling, one-storey house, built in the old colonial style—with white wrought-iron fretwork, and a red corrugated iron roof. Enormous French doors and sash windows in varnished teak opened onto a deep verandah all around, built to keep the house cool in the hot wet season. Flowering Cape chestnuts shaded the north side from the sun. There was a stand of mango trees too, some avocados, a few pawpaws.

I glanced at the house as we walked past. Even though I knew no one was there, a wicker swing seat on the verandah, a curtain whuffing in the breeze made me uneasy.

He walked to the crest of the hill and stopped. "There," he said, pointing down into the valley. He laid his racquet on the grass and sat down beside it. I sat down too.

Terraced lawns fell away from the house, down to two clay tennis courts below, and a whitewashed thatched clubhouse. Beyond that, the property was wild, stretching all the way down to a river, which ran full and brown from the summer rains. On the other side, the hills began their corrugations—green, blue, gold. Dense bush shaded the folds; smoke rose here and there from brown patches of habitation; a rooster crowed; a church bell rang.

I turned back to look the other way, the way we'd come, over the fields of cane undulating down to the sea. I had never seen both the hills and the sea from one place before. Hugh watched me watching and pulled out a cigarette.

I had no idea how the new sugar conglomerate worked, how the Stillington Estates had dwindled. But I understood now that what he had brought me to see from up here was what had once been his. I knew that he had grown up in the main house of the Estates. Then he'd inhabited one of the other houses there with his wife and sons, gone out to the bungalow only for the odd weekend on his own. His wife had detested the bungalow, and she'd been restive at the Estates. She'd wanted to live in town, where she was at home with the country-club set, with the races, with other women's husbands.

"Where does Regina's husband stay?" I asked.

He gestured over the roof of the house, beyond the stand of trees. "Down on the other side, in the old barracks. I should take you down there one day. I've had the people from the mission station teaching them how to plant vegetable gardens and keep chickens. Still, without the wives and families, the buggers take the stuff to market and sell it. Can't blame them; there it is."

A car crunched to a halt in the driveway. A car door slammed.

"Hello, everybody!" Edwina came around the corner with a tall, blond man behind her.

Hugh leapt to his feet. "Edwina! Dickie!" He held out a hand. "Ruth, this is Dickie Gibson. Dickie, Ruth Frank."

Dickie stopped and cocked his head at me. "Didn't I see you at the club the other night?"

I shook my head. "Oh no," I said, "I haven't been there since Edwina took me when we were in school."

"I don't remember taking you, Ruth!" she cried.

But I did. I remembered standing in the queue for the Sunday buffet under the eyes of the members. I remembered treading lightly into the pool too, as if they would go after my tracks with a bucket and brush. And, after that, I'd noticed the same lightness in the movements of servants as they climbed into our cars, or sat on our chairs, or drank from our glasses.

"Oh, you should go," said Dickie. "The whole *place* has been tarted up. And the food's *so* much better than it was! No more Welsh rarebit sort of thing."

I looked from him to Edwina. They were as obvious a pair as Clive and I were, and as odd.

"Let me take you to lunch at the club on Wednesday," she suggested, winding her fingers absentmindedly into a strand of well-worn pearls. "You'll see some of the old girls—Pru Lambert, Fiona Holly, all still exactly the same, might I say."

I shook my head. "I feel invisible there," I lied.

"*Invisible!*" said Dickie. "That's a new one on me." He stared up into the sky, as if there were no limits to his visibility. "Think they'll arrive before the rain, Hugh, old boy? What about a game of singles while we wait?"

· · ·

"Tell me about Hugh!" Edwina purred.

We had moved into the lounge, which was large and elegant, full of unrelated objects in comfortable harmony. Two huge old

floral couches flanked the fireplace. Persian carpets in muted colours lay here and there on the polished wood floor. A grand piano
stood in one corner. On the tables and the mantelpiece were an
old silver cigarette box, a Georgian tea caddy, a candle snuffer.
And everywhere were silver bowls of garden flowers, loosely arranged and lush.

I shrugged. I didn't want to talk to Edwina about Hugh. Catherine, I thought, must feel like this when women asked her impertinent questions about her life. It was odd, for once, to be
playing the same part as she. "Who lives here?" I asked, to change
the subject.

"Didn't Hugh tell you? No one lives here anymore. The sugar
barons use it for their meetings, weekends, that sort of thing.
That's why it's so well kept up." She twisted the pearls into a rope.
"Tell me," she said again. "What are you going to do?"

"I don't know."

Suddenly, she leaned across the couch and grabbed my hand,
held it tight between her palms. "You probably know about me,"
she said. She took a breath, as if she'd continue, but then she
swallowed, and bit her lip, and looked at her watch. "Hugh probably told you."

I shook my head. What Hugh had told me was that she'd come
into her own on D. H. Lawrence at 'varsity. A few glasses of wine,
he'd said, and she'd be rolling about on the grass or on the beach
with one man or another, invoking the moon and God knows what
else. Dickie didn't seem to notice.

She folded her arms and sighed. "Hugh's the only real gentle-
man I know," she said. "You're lucky."

People had always told me I was lucky. It was an easy thing to
say—you're lucky—easy to believe. Certainly, I had met Hugh
through Edwina, and now, because of her, I'd found him again.
But still, my luck was my own. I didn't want to sabotage it by
discussing it with her.

"Why don't you leave Dickie?" I asked.

She frowned at me, smiled to see if I were joking.

"I mean, at some point—"

Her eyes watered over, her lip quivered. "*What* point?"

I stared at her, considering the circles and circles of deception—women and men deceiving and deceived. It was hard to find an end to it, or a beginning.

Outside, a car drew up.

"*Ecce homo!*" Hugh called out from the garden.

Edwina leapt to her feet, turned to wait for me, plunged off anyway, out through the French doors.

"At bloody last!" said Dickie. "We came back up to phone you. Hey, where'd you go? Pretoria?"

Krishnah came smiling up the steps of the verandah, carrying a bunch of marigolds tied up with newspaper and string. "Listen," he said to Dickie, "can you siphon me some petrol? I forgot it's Sunday." His black eyes flickered from Hugh to me, then flew to Edwina, down to the marigolds he held out to her.

"Krishnah!" she cried. "Oh, how lovely! Marigolds!" She held them to her face, but marigolds were hardly her kind of flowers. They needed dark skin and oiled black hair. She couldn't even plunge her nose into them; they smelled acrid, awful.

He smiled softly at her. "My mother grows them. They're left over from Divali."

I stared at her, and remembered the evening they'd come to dinner at the bungalow. Her tongue curling out of her mouth at him, her legs crossed and recrossed. And the argument that was more like a quarrel, a lover's quarrel. Krishnah! How could she, even she, lover of all men, welcome the spidery fingers of such a man around her breasts, that voice in her ear, those teeth, that tongue?

Another car drew up and the American consul leapt out in Bermuda shorts, a bright green polo shirt. "Sorry, guys," he said, "I got lost!"

"Murray!" Hugh cried. "Just in time for tea."

• • •

"I met you at my sister's," I said to Murray. We sat under the thatch of the clubhouse verandah, Edwina pouring the tea.

Murray pursed his lips and nodded sagely, a practised gesture. But I saw him taking in my muslin skirt, plain sandals, my hair hanging loose around my shoulders. He was unable to place me. At Catherine's, to please my mother, I'd put on make-up, worn a good dress and heels, and done my hair up.

"Your name came up there," I said to Krishnah. "It electrified the whole dinner table."

Krishnah gave one of his barking laughs. "Not again!" he cried.

"*Got it!*" the consul cried. "The Goldmans! You were next to Chief Sibusi, you and another guy! Both of you live in the States!"

Krishnah leaned forward carefully, rested his elbows on his knees. "*Where* did my name come up?" he asked.

"Jeffrey Goldman!" the consul cried. He beamed at me. "*Gorgeous* home! *Great* folks!"

"Goldman!" Krishnah clamped his jaws together and sat back to stare at me. "Your brother? And the Chief was there, too?" he said, "How cosy!"

I flushed. "He's my brother-in-*law*." I tried sipping my tea, lifting my face to breathe in the lovely sweetness of the thatch, but still he wouldn't look away.

"Didn't you put it together until now?" Hugh asked. "Ruth's connection with the gang?"

Gang! I laughed. I loved the word. Jeffrey, with his rules of the game, his moral responsibility, his principles of leadership—the maxims with which he *thought* he ruled his family and his empire—Jeffrey as Al Capone. Long ago, Catherine had pointed out to me that it was in Jeffrey's nose for people that his real talent lay. He knew whom to trust for his own purposes, whom to look out for. Seldom, she said, had he ever been proved wrong.

"Goldman has just been put up for the club," Dickie offered.

"What?" I said.

"What?" said Edwina. Her tongue was out again, moving languidly along her lower lip.

"Well, he's an old boy of St. Andrews," Dickie said. "He's on the city council."

"Our kind of Jew," Krishnah sneered.

I smiled at him, and, this time, he seemed to begin to smile back. I noticed that his thighs and calves were muscled, sinewy, and then that he was smiling not at me, but at Edwina, who sat slightly behind me. She'd placed a hand on my shoulder, perhaps as a signal to him. And I sat between them, smiling at nothing.

"Another set?" Hugh asked.

The men stood up at once. Krishnah flittered his fingers in a wave to Edwina and me. "Bye, gang," he said.

. . .

As we turned off the freeway into the cane fields, I noticed Hugh glancing often into the rearview mirror.

"We're being followed," he said. "I'll do all the talking."

I pulled down the visor and looked into the mirror. Indeed, there was a car behind us. If we slowed down, it slowed down too. When we sped through the hotel gates and pulled in under the front canopy, it stopped at the entrance to the parking lot. A man got out and came over to us. He was thickset, blond, in a shirt and tie and a handmade, sleeveless cardigan.

"Mr. Stillington?" he bent over, looked in through the car window.

"Mr. Coetzee, good evening."

"Good evening, sir." He pulled a notebook and pen from his pocket.

Two Indian waiters came to stare at us through the glass of the front door.

"May I ask you, Mr. Stillington, from where you're coming?"

"Tennis."

The man smiled a little, cleared his throat. "But *where,* Mr. Stillington?"

"At the Estates, Mr. Coetzee."

"And the lady?" He rested both hands against the top of the car and peered in.

"On what authority—" Hugh began.

The man held a palm out to Hugh. A badge caught the light.

"Miss Frank is my guest. She is a visitor from America. She was not playing tennis."

The pulse already started in my throat. I swallowed. I had never come up against anything like this on all my visits home, never. I'd read about it, I'd talked about it, God knows. But I'd never had it happen to me. And yet what had happened? What had I done? What could they do to me? Throw me out? Send me back to Clive?

"Are either of you people acquainted with Mr. Krishnah Chowdree?"

I looked at Hugh, stared at him, willing him to hand over Krishnah if that's what it took for them to leave us alone.

"We are," Hugh said.

"And when is the last time that you saw Mr. Chowdree?"

Hugh stared up at the roof of the car, as if thinking up an answer. Today, I thought, today, today, today.

"Today," he said. "This afternoon."

"For what?"

"For what, Mr. Coetzee?" Hugh's voice was hard and cold and tight. "For tennis. Didn't I mention tennis?"

The man's face tightened too. "And how many people were playing tennis?" he asked.

"Four."

"Four, and Miss Frank here makes five."

"She wasn't with us. She was up at the house."

"Up at the house," the man repeated. He opened his notebook and wrote something down. "And who else, may I ask, was playing tennis with you and Mr. Krishnah Chowdree?"

"Mr. Murray Lutch, the American consul. And Mr. Richard Gibson."

"Ah."

I looked at Hugh, but he was black in the shadows. Motionless. If it came to it, I thought, if it came to a choice between Krishnah and me, I'd tell the man anything he wanted to know. I'd tell him about Edwina. What was she to me, anyway? What was Krishnah, for that matter? I agreed with Catherine. The whole bloody country could take a running jump.

"And Mrs. Gibson?" the man asked.

"Up at the house with Miss Frank," Hugh said.

I held my breath.

"*All* the time?"

Hugh nodded. "Indeed."

The man narrowed his eyes into the car for a few seconds. "All right," he said, drumming twice on the top of the car, "that's all for the moment."

"I thought he was after me," I babbled as soon as we were back on the road. "God, what a relief!" I leaned across and clung onto his arm, kissed it hard. It was damp and salty with sweat.

He glanced down at me. "What?" he said. "Why you?"

"I don't know. I thought they might take away my visa. God knows what."

He stared ahead silently, down the dark road.

"Tomorrow," he said, "after I drop you, I'd like you to go straight to 'varsity and find Edwina. Don't phone her—you know that."

"Their phone is tapped?"

"You can assume that."

"And tell her what?"

He pulled up at the gate and opened the door slightly. In the dim car light, he looked pale, not flushed, as I'd thought he would be. "You'll tell her what happened tonight, and to *lay off Krishnah. Stay way from him*! *I'll* speak to him. She could put him away for good, the bloody little fool! And for *what*? He despises her. Can't she see that he really despises her?" He got out and opened the gate, got in again, roared into the garage and cut the engine. "Decent of old Coetzee to warn me, I suppose," he said. "He's always been the most decent of the bunch."

# 8

Shopping still brought out the best in my mother. She was in her right mind in anticipation, miles from her first martini, even at ten o'clock in the morning.

We emerged from the parking garage onto Commerical Road, almost into the path of an Indian bus. The bus stopped, and the driver opened his window.

"No! No!" my mother cried. "Can't you see we're trying to *cross?*"

"You want to cross, you wait for the green light!" the driver shouted.

"Go on!" she shouted, waving an arm at him. "You see?" she said to me. "See how rude and cheeky they've got lately?" She shook her head. "Frankly, I don't think there's much of a future in this country, whatever they say. Hold on to your bag," she said, crossing the street and making for the short cut through Westbury Arcade. "Put it over your shoulder."

We walked out into Joubert Street and down towards Cottams, past the same old squat buildings in red brick, with white columns and arched porticoes and "Ainsley's" and "Bon Marché" and "Grenville's" spelled out in relief. The shop windows hadn't changed either. The same blond mannequins stood stiff and smiling. The same castles of shoes flanked the entrance to Grenville's—men's at the bottom, then two tiers of women's, and children's in a tiptoe circle at the top. Local stuff, my mother said, roughly made, badly cut.

She stopped at the entrance to Cottams, between two windows marked "France" and "England." "That's more like it," she said.

She had always shopped as if she were going to win a war.

The Bungalow

Behind the lists and strategies, the determined set of her mouth, lay the high excitement of a conquest. I'd noticed this in Catherine too, and in myself.

I looked around. Women walked past in pairs, white women in drip-dry dresses and white shoes stiff with polish. They carried large handbags and met for tea and anchovy toast at Grenville's. Black messengers in khaki uniforms buzzed past on Vespas. Black women, on their day off, peered into shop windows. And there were still beggars everywhere, black and Indian. An Indian woman clutching a baby to her bosom, cupped a hand out at us as we walked into the shop.

"Poor devil," my mother said, dropping a coin into her hand. "They borrow babies for this, you know," she said. "Don't imagine it's her own. But I've never seen what difference that makes. If they're hungry, they're hungry. It's a terrible tragedy."

I plunged after her down the aisle, past the haberdashery department and its knitting baskets and tea cosies and tapestry kits. A saleslady with a tight grey perm in a hair net came up to greet her. "We all miss your plays, you know, Mrs. Frank," she said, shaking her head. "Isn't it awful, the rubbish they're putting on these days?"

"Awful," my mother agreed. "Oh well," she sighed, "c'est la vie!"

She was her old self shopping, blacks or no blacks. "You know my husband had a mild heart attack? No? Well, he's better now, touch wood. Thanks to this one!" She turned to me and stroked my arm. "This is my younger daughter, from America. She brings a breath of fresh air into our lives! The house is alive again! So now we're off to find something for her to wear."

"Oh, Mrs. Frank," the woman said, dropping her voice, "you won't find the old selection anymore, you know. It's all for them now." She nodded in the direction of two black women fingering some skeins of wool. "Even in Better Dresses. Loud colours, you know," she whispered. "Isn't it awful?"

"Awful," my mother agreed, steering me towards the door. "That old duck knows what she's talking about," she said. "Been here since the year dot. Why don't we go straight to Gigi's instead of beating around the bush?"

71

Gigi was the real point of coming to town. She had started up from nothing, my mother liked to point out, a little Italian immigrant married to a stevedore. Then a crate had fallen on his head and killed him, and she'd taken up dressmaking to support herself and her child. And now look! A shop, every year two or three trips overseas. One thing you could say about Gigi, she knew her clientele. For women with Catherine's sort of money, she had the mod stuff and all that plastic paraphernalia to go with it. But for people like my mother, Gigi ordered classics. Take them up, let them down, they never dated.

My mother rang the bell and peered through the glass door, waved. "Good," she said, "we're the only ones here. She'll give me a discount for cash."

"Look at her!" Gigi exclaimed, standing back to admire me. "*Classique!*" she cried, gesturing for us to sit down. "A cup of coffee, Mrs. Frank? A cup of tea?" she asked. "Maureen! Bring two cups of tea for Mrs. Frank and Mrs.—so sorry—"

"Frank," I said. "I kept my name."

My mother shrugged. "It's the new generation," she said. "What can you do?" She looked at me and then at Gigi. "*Dr.* Frank," she said. "Did you know that, Gigi? This one's a doctor now."

"No! What kind?"

I clasped an elbow in each hand. This was not a pleasure. "Not a real doctor," I said. "The other kind."

"A professor," said my mother, accepting a cup of tea. "No sugar, thank you. This one was always clever, you know, Gigi. Prizes, scholarships—the lot!"

Gigi sized me up—denim skirt, T-shirt, brown sandals and enormous tooled-leather handbag. "How long now you have been living in America?"

"In America, eight years. Overseas, eleven."

"Poor mummy," she said.

"You said it! The daughter who is closest to me has to live farthest away! Well," my mother said with a sigh, "what have you got to show us, Gigi?"

Gigi bustled into action, opening cupboards and drawers, bringing out plastic packets with blouses and skirts, scarves to match,

even plastic bangles. Everything in the shop seemed to have something to match it, and all were in wild colours, pinks and reds and
greens and blues.

"Gigi," I said, "I prefer brown. Or white."

She stood back and folded her arms, cocked her head to one
side. I was sure she knew about me. Women passed all their gossip
through Gigi. Myrna Lipinsky was here all the time. Her parents
had a weekend house at Strawberry Beach now, just south of
Hugh's. And, although Hugh and I hadn't gone into town together
yet, her parents could have seen us in his car. Anyone could have.
They could have noticed me driving north over Umgeni Bridge,
listened to the gossip of their servants.

"After Christmas and New Year, I've got a shipment coming,"
Gigi said. "When are you leaving?"

"She's due to leave in a fortnight," my mother said quickly.
"Although she may stay on a little to see Roger on his feet again.
She can never bear to leave, you know, what with her friends out
here, and the gorgeous sunshine."

I smiled, although quite suddenly I felt in peril. For eight years,
I'd clung to my marriage as if to do otherwise were to open the
gates of hell. And now, here I was, the gates wide open. And here
was my mother, folded up on a couch, clutching her bag that
needed replacing, spending money on me so that my father
wouldn't have it to spend on another woman. So that she could say
to me in the car on the way home from dinner, or a show, "By Jove,
you look like *something* in that outfit! The men couldn't keep their
*eyes* off you!"

"Maureen!" Gigi shouted. "Bring me those new bikinis with the
pareos. Bring me the little linen frock, the beige one, and the little
scarf to match. Take that pink blouse out of the window."

"Not pink—" I said.

She smiled. "Try it for me," she crooned.

"Listen to Gigi," my mother said. "She knows what she's talking about. Darling!" she said, peering forward suddenly. "Come
here!" she whispered.

She clutched for my hand, lifted it up. "Ruth!" she hissed,
"*When* is the last time that you shaved?"

"I didn't," I said. I lifted both arms to show her. "See? Hair!"

73

Lynn Freed

Gigi fiddled with a belt, a scarf, pretending not to hear. "Mrs. Frank, you hear that the heels are going up again? Pointy toes coming back?"

"Ah, Gigi, isn't that something? I wish Roger could hear you! Since we gave up the theatre and he's home all the time, he's been after me to throw things out—clothes, shoes, the lot. I must have twenty or thirty pairs of Maglis I've collected over the years! I keep telling him that I need the *height!* Anyway, who would I give them to? Israel won't take high heels, you know. They don't seem to wear them over there. And what African woman can wear a size three and a half?"

Gigi smiled. She walked over to my mother and laid a hand on her shoulder. "You keep them, Mrs. Frank, you hide them away. Here," she said to me, holding out the pink blouse, "just try it. Buttons in the back."

"Is that day or evening?" my mother asked, reaching up to squeeze Gigi's hand.

"Oh, Mrs. Frank, they're wearing anything these days! In Europe, they wear a sundress to a wedding. Just put the jewelry, the scarf, the belt, the right shoes. You should see what they're wearing in Europe, Mrs. Frank!"

. . .

*My wedding provided my parents with their first trip overseas since they had married. They accepted it, quite naturally, as a gift. "We've got this one to thank for bringing us over here," my mother told the saleslady in the glove department of Lord & Taylor. She was searching through drawer after drawer, pair after pair for just the right shade of tobacco. "By Jove, you have a selection in this country!" she said, fishing out a glove and holding it up to the light. "Did I tell you we've come all the way from South Africa?"*

*"Oh my."*

*My father stood back, waiting, in his standard summer uniform— Indian Army shorts, long yellow socks, Crocket and Jones shoes, and a short-sleeved white cotton shirt. His face, neck, arms, and knees, almost black from years of golf under the African sun, seemed cast in shadow. Wherever we went, New Yorkers, who would stare blankly*

74

*through the antics of the local street lunatics, turned to look at him, and smiled.*

It was the hottest July on record, he had reported to us that morning, turning from the television. He'd fallen in love with television—with cartoons and with the news—but most particularly with the weather report, which he found vastly entertaining. I tried to explain that Americans loved records. Record this and record that. Still, this record impressed him greatly. "Ninety-two today," he said, as we plunged back out into the street. "This is certainly some record."

After lunch, while my mother and I shopped for sheets and towels, he joined a line behind a cashier, to divest himself of the irritating collection of coins that had been accumulating in his pocket. He had collected in his hand eight quarters, twenty dimes, and a dollar's worth of nickels to convert into notes. When he reached the front of the line, he assembled them in piles and held them out to the cashier.

"Pardon me, my dear," he said to the cashier, "but I have here a collection of coins that I wish to convert into paper. A five-dollar bill should do nicely, I would think. As you see, I have here—"

The cashier banged furiously at a bell next to the register. A staccato code of dings rang out overhead.

"So that's what the bells are all about!" my father exclaimed. "I'm rather surprised that you Americans, with all your marvellous conveniences, can't come up with something a little less annoying to your shoppers."

A floor manager arrived to find out what the matter was.

"Got some sort of nut here!" the cashier told him. "Get him out of here, will you? Can you look at the line?"

When my father found us, he was full of complaint. "Jolly rude, these Americans, I must say," he said. But, really, he was wounded to have failed so unexpectedly with a woman. "You should just take a look at her," he suggested. "I think, perhaps, she's a Coloured."

"One can't tell, of course," my mother said, "because they sound just like Americans over here."

"They are Americans," I said.

"Certainly they are," said my father. "What would you expect them to sound like? Our Zulus? Let's go and find the men's shoe department."

Lynn Freed

*The night before, my father had put two pairs of shoes in the hotel passage to be polished. When they didn't reappear in the morning, he phoned down to the front desk to inquire. But the concierge wouldn't seem to understand just how he had expected them to get polished by putting them outside the door; just what he was supposed to do about it now.*

*My father's nostrils had begun to flare. He'd covered the mouth-piece and handed me the phone. "Sounds like a blithering idiot to me," he'd said. "You deal with this, you speak their language. Tell him I want my shoes back pronto, polished or not."*

*But the shoes didn't come back. And his Crocket and Jones street shoes wouldn't do for the wedding. So off we went to the shoe department, where my mother and I entertained each other by encouraging him to try on patent-leather dress shoes with bows, wing-tips, loafers.*

*In America, together, we were the happiest we'd ever been. Except for Clive's mother, the Brasch family itself, my future tied to people they despised, the whole idea of the wedding was a great success with my parents. For the first time in forty years they were going to Paris. And then to Florence. And then to Rome. Not even Flo Brasch could upset my mother's delight in being lifted so miraculously into the real world. In having a daughter married and living overseas. Letters to read out to the family on Friday night. Parcels to send. Biltong to smuggle. Anchovette. Golden syrup. Mrs. Ball's chutney. All the paraphernalia of separation and nostalgia.*

· · ·

At the parking garage, my mother planted herself in the queue, with the ticket and the money ready in case I tried to pay. I hung back next to a pillar, watching a small boy in shorts and sandals whine around his mother's skirt.

"Mummy, can I have a Super Moo? Please! Please!"

The woman smiled at me and rolled her eyes. "No, Gavin," she said, "we're going home for lunch."

"*Please!*" he cried, pointing to the parking-lot café. "A curry pie, then! *Please!*"

Someone pulled at my own skirt. I looked down, smiling still, into the face of a legless Indian beggar.

"Madam! Please, madam!" He cupped his hands together, opened his toothless mouth to reveal a bright pink tongue. Then, he began to raise himself onto his black and filthy stumps. The dusty tip of a penis flopped out of his rags. "Ten cents, five cents," he said, grabbing again for the hem of my skirt.

Suddenly my mother was at my side. *"How dare you!"* she boomed at him, her voice lowered to its old stage tone of menace. "Let go of my daughter's dress *this minute*! She began to wind the strap of her bag around her hand, ready for a swing.

The beggar shrank back, shielding his face with an arm.

"I'll call the po-*lice*!" she shouted at him. "Dirty, filthy creature! How *dare* you touch my daughter?" She turned on me as I dug into my bag for some coins to give him—for the sake of the crowd watching from the queue, and because I wanted to end the scene at any cost. "And don't you go giving him any money, you stupid little fool!" she spat out, her face contorted, nose, mouth, eyes.

In the lift, she grabbed at my arm. "Don't *touch* the part he touched!" she snapped. "*God* knows what sort of germs that creature could be carrying! We're going to have to give that dress to Grace to wash."

# 9

Catherine was driving me out to the bungalow for tea. She seldom drove out of town. She drove her children to school, and then picked them up again. She drove to the dry cleaner and to the market and to a special shop for fish, another one for vegetables. And then, in the afternoon, she drove the children to the barber or to the dressmaker or to rugby.

Other women had drivers. But Catherine didn't trust Africans to drive her children, or even to feed them. She herself had cooked her children's food, and fed it to them while the nanny stood by and watched. This she considered normal. In fact, she loved the whole idea of normal—normal children, normal families, normal people. Driving her rounds in the car, with Frank Sinatra crooning on the cassette player, she dreamed of living a normal life somewhere far away.

We turned off the highway and wound through the cane. She drove fast, breathing lightly.

"Isn't it lovely here?" I said.

"It is, it really is."

"Cath," I said, "what am I going to do?"

She glanced sideways at me. She seldom gave advice, and never asked for it. In fact, she seldom asked for more than a recipe or a measuring cup in ounces, unobtainable from the local shops. She just waited, bound up like a mummy in her own discretion. And, even then, I had always had the feeling that she didn't want to know.

"Be careful, old girl," she'd said when I had told her about Hugh. Apart from Clive, my future turned upside down, a lover beyond the pale of the community, she'd meant, I thought, that I should be careful of Jeffrey. She herself had only me to be careful of. With every visit, Jeffrey grew more wary. He complained to Catherine that, when I was there, she wasn't the same. She was cocky, he said. She laughed a lot about stupid things.

"If you were me," I persisted. "Given the situation. What would you do?"

"It's hard to say."

If I had asked her where to find an asparagus dish, she would have bought me one. She would cry when it was time for me to leave for the airport, and so would I. I loved the familiar curve of her nostril, the way she sniffed, the sight of her foot in a sandal, how she soaped herself in the bath.

"If you told Jeffrey," I said, "then what?"

She shrugged.

But we both knew. As the only child of a silly, uneducated woman and a self-made man—a man of lusts and furies and raw charm, a man who gave and took without scruple—Jeffrey took great pride in having scruples himself. And in lusting only for his wife. He had a horror of women like Tanya Kaplan—tricky women who couldn't be trusted, who schemed to get things from their men, and would tell each other everything, every secret thing, behind their husbands' backs. Catherine was nothing like these women. She didn't belong at their bridge tables or tennis tournaments. She was refined, everyone knew that. Except for me, she didn't have a friend in the world. She didn't need one. And Jeffrey liked it that way.

.  .  .

We sat on the verandah, waiting for Regina to bring tea. A hot wind blew in from the sea, clouding the air with salt. It smelled sweet with Beaumontia, sour with rotting vegetation.

Catherine sat stiff and quiet, like a captive, holding the arms of the chair. She wore a lavender sundress from Gigi's, with lavender bangles and earrings to match, lavender high-heeled sandals. Already, I knew, she was worrying about getting back, and how she'd account for her time to Jeffrey.

"Isn't it lovely here?" I asked again, reaching back to pluck off a Beaumontia bloom.

"Are you quite sure, old girl," she said at last, "that you're not confusing the romance with the place? Or vice versa?"

"You have a point," I said. But I felt as if the afternoon were over already and I standing at the gate, waving her back to the normal life.

Regina appeared with the tray. She'd put out the best tea set and a starched doily under the scones.

"Regina, this is my sister, Mrs. Goldman."

Regina smiled. "Your sister she's beautiful," she said.

"She's a friend of Chief Sibusi!" I burst out. "*Big*, big friend!"

"*Hau!*" Regina glanced quickly at Catherine, but Catherine looked out to sea, smiling, as if she hadn't heard.

"I'm go to the Indian supply for eggs," Regina said. "Master he say Yorkshire pudding for supper."

"Listen, old girl," Catherine said when she was gone, "keep Sibusi under your hat. The word will get out through the bush telegraph and we'll have them storming the gates." She still smiled, but her lips quivered.

"How stupid of me," I mumbled. I felt like an idiot, cheap for using her connections to show off to the maid.

"It's this bloody country," she said, taking her tea. "You're just not used to it."

It was always this bloody country. The things you couldn't find in the shops, the phone not working, a strike at the factory, winter in July. I looked at her eating her scone. She ate daintily, taking up small pieces with her fork. She'd let herself go, my mother said, she should take herself in hand. But I loved Catherine's plumpness. Her roundness went with the colours she wore, with the height of her heels, the way she undulated as she walked. Men, white and black, turned to look at her in the street. Regina was right. She was beautiful, more beautiful than ever.

"Someone should prune the Beaumontia," she said, "or it won't bloom properly again."

I nodded. But, in fact, Hugh's domestic arrangements never came up between us. And, anyway, I quite liked the place the way it was. The lawn now was not much more than leggy runners of kikuyu grass across red earth. On the north side, the gula-gula and mango trees had spread their shade so far that the grass didn't grow there at all. Half-eaten fruit rotted on the ground, where the monkeys had dropped them.

"The new gardener is hopeless," I explained. "All he does is mow."

"Hello? HELLO?"

We both sat up as a tall woman in walking clothes and her grey hair in a bun came around the garden.

"I rang the bell," she said, "but no one answered. So I thought I'd come round and see if anyone was home. I'm Lily Diamond." She climbed the steps and addressed herself to Catherine. "I used to know Sir Liege."

Catherine gestured to a chair. "Would you like some tea?" she asked. "We're just having some. I'm Catherine Goldman. This is my sister, Ruth Frank."

The woman frowned at Catherine. "Roger and Sarah's daughters?"

Catherine gave a thin smile. The association followed her everywhere she went, even out here.

"I knew your mother as a girl," Lily said, settling herself onto the swing seat and kicking off her shoes. Despite the heat, she wore stockings. And she carried an enormous crocodile handbag. Her hands and arms and legs were long and elegant. Her face was beautiful, her cheekbones high, her mouth wide, with strong, white teeth. And her skin, taut rather than loose with age, was translucent, like the teacups. She looked up at me, poised with the teapot on my way inside, and said, "You must be the one who went overseas—wasn't that you?"

"Hugh," said Lily, when I came back, "is very like his grandfather, face and figure. I am quite unnerved to find myself an old woman looking upon a ghost."

Catherine smiled warily. Lily Diamond, whoever she was, was certainly not normal. If she'd had a husband, she didn't seem to have one now, nor to want one either. Friends were mentioned, a trip down the Nile with one. Another who had a house in Lisbon, a hunting lodge in the Pyrenees. And, although there was money behind her—the handbag, the travelling, her turn of phrase—she was staying at the Umgeni Beach Hotel, which, she said, for all the appalling food and boozy clientele, at least had the smell of Africa to it. More than you could say for the Majestic these days.

"You must both come and visit me there," she said. "There's a sea pool down on the beach. Frightening at high tide, but superb in the early afternoon." She clicked open her lorgnette to scrutinise the silver mark on the sugar spoon.

Catherine stood up. "Please excuse me," she said. "I have to go."

I stood up too, hoping Lily would stay. Her presence, somehow, gave licence to my own. I'd told my parents Hugh lived with a woman, a Belgian anthropologist called Monique. That I slept in the spare room, a room with a lovely view of the sea. They didn't believe me, of course, but I clowned around their questioning. It was the way I'd always kept my secrets intact—playing with them like children, as if their happiness depended—as indeed it seemed to do—on the distance I kept between them and the truth about myself.

. . .

After Catherine had gone, Lily suggested I walk back to the hotel with her, along the beach. I hadn't been down to the beach yet. Its wildness had always put me off—the way the bush grew right down to the edge of the sand and the surf came in so fierce and high that it seemed it wouldn't stop at the water line. Last year, Hugh said, an Indian, half eaten away and rotting, had been washed up there like a log, with crayfish feeding off the corpse.

"Now where are the walking sticks?" Lily muttered, stalking through to the front hall and then back again. "What's he done with the walking sticks? Oh well, we'll just have to manage without them."

The path down to the beach—eighty-four steps cut zigzag through the bush—was overgrown now, almost invisible. We made our way by holding on to branches and vines, and sliding our feet over the sponge of rotting leaves that covered the ground.

"It's a shame," said Lily, "that he's let the place go like this. In my day, it was a gem, an emerald."

"Did you stay here?" I asked. I had to shout above the roar of the surf.

She stopped for a moment then, and smiled up at me. "I think we'll be friends," she said.

The beach was indeed a mess of plastic bottles and rusted tins, seaweed, yellowed foam, and traces of oil washed up. Dead fish lay rotting here and there. The tide was in, misting the air with salt. Lily had found a rock and sat down to roll off her stockings. "Ah!" she said, standing up and stretching her arms wide to the horizon. Wisps of hair hung down from her bun. She looked like a witch, a beautiful witch.

"We'll have to clamber a bit," she said, stuffing her stockings and shoes into her handbag. "Unless you want to wade."

"I'd rather clamber."

She led the way, heading into the wind. We took a path, up and over a small bluff, down onto the hotel's beach. From there, the hotel looked much grander than from the road, white and gleaming in the sun, with columns and balustrades, palm trees, and stairs meandering down the cliff. There was a lighthouse, too, that I hadn't seen before. It had been built into the rocks at one end of the beach, all white except for an orange turret. It caught the sun now on its way down behind the cliff.

"I think the architects must have had this view in mind when they built the place," Lily said, stopping on a flat-topped rock. "Imagine what it must look like from the deck of a ship."

I sat on the beach and took my sandals off. The sand was coarse and full of shells, still warm from the sun.

"Liege said that to me once," she said, settling in beside me. "He said, 'Lily, you see this country from the deck of a ship.' And he was right. I'm an awful old fake."

"So am I."

"I'll tell you a secret," she said, "I knew you were at the Stillington bungalow. I phoned Hugh this morning—I always phone to say hello when I come down—and he went into a rigmarole about being caught up with an old friend from overseas. By which I gathered he had a new woman. Are you married?"

"Yes."

"Aha!" She gazed across the curving coastline towards the faint skeleton of the city. "And the husband doesn't know. And you're not in love with him, probably never were. You're—what?—about twenty-eight or so? And—do you have children?"

"No. That's—"

"No children, hmm." She traced a pattern in the sand, circles and triangles. "Let's go up for a drink," she said suddenly, heaving herself to her feet and holding out a hand for me. "I must admit to an enormous curiosity. Do you believe in reincarnation? I do. Horrible as it seems, I know I haven't worked through very much so far." She strode across the beach toward the stairs, with me beside her. I wondered whether anyone watching could mistake us for mother and daughter. And I was glad we weren't. With such a mother, there would be no hiding places. She would dig things up, call them by their names. Coward, fake, embracer of the mediocre. This way, however, she could call loudly for the waiter, or offer me her jersey when I shivered, like the witch she was. There was no question of giving or taking comfort. We were comfortable already. We knew each other well.

# 10

"You'll be delighted to learn that your mother-in-law, the Hunchback of High Wyckham, has extended her stay in America," my mother announced. "Ettie Goldman took it upon herself to give me the good news."

She sighed. Mention of my mother-in-law, or even of Catherine's, distasteful as it was, put her in mind of the danger my marriage was in. She'd given up asking me if I thought it wise to spend so much time out at the bungalow and why I didn't phone old friends like Myrna Lipinsky anymore. When I told her I'd extended my ticket, she didn't say, "That's marvellous, darling!" She asked if I'd be in for dinner that night, and what my plans were for the rest of the week.

I carried my bag up to my room. I needed sleep. Over the years, I'd lost my talent for it, even here, in my old bed. It was too narrow now, or too tightly made. And I could hear every little sound. The clock ticking, a toilet flushing, Grace creaking upstairs with early-morning tea. At the bungalow, it was Hugh's arm behind my neck, his breath in my nostrils. I thought, perhaps, I'd sleep better on my own, in the spare room. But I couldn't find a way to tell him this. It had taken me years to move out of Clive's bed and into my study. And, even there, night after night, something jumped me awake on my way down into sleep. Something I'd been groping for, something still murking in a haze of disconnected images. Sometimes, on my drives out to the bungalow, with the music blaring, the sun glinting off the sea, this something seemed to billow under my ribs, quicken my breathing, give me hope. When I was ready, I thought, it would come into my palm like the handle of a knife. And I would know just how to use it, where to begin.

The morning sun shone full onto the venetian blinds, which riffled in the breeze. Down the passage, Nicholas and Grace shouted and laughed over the noise of the Hoover. Soon, my mother would call upstairs to ask what I wanted for lunch.

When Hugh had dropped me off, he hadn't asked when I was coming out again. I'd watched him back out of the driveway—a cigarette hanging from his lips, the sinews of his neck pulled taut as he looked back over his shoulder—and, for one fierce moment, I'd understood how emigrants feel when the boat pulls out. A pain burned across my chest like a gunshot wound. It felt like something that would leave me crippled for life. Something sour, harsh, hopeless, full of blame.

"Ruth!" my mother called. "What would you like for lunch, darling?"

When I'd phoned Clive to ask about staying on, he'd told me that some nut had reported him to the Anti-Vivisection Society and that the university wanted me back for the spring semester; they needed an answer within two weeks. The Cambodian next door had been mugged in the elevator, he said, and now the tenants were forming a committee. There'd been the usual Christmas party at the lab. And, would I bring him a supply of Hermesetes? He was going on a diet.

I sat down at the dressing table and stared into the mirror. Already, I could see my mother in my face, the pull of gravity, the grey around the eyes. She was climbing the stairs now, calling my name. She'd be carrying her martini with her, and would settle into my armchair for a chat. How about an omelette at the Majestic tonight, she'd say? What about a show if there's something worth seeing? She'd open my wardrobe. Why not wear this tonight? Why not do your hair up for a change? At the Majestic, my father would lay his hand over mine. Order whatever you wish, he'd say, it doesn't have to be an omelette. People would wave at us, or stop on their way out or on their way in. They'd say how glad they were to see my father up and about, and how long was I out for this time?

"Have you heard of a woman called Lily Diamond?" I asked my mother.

"Good God! Lily!" She leaned back in the chair and closed her eyes. "Lily Gershin! What a vision she was! Grey eyes, and that Titian hair in a gorgeous, long, thick plait hanging down her back—"

"She's staying at the Umgeni Beach."

"*What* a voice she had! Even as a little thing. I remember the concerts she gave when she got back from London, during the war—Diamond, of course, is her stage name—and then she seemed to disappear. The *Umgeni*! She must be down on her luck, poor thing!"

The front door opened and closed. My father stepped across the hall, tossed his keys into the brass bowl on the kist.

She drained her glass and sighed. "Well, *he's* home! I suppose I'd better go and find out what he wants for lunch."

• • •

*After the wedding, the last morning of my parents' stay, I tried to comfort myself with the thought that now, at last, I would be able to break the awful deadlock of belonging. Someone's daughter. Someone's child. I reminded myself of what Chinese parents told their daughters. "You are a guest in this house. You will leave us soon to become the mother in someone else's house and contribute to his lineage."*

*But, planted between Clive and his mother, looking across the table at my parents' sad eyes, their luggage ready and waiting in the hall, I was strangled by misery. I pushed the egg around my plate, picked up my coffee cup, put it down again.*

*Clive's parents were staying on with us in New York for six weeks or so. They were sleeping on the foldout couch in our living room. I tried to remind myself that this was life, that this was normal life. But everything about Flo Brasch offended me, even the sound of her breathing. Nor could I stand the way she slipped packets of sugar and salt and pepper into her handbag at restaurants and never offered to pay.*

*My parents couldn't either. "Your father never could stand a coarse woman," my mother said. "I can only marvel at Alfred."*

*But, if ever Alfred Brasch had been whole and spirited, as Clive*

*claimed he had, he was now broken and tamed. After a heart attack
nearly killed both him and the patient whose uterus he had been
removing, Flo Brasch had put him to use as her hairdresser, or sewing
moccasins from kits, or finding the cheapest ticket to get from one
place to another. In fact, she had come into her own as his keeper.
She ordered what he ate and when he slept; whether he took an
umbrella, when he put on a hat.*

*"Alfred!" she screeched. "This coffee is cold as ice."*

*He turned to look for the waitress, and then there she was, come
to announce the cab. My father placed his fingertips on the table and
said, "Well, then!" And my mother closed her eyes and put down her
napkin. I put mine down too, and started to stand up. But, just then,
Flo Brasch closed a hand around my arm and held on tight. She
brought her face up close to mine. "We are your family now," she
grinned. "In our family we don't use the word 'in-law,' Ruth."*

· · ·

"I've been thinking," my mother said, sipping her tea, "why not
write a book?"

I smiled. Since she had stopped working herself, her ambition
had been attaching itself, quite naturally, to me.

"Didn't you used to write the odd thing in school?" she asked.
"English essays, that sort of thing?"

"For God's sake, Ma," I said.

"So *what!*" she cried. "You have to start *somewhere!*" She cosied
up in the corner of the couch. "I can't say I'm sorry that you gave
up lecturing, you know. Frankly, I could never quite see you in a
classroom."

"I couldn't stand it," I said.

"*I know!*" she cried suddenly. "Why not turn your hand to a
*bestseller?*" She beamed at me, triumphant. "Now *there's* an idea!"
she said.

I laughed. Somehow, the absurdity of the conversation cheered
me up.

"Writers can make a *fortune!*" she cried. "They can live anywhere they *like*, all over the world. I've always said, you know, that
you should be living in London. You should be living in the *hub!*"

But the idea of London had no appeal for me. The string bag

with one tomato, a tin of soup, perhaps, the sun at a slant, or no sun at all. And the English with their beige skin, beige clothes, beige thoughts. Oh God! "What about Clive?" I asked.

She set her cup and saucer on the tray. "Darling," she said, "I don't think you're very happy in America."

"I am happy," I mumbled.

"I have eyes, you know, although they don't do me much good anymore. I wasn't born yesterday." She sighed. "I think that London might give you two a second wind. All sorts of writers live in London. Bournemouth too."

"But I'm not a writer," I said.

"Well, just make up your mind to *be* one! Mark my words, once that *mind* of yours is occupied, and you're in the right place, you'll find yourself pregnant in no time. Sure as eggs."

# 11

Lily and I sat at the hotel pool—me in, she out of the sun. She waved her hat at a waiter, who was lolling over the ballustrade. "Waiter! Hoy! Two teas, please! Down here!"

This much I knew: as a girl, she had gone to train as a singer in London. Then, she'd joined the opera in Munich, fallen in love with an admirer, and run off with him. He'd turned out to be a gambler and a womaniser. They'd lived in Paris, in Geneva, in other places too. Everywhere they'd gone, he'd had other women, right from the beginning. Then the war had broken out and she'd left him, sold her jewelry, and come home.

"A woman needs money," she said to me. "Real money, that is. I'm not talking about an allowance or a salary."

I thought of my mother, my mother and her piffling dividends that paid the household bills, bought shoes, a frock from Gigi's— that little bit of independence that made all the difference in a woman's life, she said. But how little did the difference have to be? And how did they think it would just happen? How had it happened for Lily? "Did you have your own money?" I asked her.

She brushed her fingers through the air, as if sweeping away the details of history. "Some. Later. A small sum from my father, and because Liege knew what to do with it."

Sir Liege was still an assumption between us. She'd been more than a mistress to him, Hugh had told me that. She'd lived at the bungalow for a while, travelled with him, inherited from him. But still, I didn't know exactly what to assume, how close she'd been to a wife.

"For you," she said, "I don't think it'll be a man."

My heart leapt. This I had never heard before. And, hearing it

from her, I didn't doubt its truth. Even so, her words surprised me
with hope—hope attached to nothing but the assumption that
Lily made on my behalf: "For you, it won't be a man."

The waiter wound down the path from the hotel, carrying a
tray. The tide was coming in. Waves began to wash against the sea
wall, spraying us lightly.

"How long were you with Sir Liege?" I asked.

She threw back her head and laughed deeply. "*With* him? I'm
still with him, my dear. I'm quite sure he slammed the door of my
room the other night. It was very like him, you know, slamming
doors. I was lying back in bed, reading *Wuthering Heights* and
thinking to myself that there was, after all, much comfort in being
through with all of that, when Liege slammed out of the room."

She chuckled to herself as she poured the tea and handed me
my cup.

"Once, in a fit of temper, he left the bedroom and slammed the
door. But the door didn't slam—it still doesn't, have you noticed?—so I had to go after him and slam it for him myself, turn
the key. Ha! Ha! Ha!"

"When did he die?" I asked.

But, just then, a strong wave arched over the wall and drenched
us both. Lily whooped with delight. A wedge of yellow cake floated
off its plate and onto the tray. I wiped the salt from my eyes, and
began to gather up our sandals and our clothes.

"Leave the towels," she said. "The sea's always claiming them
for its own. Anyway, these are bald. It's high time the hotel provided better ones. Come, let's go up to change."

· · ·

I changed first, and then sat in her armchair as she dressed in the
bathroom. She was strangely modest. My own mother rolled down
her corset and unhitched her bra in front of us without a thought.
She climbed into the bath and scrubbed with soap between her
legs, or lay on her back and kicked her legs in the air for exercise.
Her body was as opulent as Lily's was spare. It was pink and white
and rounded, with a large, protruding belly, full, pendulous breasts,
shapely legs. It was innocent too, vulnerable, always a surprise in
contrast to her weary face and ropy, sharp-clawed hands.

"I've never had a sister," said Lily, coming out of the bathroom. She wore a long black skirt and white silk blouse, and sat at the dressing table to apply some rouge. Her face was soft in the evening light, her hair gleaming in its complicated bun. "That's what you feel like to me, you know," she said. "A sister."

· · ·

Hugh was waiting in the lounge, sipping Scotch, when we came downstairs. We hadn't seen each other all week, and now I felt shy with him in front of Lily. I'd dressed up for the occasion in a white, low-backed dress and high-heeled sandals, tied my hair back into a knot, and worn eye make-up, and a pair of antique gold drop earrings—twin Byzantine spheres studded with seed pearls and turquoise that I had found in an antique shop in San Francisco.

"Drink?" he said, signalling to the waiter.

The lounge was noisy with people. They sat in groups, half drunk already—old men with florid faces, white hair, handlebar mustaches, their women in short, tight perms, glass beads and marcasite. "Cedric, what's your poison? Marjorie?" "Chin-chin everybody!" The place smelled ripe with liquor, salt air, old carpeting, furniture polish.

The manager came over to greet Hugh. So did the Indian maître d'. "Long time no see!" they said. And, "Welcome back!" People turned to look at us. What did they see, I wondered? Husband and wife? Mother and daughter?

"You look gorgeous, darling," Hugh said. "Lily, what do you think? Should I have her portrait taken at the bungalow?"

Lily snorted. "Wearing the sari? From the collection?"

I looked from him to her. The sari? The collection? She accepted her drink from the waiter, swizzled the olive around and then ate it. "If you don't hire a decent gardener soon," she said, "the whole place will return to the bush."

He laughed, raising his glass to her. "Speaking of saris, you should see what I found in the kist the other day. Did Ruth tell you? An ensemble for the seraglio! Bloody *marvellous*! Silk, I'd say, wouldn't you, darling?"

I smiled, but I had no idea how to cope with the question,

remembering the performance I'd given for him, the look on his face.

He grasped his jaw between the thumb and forefinger of his crippled hand and contemplated me. "No," he said after a while, "not the sari, definitely not. She's more like an odalisque with that profile. What do you think? Something wound around the head, perhaps, nothing else, just those earrings—"

"Hugh, I'm starving," Lily said, draining her glass. "What do you say we go in?"

. . .

Hugh's eyes were blue-black in the candlelight. His shirt shone very white. He looked up without opening his menu. "Oysters to start?" he asked. "Oysters all round?"

The oysters were brought, and Champagne. We lifted our glasses to each other and toasted and drank. The band began to play.

"Why don't you two dance?" Lily suggested. She turned to look out to sea. "Go on, go on!" she said, flapping a hand at us. "I'll watch."

But I didn't want to dance, with Lily sitting there. "You two dance," I said. "Please."

Hugh pushed back his chair, held out a hand to Lily. I watched her turn to face him on the dance floor, a slight smile on her face. He said something and she laughed, and I thought it must be something about me. So I, too, turned to look out at the sea, which was black as ink, silver in the beam of the lighthouse.

I smiled now to think of my portrait taken as an odalisque. And at me, the pagan odalisque, standing at the edge of the verandah, admiring Hugh's peacocks. Me, training his binoculars on a ship moving north to Suez, on a monkey, on a snake, while he stood behind me, his breath on my hair, watching, with the careful attention of a missionary, for signs of my conversion.

"Krishnah is right," I said casually, when they returned to the table. "Hugh likes to play Tolstoy."

"Krishnah?" said Lily, cocking her head.

"Krishnah Chowdree," Hugh explained. "You remember the flap over his book?"

Lily closed her eyes and nodded. She was flushed from the dance, happy. "Unreadable," she said, twirling one hand in the air. "Occasionally our censors do us a favour. It's polemical rubbish."

I beamed at her. I wanted to laugh.

Hugh shook his head. "One can read past all that, if one wants to," he said.

"But one doesn't want to," said Lily.

"Touché!" I said.

One afternoon, Hugh had reached into the bookshelf and pulled out Krishnah's book, carefully disguised by the jacket of T. S. Eliot's *Collected Poems*. "Here," he'd said, "perhaps this will shake you up a bit." But, stretched out along the swing seat in the afternoon heat, with the spitting bugs singing in the trees, I'd found the book growing heavy in my hands, weighed down by lost causes and constitutional dispensations, recriminations leading to normalisations. I had set it aside and fallen asleep.

Hugh smiled at us indulgently. "You're ganging up on me," he said. "I feel exposed."

· · ·

*In America, I discovered a new kind of privacy.*

*Coming back to the apartment after my first day out, I stopped dead in the living room. The place was in chaos. Clothes lay strewn across the floor, just where I had dropped them. Drawers that I'd left open hadn't been closed. The bed was unmade.*

*I stood still for some moments, waiting for the fright to subside. Then I began to pick up the clothes and put them away, I pulled the bedclothes off and made the bed completely, put on the bedspread. I went through to the kitchen. There were dishes in the sink, food out on the counters. I cleaned it up and went back to the living room with a mug of tea to consider the possibilities of my new life.*

*If I opened the drawer to Clive's desk, looked through his letters, and then put them back again, who would see? No one. I could also climb onto a chair and bring down his box of memorabilia from the shelf in the closet, spread them out on the bed, and examine them closely. What's more, if I talked on the phone, no one could overhear. I could fall asleep without warning anyone not to wake me up. I* could take off my clothes. I could walk around naked if I wanted to, day and night. I was free.

"For God's sake," Clive said, coming home that night, "put something on." He couldn't bear to look at me naked. But I couldn't bear not to be looked at. I pranced into the kitchen and back out again, squatted at his feet, twisted this way and that way as he turned up the volume of the TV to hear how many thousands had been killed that day in Vietnam.

I put on my shorts and blouse and came to sit next to him on the couch. I liked the ads. Every night, between bouts of news, smiling white women vacuumed their houses, washed their clothes, their cars, their faces; they polished their furniture and their floors, fed their dogs and their children. At home, it had been different. The ads had come over the radio; there was no face to the voice. At home, there was no joy to cleaning. Every morning, the servants dusted the house, they Hoovered, they cleaned the bathrooms, made the beds from scratch. Monday was wash day. Friday, the silver was polished. Once a month, the books were painted for bookworm, the hairbrushes were soaked in ammonia and then laid out in the sun. Every now and then, my mother had run her finger along a windowsill or over a lampshade. Then she'd rung the bell for the servant so that she could tell him to do it again, and properly this time.

I consulted the Hoover manual and found out that there was more than just the floor to consider. There were places underneath the furniture, and underneath the cushions on the furniture, picture mouldings, invisible flakes of skin that filtered down into the mattress. Nothing, however, was said about windowsills as such, where the dust was not dusty, but stuck to the paint like glue. Nor could I find a solution for the pots and pans that gathered oily grime. Nor for the seam of thick, black slime that kept returning, week after week, between the toilet and the floor.

When I mentioned this to my new friend, Anna, she just laughed. Why bother, she asked? The sky won't fall in if you don't vacuum, or clean the toilet. Who cares? Who's going to see?

· · ·

When we reached the bungalow, lights were on in the backyard.

"Master!" Regina stood at the gate in a pink petticoat and bare feet. Small plaits stood out all around her head.

"Go inside," Hugh said to me. "I'll join you as soon as I can."

"Well," he said, coming in through the kitchen. "That's that. Cognac, darling?"

"What happened?"

"They've arrested him for the last time. He'll be sent back to the reserve."

"You can't do anything about it?"

He shook his head, lifted the decanter to check the level. "Nor shall I. I give up."

"That's the second time you've given up tonight," I said lightly.

But he didn't smile. He poured two snifters and came to the couch. "What with that bugger of Regina's pushing me to the limit, Krishnah's perversity, and Edwina's blithering, unimaginative, pigheaded selfishness, I've had just about enough of this bloody country," he said.

There was nothing to say to this. He wasn't even talking to my audience. When I'd found Edwina at 'varsity, and told her about the policeman, she'd gone pale and bitten her lips. "What am I going to do?" she asked. "I love him. I'm not going to give him up."

Hugh loosened the knot of his tie, pulled it off, rolled his sleeves up to his elbows. "I think I'll stay home tomorrow," he said. He stretched out a hand and pulled me over so that I lay awkwardly across his chest. "I'd like you to do something for me," he said. His voice rumbled deep in his chest.

I knew what he wanted already. It seemed quite normal now.

"Put on that outfit for Lily," he said. "I want her to see you in it. Would you do that for me?" he asked.

# 12

Almost every day now, I was at the bungalow. When I didn't stay overnight, I drove out in the morning in the Rover, stopped at the hotel to fetch Lily, and then at the Indian shop, perhaps, to buy things for lunch and supper. Regina seemed quite happy to see us. She even laughed, now that her husband had been sent back to Swaziland. Sometimes we all stood in the kitchen, making things together. But, soon, Lily would wander off to put on a record, or to lie on the swing seat and rest. "Old Madam Lily, she don't like the cooking," Regina would confide. "Old Madam Lily, she too *old* now for the cooking."

"In old age," Lily said, trailing one leg off the swing seat, "you have a kind of leprosy. It's particularly awful if you had a full and romantic life as a young woman."

I knew better than to contradict her with cheap assurances. It was she who was first to suggest the dress-up sessions after supper, she who lit the candles, switched off the lamps, called Hugh into the spare room to choose what I should wear. She chose the music, too. Mostly Schubert, but also Debussy, Satie, Duke Ellington, Louis Armstrong. She would stretch out on the couch and he'd sit on the floor beside her, her long fingers in his hair. On the table next to them was the sherry decanter, or a bottle of Champagne, or wine. They watched in silence as I came in and went out again. They made me stop and turn, they smiled at each other. And I was drunk on their attention, drunk with Lily, drunk with Hugh, even with the thought of Hugh.

"Men don't see beyond the body," she explained. "But, it is only the body that changes in old age. The soul and the spirit are exiled within."

I looked at her stockinged feet with their bunions and crooked toes. Perhaps, I thought, it was only her age that made her modest about her body. My body seemed to delight her, as if it were her own. I'd even heard her thank Hugh when he praised my skin or my shoulders or my hips. And yet, she was nothing like me. She was fair, long-boned, with small breasts and narrow hips.

"Well, how about some Champagne?" she'd say when it was time to stop. And I'd flop down on the floor, or on the couch, and Hugh would get up to pour. She'd run her fingers through my hair, or stroke my arm. "The skin is like velvet," she'd say to him. And then, when she'd finished her Champagne, she might get up to dance. Sometimes, she would unpin her hair and let it stream down her back. And then, with her long arms reaching out into the shadows, her head tossing and swaying to the music, she looked, indeed, like an exiled spirit.

"Shall we walk to the hotel for a swim?" she suggested, sitting up. "Then I can change for dinner, and Hugh can fetch us on his way home."

. . .

But Hugh wasn't in his office when she phoned, and he didn't return her call.

"There's hardly a moon tonight," she said. "Let's take a torch and walk along the road."

The idea didn't thrill me. "The first night I came out here, I banged into Regina's husband," I told her.

"Banged?"

"I didn't see him, it was dark. I stopped, but he ran off."

She examined the lie of her pearls in the mirror, put in one earring and then the other. "We haven't got much longer here, you know, before we enter a state of chaos. In fact, we're there already, except that people are making so much money, they're deaf and blind. Look what's happening in Angola. It's only a matter of time."

Watching her mouth, "It's only a matter of time," as she applied her lipstick made me think she had something else on her mind.

"If you're going to stay on," she said, turning around to face me, "you'll hang on to your American passport, I hope. Thank *God* you're not the sort to think of going native."

·  ·  ·

She was in high spirits as we set off along the road. "Oh!" she cried, as we rounded the bend, out of the hotel lights. She switched off the torch and stood on the verge of the road, looking out to sea. I stood next to her, watching things reveal themselves in the dark. A moist wind blew off the sea. The bats were out. Ahead of us, the lights of the Indian houses twinkled gaily.

"Did you never want a child?" I asked.

She threw a bony arm around my shoulder. "I *am* the child, my dear," she said. "Curiosity has never led me up that particular path."

If she'd told me she were a man, it would have seemed as ordinary. Like Hugh, she exposed my own small ambitions, the ones that had informed my life so far—husband, child, a life overseas—as threadbare abstractions, cartoons of the happy life. I thought of my friend Anna, whose parents had wanted a normal life for her, a normal husband. But then she'd met an Indian at the foreign-student centre, and there he was, the one she wanted. He had a black beard, and wore a turban, and was scornful of everything—Jews, New York, America. Her father offered her money if she'd forget the Indian. She was beautiful, she was bright, she could have any man she wanted, he said. But she married the Indian anyway, and went off to live in India. She wrote me letters from there. Things were difficult, she said. Her Indian husband left her at home and went off with other women. "Why don't you leave him and come back?" I asked. "Because," she wrote, "I feel at home in India. For the first time in my life I feel at home."

We arrived at the front gate of the bungalow quite quickly. The place was dark, and Hugh's car wasn't there.

"Let's go around to the kitchen," Lily suggested.

But the kitchen, too, was dark, the door locked. We called for Regina, and knocked, but no one answered.

"Here," I said, "I have a key."

Lily shone the torch at the lock, and then into the kitchen while I searched for the light switch. Clearly, Regina had been preparing dinner before she'd left. A leg of mutton stood dressed on a rack, potatoes peeled in a bowl of water, mint in a colander.

"Funny," Lily said, going out into the hall. "It's half past seven already. He's usually home by six. Seven at the latest."

She switched on the lamps, the verandah light, checked the doors and windows, and then walked through to the dining room. It was a small room, choked with furniture—a sideboard, a large, square table, and six squat, round-backed chairs, all painted white and then neglected. An etched glass chandelier cast a dim light over the table. The table was laid for three as usual, with a cloth and candlesticks.

"Champagne glasses," said Lily, touching things on the table—a knife, a glass. "Something funny's happened."

She walked back out into the hall, into the lounge, me following. A peacock shrieked. "Good God!" she cried, jumping back against the bookshelf. "What's that?"

I laughed. "Just one of the peacocks. Do you want a drink?"

We sat in silence, sipping Scotch.

"She only uses the Champagne glasses if we're three," I said. "They're the only three that match."

"What?"

"The glasses on the table—they don't mean Champagne."

But Lily swilled and swilled her Scotch, staring down into the vortex.

"Shall I put on the lamb?" I suggested.

She clicked her teeth together. "Ruth," she said, "I'm going to phone the Estates. Do you have the number?" She stood up, swaying a little. In the dim lamp light she did indeed look old, unsprung, her skin grey, spotted with age, her eyes loose in their sockets.

The doorbell rang, and she jumped again.

"That must be Hugh," I said, getting up. "Perhaps he forgot his keys."

• • •

*One day, a week after the wedding, the front-door buzzer of our apartment sounded. I recognised the noise from the time Clive had*

*forgotten his keys, and raced to the grid in the kitchen. "Who's
there?" I shouted.*

*"Your fire-insurance man."*

*I pressed the button, and flew off to the bedroom to dress. Re-
membering Clive's warning that Americans thought bare feet bad-
mannered, I grabbed my sandals. But, before I could buckle them, the
doorbell chirped, and I ran barefoot to answer it.*

*A short dark man in a seersucker suit and wing-tip shoes stood on
the mat.*

*"I didn't know you were coming," I said, glancing at my feet.*

*But the man seemed too hot and cross to notice. He walked past
me and into the living room without being asked.*

*"Would you like some coffee?" I asked. "Or tea?" No one but Mr.
O'Grady, the superintendent, had come to the apartment before.
And he'd taken his tea in the kitchen, standing up, like a servant.*

*"Coffee sounds good," the man said.*

*When I returned from the kitchen with the tray, he had his brief-
case open on his lap. "I need to ask you a few questions," he said. He
took out some papers and a gold pencil. "I need to know when you're
in and out. You and your husband. Both."*

*I put down the tray and sat opposite him. "We don't know yet,"
I said. "We won't have our schedules until the semester begins."*

*He looked around at the fake colonial furniture, squinted through
to the bedroom. "You own all this?"*

*"Oh no! Only that worthless old piano. This is graduate-student
housing—"*

*"TV?"*

*I pointed to the bedroom.*

*He looked up at me for a moment, and took his coffee. "Stereo?
Camera? Jewelry?"*

*I waved my wedding band at him and touched my ears. "This is
about it," I said.*

*"Ever have a fire?"*

*"No. Never. I've never even seen a fire—except once, mind you,
from the balcony of my old house. Fires are very rare where I grew up.
The houses are built of stone and brick. So you can't hear every word
your neighbour says through the walls!" I laughed. Two days before,*

*the neighbor had knocked on the door and asked me please to stop playing the piano, her father had just died. I wanted this man to know, this stranger, how strange I felt here. He was, after all, my guest. He was sitting on my chair, drinking my coffee out of my cup.*
"Another biscuit?" I asked.

He drained his coffee in one gulp, closed his briefcase and stood up. "No thanks," he said. "No time. I must be going."

That night, when Clive came home, I told him the story.

"Fire *insurance* man!" he sneered. "Fire *insurance*, for God's sake! Don't tell me you believed that crap!"

But, in the dark of the bedroom, he made me tell him again. He asked me questions, tried to trip me up.

"Fire *insurance* man!" he laughed. "Do you realise what he could have done to you? Do you realise how lucky you are?"

He ran a hand under my nightie. "Come here," he said. "Tell me again."

"Not again," I said.

He heaved himself onto me. His panting grew more urgent. "What else?" he said. "Tell me!"

"I'm lucky!" I said. "I'm very, very lucky!"

"Tell me!" he rasped. "Cry! Tell me how wonderful it is!"

"It's wonderful!" I cried. "You're wonderful! You're driving me out of my mind."

. . .

The policeman stood in the light of the front door. Another stood in the dark behind him, holding an Alsatian on a tight leash. "Where's the girl?" the first one asked.

"We don't know," said Lily, folding her arms. "What I want to know is what's happened to Mr. Stillington. In fact, I *demand* to know."

The policeman stared down at his boots. "We can't say, lady. I'm very sorry. We can only talk to the relatives."

"Well, who do you think this is?" Lily turned fiercely to me. "This woman is his fiancée."

The policeman glanced at me with small beige eyes. He was about my age, bat-eared, and very ugly. "Do you have proof?" he asked.

"Proof!" Lily snorted. "What proof? She has keys to the house, isn't that enough? Here"—she pulled off her diamond ring— "Here, here's your proof. I'm the aunt. It was to be my gift to them. I'm staying at the Umgeni Hotel. Lily Diamond. Ring them up!"

"O.K. O.K., lady." He took off his hat and smoothed it with one hand. "I'm sorry to say, lady, that Mr. Stillington has been murdered."

Lily closed her eyes and pinched the bridge of her nose. "Oh God!" she whispered.

"My sergeant here, he'll take you ladies back to the hotel," the policeman said. "We have to search the premises."

# 13

Jeffrey paced up and down, from the bookcase to the window and then back again. He opened the door to the verandah and walked out there, walked back in again followed by a cloud of mosquitoes. "The thing is," he said again, slapping at his forehead, "basically, you are a foreigner." He stopped in front of me, plunged his hands into his pockets. His lips were white, his hair falling in strands over his face. "That's one thing to remember."

I nodded, although I couldn't see the point. But he'd been kind to me in the car, driving me back from the hotel. When I'd asked him to slow down, he'd done so immediately. And, when we got home, he hadn't run off to his study as usual, leaving Catherine and me to ourselves. He'd started this pacing up and down, up and down, stopping every now and then to point out that I was a foreigner.

"Darling," Catherine said, "what's the significance of her being a foreigner?"

He stopped then, and gave her one of his sardonic looks, knitting his eyebrows into a "V." "Catherine," he said, "I'm surprised at you. Weren't you supposed to be clever at school?"

She smiled back. This was a game between them: her cleverness at school, his cleverness at life.

"Can't you guess?" he asked, turning to me.

"No." My heart began to shiver in my throat. I coughed.

He fell into an armchair and reached into the sweet dish for a chocolate. "You had to get a visa to come in, right?"

"Right."

"So, that visa can be withdrawn. Permanently."

Suddenly, I felt nauseous. The tea I'd just drunk rose to my throat, soured. "But why? Why should they?"

He smiled. I remembered his nose for people. Anything was possible in this place; there was always more to everything. It was a national sport. "Rumour has it," he said, "that the Stillingtons have been siphoning in terrorists from Mozambique."

"So?" said Catherine. "Why should that involve Ruth?"

"But, that isn't the case!" I shouted. "Hugh is interested in agrarian reform. His only interest in Mozambique is academic!"

"*Was.*"

I stared at Jeffrey, thinking of Hugh, the particularities of him— the fuzz of hair on the curve of his ear, the smell of gin and sweat when he came in from the Estates, his teeth, his smile. And, for the first time that night, I was in tears.

"Here," said Catherine, handing me a hanky, "it's clean."

"So, the point is," said Jeffrey, "to keep the rumours down, I'd advise you to go back to New York, maybe Friday."

"Friday?"

"Catherine can arrange with the travel agent to fix the ticket."

"But, darling," Catherine crooned, "I still don't see how that will affect any rumours. If they're going to cancel Ruth's visa, why shouldn't they do it now? Or the next time she applies?"

"Because," said Jeffrey, "if she goes back home, back to her husband, there'll be less speculation. That's all." Colour had risen to his cheeks. I knew he was lying. He wanted me out of there for his own reasons.

"The thing is," I said, "I'm not leaving on Friday."

Jeffrey's eyebrows shot up. His face flushed. "Why not?"

The sound of my voice, the words too, comforted me. "I'm not sure I'm leaving at all. I may even jettison my American passport. Who knows?"

He glanced at Catherine.

"Look," she said, "it's been a hell of a night. Let's all go to bed."

•  •  •

The spare bedroom I slept in was enormous, half the size of our apartment in New York. Catherine's decorator had redone the room and it was not itself. Curtains, wallpaper, bedspreads, couch, and chair were all co-ordinated in peach and yellow stripes. Edge-to-edge peach carpeting covered the old wood floors. Along one wall, peach-lacquered cabinets rose floor to ceiling, with mirrors shining out of unexpected places. A luggage rack with matching peach and yellow straps stood open at the bottom of each bed. Fabric, light fittings, door handles, coffee table—all had been imported at enormous cost from Italy. On the coffee table downstairs, there were magazines with pictures of just such ensembles in houses on the Italian Riviera. Holiday houses in whitewash, with the Mediterranean in blue, and yachts, and sun. Not stone mansions built to outlast the Empire, with formal rooms, and back stairs for the servants, and holidays spent skiing in Gstaad.

I opened the curtains to the balcony, and fastened back the French doors. Traffic noises echoed up from town. Mosquitoes floated in on the breeze.

Already, there were things I'd forgotten about Hugh. That first time, years ago, when I'd met him at Edwina's engagement party—whom had he been with? All I could remember now was the triumph of his taking her home first, then coming back for me, his car purring in the dark of the driveway, his hand on my thigh as we wound through the cane in weightless silence.

From the start, it had been one betrayal upon another, light as air. Lying in bed one morning, we'd discussed Clive's solitary testicle. I'd made Hugh spread his legs so I could see for myself what a matched pair looked like. And they looked wonderful to me, bizarre, enormous. Smiling down on him, I remembered thinking that he looked like a satyr, with all that massive apparatus nested between his massive haunches. I remembered thinking, too, about happiness. That, for once, it was happening in the present tense. Oh God!

I turned back into the room and drew the curtains, pulled back the bedspread, and sat down.

The door opened slightly. "Hello, old girl," Catherine whispered. "I forgot to give you towels."

I stood up, my face streaked and stiff with dried tears.

"Is there anything you want?" She closed the door softly and stood there in her gown and bare feet, holding a set of matching peach towels.

I smiled. Her life seemed so impossible to me.

"Jeffrey's asleep. He's been exhausted by this strike they've had."

I knew she was excusing him, although I understood now there was nothing to excuse. I *was* a danger to his world. I took Catherine to places where murders were committed, where people siphoned in terrorists, dressed their women up in strange clothing, and God knows what else.

She laid the towels on the spare bed and sat down beside them. "Perhaps it isn't a bad idea to cut your losses and go back," she said. "I understand the situation. Believe me, I understand. But it can only complicate things if you stay on now. My advice is to go back to Clive and work this thing out once and for all. One way or the other." She looked up at me. She was asking me to go. It wasn't a suggestion.

"The thing is, Cath—" I was breathing so lightly that the words petered out. "The thing is—" I tried again.

She stood up. "Why not let me give you a couple of aspirin? Or a sleeping pill?"

"The thing is, Cath, I'm pregnant." I turned back to the balcony, hearing the word dropping and dropping into silence. I was embarrassed at the delivery of the phrase, at the phrase itself, the pauses that preceded it. It sounded like the last line before the final curtain. Ta-da!

# 14

My face looked dead. Grey and yellow, very ugly. I grabbed a towel and hung it over the dressing-table mirror. When Catherine came in with the tea, she would notice, of course. She'd think I'd gone off the deep end, covering mirrors like an old Jew.

"Aren't you stifling in here?" she asked. "Shouldn't I open the air-conditioning vent? Or, at least, a window? It's like hell in here."

I watched her at the windows, pulling furiously at the cords, unlatching and pushing open the windows. She wore a sundress with a built-in bra, and her bangles and hoops, her high-heeled sandals with the bag to match.

"There!" she said, turning back. "Whew!"

But the room had been better dark and close, sealed off from the servants' shouting, the dogs, the traffic straining up Athlone Road. Downstairs, the Hoover started up. In the room next door, a maid was listening to "So Long the Day," the morning soap opera.

"Look, old girl," Catherine said, handing me a cup, "Ma's driving me up the wall. Unless it's really out of the question, I think we'd better have them over for drinks tonight. Or supper. Will you come down?"

I'd known the hours and days would add up against me. I'd known that. "I'd only begun to miss him," I said, "and then he was dead."

I saw her watch me pronounce each word, and knew that I must sound mad to her. But what she thought didn't concern me. Nor did the others who had come in to see me. Jeffrey, shifting around in the doorway. My parents, too, whispering down the passage. Day and night, I'd heard the door squeak open and click shut. I wasn't properly asleep, though, just wanting to sleep, or woken up from a half sleep. And then, Catherine had given me the pills, and I'd slept a whole day and a night in a row. And, if I'd dreamed of going back to New York as usual, leaving again as I had always done, I'd forgotten the dream on waking. Because, after such a sleep, everything seems different.

Now, drinking tea in that acrid room, I saw that it would, indeed, seem normal to leave, even if one didn't really want to. Had I ever wanted to leave? Every time, *every* time there were tears on the plane, me staring out of the window at the clouds, or the darkness, whatever was out there, and wishing I could go back. If there was to be a child, so much the better. It would give me more reason to return. Even Clive would have to understand that. Clive, standing at the customs exit as usual, with his shoes worn down on the outsides because his feet were problematic—would he notice, perhaps, how ugly I'd become?

"Let's go to Ma and Dad's for lunch," I said lightly.

She frowned and raised her eyebrows.

"Have you spoken to Lily?" I asked. Every day, I asked her this, because she was the one who phoned Lily for me. And sometimes Lily phoned her. I never spoke, though. I hadn't wanted to.

"She sends you her love. They have the man in custody—the maid's husband."

"How many days has it been?"

"Five," she said. "This is the fifth."

"What I meant was, when I left the bungalow, I had begun to miss *him*. Hugh. Do you know what I mean?"

She nodded, but clearly she hadn't a clue. "Look," she said, "it's actually four o'clock. I have to go and pick up the fish for supper. Do you want to come with me?"

"No."

I liked saying "no" to her, without explanation. Going with her to pick up her fish would be far more hellish than staying in the peach room.

"Why not have a bit of a walk in the garden then?"

I put down my teacup, but it slammed by mistake, slopping into the saucer. "Cath, what were those pills I took?"

She stood up, hooked her bag over her arm. "I suggest you have a nice bath and come down for supper tonight. Wear your dressing gown—it's just us. The children are eating early. I'll tell Ma you'll come for lunch another day."

But I was mad now to have her stay with me. "How do they *know* it was Regina's husband?" I insisted, standing up too. "How did he do it?"

She fished in her bag for her sunglasses. "Stabbed," she said. "Don't worry about it. You can be sure they've locked him up."

"Hugh?"

She flexed her jaw and sighed. I was wearing her down. "No, not Hugh," she said steadily, "the maid's husband. Ruth, are you putting this on?"

"Cath—" I cleared my throat. I reached into the pockets of my gown for a tissue so that I could cough or blow my nose to convince her I wouldn't cry. We were the same with crying. It embarrassed us. Still, we always cried when I was leaving—right at the end, when I had to go through to the plane. Each of us was like a mother, like a child. One child sent off, the other left behind. Now, though, I was far from tears, and she was annoyed. "Cath," I said quickly, "look, I've been thinking. Maybe you're right. Maybe I should go back."

She turned away, but I could see her smiling, the way she flicked the towel off the mirror, folded it, and laid it down. And then looked around for a way to start ordering my life. "What about some Badedas?" she said, making for the door. "I'll fetch it from my bathroom."

And, really, she was right, the bath was nice. I ran it hot, and stayed in for an hour, and, when I came out, and dressed, and dried my hair, I still looked thin, but less ugly. And I did go for a walk in the garden. There were places there where nobody but the gardeners went, and things I hadn't seen before. A thick-leaved bush with waxy flowers that smelled like fresh meat. A column of giant red ants, snaking up the trunk of the mango tree. One of the children had built a tree house up there, with a knotted rope hanging from it to climb up. There was a giant bread tree with leaves like teeth, growing in a corner. If Hugh hadn't been murdered, I'd have seen none of this.

At supper, Catherine's fish was delicate and sweet. I asked her how she'd cooked it, and Jeffrey excused himself because he couldn't stand the sight of women in dressing gowns, Catherine whispered. But, really, it was because she was so pleased with telling me about the fish. Too bad for him. She and I had the evening to ourselves. The pills I'd taken were harmless, she assured me, nothing to worry about, baby or no baby. And did I want her to get me some curry powder to take back? Biltong? Tea? Golden syrup?

. . .

"I only hope," my mother sighed, "that they don't involve this child in this terrible business." With Catherine, my mother always referred to me as if I hadn't yet learned to talk. "Just *look* at this! It's *still* all over the front page! Photographs, the lot!"

I hovered out of sight in the hall, on my way back from phoning Lily.

Catherine twitched one foot and looked out of the window. For her sake, I had gone with her to Albie Stern, her gynaecologist. To confirm things, as she put it. But I knew already it was exactly five weeks before that Hugh had said, "Bugger the diaphragm, come here." I knew what I knew.

"Who knows what's going to happen in this country," my mother said. "Where's it all going to end?"

"Ma," I said, "there are far more violent places in the world to live."

"You're telling *me*!" she cried. "And New York is one of them!"

Catherine gave me a thin smile and stood up. "I have to go," she said. "Listen, I'll phone you later. Are you sure you're all right?"

I picked up the morning paper and read the headlines again. BOSS BOY'S REVENGE IN STILLINGTON MURDER. There was a picture of Regina's husband, and there was Hugh, an old studio photograph of him in a jacket and tie. At the bottom of the page was a front view of the bungalow. With its ornamental fretwork and columns, its wide verandah, and the expanse of lawn to the edge of the cliff, it looked much grander in the photograph than it really was.

I lay back along the couch, pretending to read the paper. When

Lynn Freed

the policeman had asked the night of the murder if I would come in to the morgue and identify the body, Lily had grasped my arm hard and said that was quite unnecessary. Unnecessary? Why had she said that? Perhaps Hugh had told her I was pregnant. When I'd told him I thought I was, he'd swallowed his Scotch in one gulp and then looked up at me, a perfect cinematic gesture.

I closed my eyes. For the first time since the night of the murder, my throat ached with tears. They were tears of pity for myself. Myself claimed back by this ordinary life. Hugh was dead—I saw the truth of that now—and Regina's husband would be hanged because of him. So, why hadn't Hugh seen that coming? Who the bloody hell did he *think* he was? Who was he? I stared through swimming eyes at the picture in the paper. Hugh Stillington. The father of my child. But the words were nothing to me. Father. Child. Nothing.

My mother pulled my feet onto her lap and ran her fingernails lightly across my skin, around my ankles, up my shins. "Oh, Ruth, Ruth, Ruth," she cried. "What are we going to do about you?"

I wiped my eyes and put the paper down. I had left a message for Lily at the hotel. I wanted to speak to her. Suddenly, I was desperate to speak to her. Perhaps there were things they weren't telling me, all of them, even my mother. Lily could have left the hotel. She could have gone to London, gone to Rome.

My mother clapped her hands. "*I* have an idea!" she said brightly. She grabbed the paper and flapped it at me. "Why not write a *murder* mystery? Something for the *American* market?"

"What?"

"You could change things around, of course, bring in all sorts of wild animals, that sort of thing. You know how mad Americans are about wild animals? Make it *exciting*, make it *romantic*!"

My father's key turned in the front-door lock.

She reached for the magnifier to look at her watch. "Already?" she said. "But it's only half past ten."

"It's a scorcher out there today," he said, making for his chair. "The air conditioner packed in at the recording studio and I thought it sensible to come home." He breathed deeply as the doctor had told him to do in times of stress and then lifted his feet onto the footstool to improve his circulation.

112

"What about a drink?" my mother suggested cosily. "Slatkin said a drink would do you good now and then." She looked around. "Why don't we *all* have a pre-lunch drink?"

"Now? Certainly not!" He closed his eyes to shut her out.

She sighed and clicked her tongue. "It might interest you to notice that your younger daughter is up and about again at last. She is sitting to your left."

He sat up then and blinked at me. "*Chopsticks!*" he cried. "Come here! Let me have a look at you!"

"And it *might* please you to know that your second favourite phoned this morning. She wants us all for dinner Saturday night."

He looked at her. So did I. "Who?" I said.

"Can't you guess? Ettie Goldman. Ha!"

"Out of the question!" my father snapped. "Didn't you tell her I'm still recuperating?"

"You can climb down off your high horse! What do you take me for?" She began to heave herself up for the journey to the liquor cabinet. But then, having made it onto her feet, she stopped and turned to him. "Are you sufficiently recovered to fetch me a gin-and-it? Or are we all going to be enjoying your ill health for the rest of the day?"

Slowly and deliberately, he leaned over to one side, retrieved his pocket watch, and pulled it open. "You might be interested to know that it's twenty-five minutes to eleven, ante meridiem."

"Hmph!" she snorted, walking off. "One of these days, you might consider taking a proper job. Making some money for *us* instead of sitting on the phone selling raffle tickets for so-called good causes."

He turned to me, his nostrils flaring. " 'So-called'! One day, I'm going to strangle that woman, and bugger the consequences!"

I looked away. There was no longer any sense to be made of their old age. My presence, far from helping, seemed to make things worse. They had simply turned me into an audience for their despair. He was even trying out his new vocabulary on me. Dr. Slatkin had advised him not to bottle up his emotions, and so he'd taken to saying "bugger" and "crap" if the occasion arose. Still, as far as I could see, stepping out of character only made things worse for him. For any of us. It allowed her to laugh, hard and cold at his threats, and to point out that, despite appearances, he'd never been much good as a villain, even on the stage. He was stiff as a poker, and had only two expressions, this one and that one. What could one expect, anyway, of a tailor's dummy? A Jekyll and Hyde? A ninny who had a so-called heart attack when his wife cut him out of her will?

"Perhaps we can have one of our little chats after lunch," he said to me, "when your mother is snoring her head off."

• • •

As soon as they arrived for the wedding, my parents set about rearranging what I had already arranged. The service, for instance. My father objected to an organ in shul. He also objected to Bach. Why Bach, he asked the rabbi? Wasn't it a bit much to play a German composer at a Jewish wedding? We were a traditional family, he explained, Orthodox, in fact. Couldn't we have the baruch abo?

The rabbi smiled. He had red hair, a retroussé nose, and freckles. His name was Ashley Shepherd, and his wife, a graduate student in music, was the organist. "Things are a little different here," he told my father, who was smiling too. "We consider our service eclectic."

But I knew my father's smile. It was the one he wore in the face of barbarians. "I think we'll do without the organ nevertheless," he said. "We would like the baruch abo," he added genially. "And, of course, there has to be a chuppa."

Rabbi Shepherd's mouth twitched at the corners. "We don't use a chuppa in our weddings," he said. "We don't even have one, I'm afraid."

My father nodded sympathetically. "That might be difficult," he said. "Of course, there can't be a wedding without a chuppa."

"Perhaps the pole holders can hold up a scarf," I suggested.

Ashley Shepherd nodded. "There's a possibility," he said.

But my father grasped his chin as if deep in thought, an old stage trick. He was ruling the moment, holding his audience. Finally, he looked up. "You seem like a resourceful sort of chap," he said. "What about borrowing one?"

The rabbi grabbed an address book on his desk and began flipping through it. "Wait a moment," he said, picking up the phone.

114

# The Bungalow

And so a chuppa was to be brought across town in a truck. And baruch abo sung by someone from the music school, not played. And I would wear a proper wedding dress, not the long skirt and blouse I had bought already.

When I went for the final fitting, my father sat downstairs, while my mother supervised the alterations in the dressing room.

"What a job you've done!" she cried. She had always had a way with alteration hands. A little flattery and they'd do it right, she told me. "Perhaps—what do you think?—the hem can be lifted just a little over there?" she asked. "And the sleeve is a little long, don't you think?"

I, on the other hand, couldn't stand the woman creeping around me. Nor did I like the dress. I had chosen it because it was cheap. It had been modelled for a bridal magazine, the saleswoman had told me, and brides were superstitious about such things, wasn't that silly?

"I sewed a daisy here on the veil," said the woman. "See? To cover that little tear."

"But it doesn't cover it," I complained. "Look! The netting's all bunched up." I looked at myself in the mirror. I was fat. For the three months since I'd arrived, I'd been eating furiously. Every day I discovered new foods, things I'd never tasted before and couldn't do without. Fig Newtons, Sara Lee cheesecake with cherries on top. I ate before meals and after, in the middle of the night. My skin was bad, my face was full, my breasts and hips and thighs all bulging. "It looks ridiculous!" I said, wrenching the veil off my head.

My mother came over and took the veil from me, placed it back carefully on my head. "Come on, darling," she whispered, "she's doing the best she can. Really, she's done a fine job."

The alteration woman sulked around the hem with pins in her mouth.

"Why don't we call Dad up to have a look?" my mother asked.

I shrugged. "Who cares?" I said.

She went out into the hall and waved down to him. I knew she was coaching him to be bowled over. "By all means," I heard him say. And then there was his rat-a-tat-tat at the door, and him, standing to attention outside it.

115

*"Turn towards him, show him," my mother coaxed.*
*I turned and glared.*

*But he only stood there, saying nothing. His eyes filled with tears, he took me by the shoulders. "Forgive me," he half whispered, his voice cracking. "Forgive me, but you are so beautiful, the most beautiful of my brides. I only hope this man realises how lucky he is."*

• • •

My father and I sat in the shade of the pergola at the far end of the verandah, sipping our Nescafé.

"This whole business can't be very pleasant for you," he suggested.

My lip began to quiver. I reached up and pulled off a bougainvillaea bloom, pretended to examine it. I wanted Lily. I wanted to believe what I knew had happened. I wanted to see Hugh's body.

"The point is," he went on, "whatever your relationship was with Hugh Stillington—and it's pretty clear to me what it was—for your own sake you should try to return to your normal life now."

He began to stretch a hand out in my direction, but I turned away to inspect something invisible on the sleeve of my blouse. "Normal," I mumbled, "what's normal?"

"I would hope," he said, "that things are all right in the physical department with Clive?"

It was a question he'd been asking since I'd got married. He'd asked Catherine too, she said, and it was none of his bloody business, ugh!

"I should like to think," he said, "that all you girls have rewarding sex lives. Without a rewarding sex life—"

"Dad," I said quickly, desperate to silence him, "Clive can't have children."

"What?"

"Children are out of the question with him. He's sterile."

It was done then, and so easily. He frowned down at his knees and cleared his throat.

"What are you two up to out there?" my mother demanded, swaying slightly in the doorway.

Slowly, he pushed himself up from the chair. He touched my shoulder and then glided past her without a word.

"What's come over *him?*" she asked, turning to follow him inside.

I walked down the steps into the garden. The flowerbeds were overgrown, and the grass full of weeds. Since her eyes had gone bad, the gardener spent most of his time weeding near the street so that he could talk to other gardeners. But there was a lovely pink Tibouchina in full bloom, and an ornate birdbath with Indian mynahs splashing around in it. I took off my shoes and sat on the grass in the shade. There were freighters on the sea, a light afternoon breeze had picked up. I closed my eyes and tried to think that I was waiting for the moment to leave for the airport, my suitcases ready in the hall. But there was nothing to the thought. Like a thief, I mapped the route out carefully instead: up the driveway, through the gates, right onto Burnham Road. Then along the ridge, and down, down through Umbilo Crossing to the lagoon, left onto the bridge and up the northern thruway past the Victoria landing strip, past the filling station and the "Hou links, ry regs verby" sign to the turning. Then down through the cane, hooting at the bends, till the hotel, and left onto the coastal road, not quite three kilometers, to the bungalow gate.

That was where I wanted to go. Nowhere else. Here, in this rotting place, I felt exiled. Like Lily within her body. Surrounded by noise. Cut off. And without hope.

"Darling!" my mother called from the verandah, shading her eyes against the sun.

They stood there together—she in her old tight-fitting, sleeveless sundress, belted at the waist to show off the figure she'd once had. And he in his wide shorts, golf stockings, and voile short-sleeved shirt.

"Come in for a moment, darling," my mother called. "We want to have a word with you. Let's all have tea."

# 15

Lily had made the arrangements. She'd gone to see the Stillington solicitor and found out that Hugh had recently made some changes in his will. He'd made allowances for the maintenance of the bungalow, a maid, a watchman, and his car for as long as I stayed there. There was also a small trust for the education of the child. The bungalow itself, however, was tied up by the Stillingtons for themselves. The place now belonged to his oldest son, on condition that he came to live there. Until and unless he did, I had full occupancy rights. If he didn't, it went to his first son's son, if he had one, on the same condition, or, if he didn't, to Hugh's second son, and so on. "And by that time," Lily said, "we'll all have been driven into the sea. So let's have a drink."

Lily had suggested she stay for a few days while I settled in. She'd spread her bottles and sponges and bags of cotton wool around the bathroom. Her stockings and a pair of old-fashioned satin panties hung over her towel to dry.

"Josefina!" she called. *"Buyisa lo ayisi!"*

All Lily would tell me about Hugh's body was how his feet had looked—sticking out of the canvas, still neatly laced into his shoes, like feet off the edge of a bed. When I asked her for more, she waved a hand in the air, put an arm around my shoulder. Death is nothing, she assured me. It is simply an absence.

But, by sundown, Hugh's absence had settled itself into the hollow of my stomach. In an instant, I knew it could be at my throat or my eyes. And for this, Lily could do nothing.

At first, I had moved carefully among his things, as if he had just left the room and would come back again. But, after a while, their silent presence, day after day, seemed like a mockery. I gave

The Bungalow

his boots to Josefina to polish, inside and out. And then I put them in a box and pushed it onto the top of the wardrobe. I moved his chair to the other side of the room, unhooked the binoculars, and adjusted them for my eyes. Still, there was his smell in everything. Smoke in the slipcovers, half a bottle of gin left, and the sherry in the decanter. Even in the spare room, there was the camphor and the coir matting, the sharp fragrance of the dress-up clothes.

I went to the edge of the verandah to watch two hadedahs stalking across the lawn. The peacocks were gone—caught and eaten, no doubt, said Lily, when the word went around.

When I drove along the road now, blacks turned to watch me. So did the waiters at the hotel. The Indian at the supply store looked shy when I stopped in for fruit. "Sorry to hear about the boss, madam" he said. "I hear they got that tsotsi and all in jail." In a matter of months, I would be the talk of Gigi's. All over town, around swimming pools and dinner tables, they'd be counting the months backwards and forwards. They'd turn to look when my parents walked into the cinema or waited to be seated at the Majestic.

It seemed like years, not months, since I'd left Clive standing with his parents at the entrance to our building. Flo Brasch had hung on to the shopping cart with one hand, grasped Clive's elbow with other. His father had sported a foldup travelling hat. Standing there, they had looked like people I hardly knew, even Clive sucking in his stomach, wearing the same smile he'd worn as a fat, unhappy boy in family photographs. When I'd waved to them from the taxi, I'd felt as if it were I who had come to visit, and had stayed too long, and were now going home at last.

My parents blamed the Brasches for everything. "I always thought," said my mother, "that there was something deficient about that Clive. But I put it down to the parents, that mother in particular. Who would ever think of testicles?"

The word "divorce" was never mentioned. When there was a pause in the conversation, they looked at me to save us all from it. "Don't they do particular things these days with anonymous fathers?" my mother asked, ringing the bell for tea. I could have told them then, but I grabbed for the marble ashtray instead, traced around and around its familiar shape with my finger. Then Nich-

119

olas knocked and came in with the tray. And I told them I'd be staying on for a bit, that I was applying to have my visa extended. And that I'd be moving out to the bungalow with Lily Diamond.

   • • •

Josefina carried out a bowl of ice on a tray and placed it between us. She had appeared at the back door soon after our arrival—sent, no doubt, said Lily, by the bush telegraph.

"I'll have to show her the ice bucket," she said, fingering a cube into each of our glasses. She shook off her shoes and lifted her stockinged feet onto the swing seat. "Ruth,"she said, "the husband must be told."

By now I was used to having my anxieties—still slipping around my intestines—given voice by Lily. I half expected her to put on her shoes and march to the phone herself. In fact, Clive would have accepted her word, her version of things. He could relax in the company of a woman too old to be considered womanly.

"The truth will do," she added. She peered at her watch over the top of her glasses. "It's six o'clock," she said, "what time is it in New York?"

"Lily," I said, "I'd rather write."

   • • •

"My dear Clive," I wrote, underlined, retraced, and then abandoned to go and look out of the library window. I had never loved a university. There was a smell to them that I disliked, special to their building materials and cleaning fluids and substances used to stop the rot of books in libraries. I disliked libraries too—row after row, wall after wall of books, like money in the bank. I had no stomach for electric bells. Nor for students swarming, their voices raised in argument over big ideas.

The university had spread its ugliness all across the ridge and down both sides of the hill, building after building in cement and brick. There was a utilitarian spareness to the conglomeration, and also a carelessness of purpose. It could have been anything—government offices, shipping headquarters, even a hospital. The wind blew in from the sea, raising clouds of red dust, mixing with the fumes of African diesel buses grinding up the hill.

In the parking lot below, students milled about, or walked along the verge of the road. There were men with long hair now, some in ponytails. Women wore African print dresses and Zulu beads and handmade sandals. Someone strummed on a guitar.

"Miss Frank?"

I turned back into the gloom of the library. There stood Krishnah, hands in his pockets, quite unsmiling.

"Hello, Krishnah."

"Would you like to come to the union for some tea?" he asked.

It seemed like a real question, without a sting in it. Still, I didn't want to go. "I'm supposed to be going about turning my dissertation into something of a book—" I started. I heard myself fall into an Indian sort of rigmarole of present participles and qualifying phrases, and hoped that he hadn't heard it too, wished he'd go away, wondered why on earth I couldn't just say no.

"I wanted to phone—what can I say? Hugh was—shit, man! He—" He looked around at the empty library. "It's difficult to talk here," he said.

His presence there—that voice, that jaw—were like Hugh's boots, the binoculars on the hook. "Oh, don't worry," I said. "It's fine."

"Edwina told me I would find you here. She said you're meeting her for lunch."

Clearly he wouldn't go away. He was determined, for some reason, to take me to the union. I gathered up my writing pad and pen and put them in my bag. But I looked at my watch to make it clear it couldn't last.

"What was the subject of the dissertation?" he asked, loping along the road beside me.

" 'Jane Austen and the Economics of Middle-class Marriage.' "

"Ah! 'Masterpiece Theatre'!"

Here we go again, I thought.

We'd come to the steps of the union. Students sat around in groups laughing and talking. They looked up as we appeared. "Hi, Krish!" someone said.

He tripled down the steps, beckoning me to follow. The union smelled of curry and sweet, hot oil. Coloured women in hair nets stood behind the counter, filling orders and shouting to each other.

One woman fished koeksisters out of a vat with a pair of tongs and piled them, one by one, onto a wire drainer. When she saw Krishnah, she held one up and flashed him a toothless grin. "Hey, Krish! Look what I got for you!"

He ordered two, reached across the counter to squeeze the woman's arm, looked back to see whether I'd noticed, and then went on. Two pots of tea, cups and saucers, spoons, paper serviettes. At the cash register, he dug into his pocket, laid some coins out on the counter. I dug too, but he waved away my money.

"This way," he said, leading with the tray to a table in the corner, by the windows. He set the tea things out with care, placed the plate of koeksisters between us.. His hands tapered into long, thin fingers with tiny fingernails. His skin was grey as dust, his palms very pink. "Look at all the tankers out there," he said, saliva running in his mouth as he spoke.

I turned to look. There they were, as always, lined up and waiting to come in. "Where are they from?" I asked.

"Iran, all over the place." He nudged the plate of koeksisters towards me. "Remember these?" he asked.

I took one that was still warm and bit off the tip. "What did you read at Oxford?" I asked.

"PPE."

"Do you, by any chance, know Maya Chowdree?"

He grinned, picked up his koeksister delicately, between two spidery fingers, keeping his eyes on me.

My ears and cheeks caught fire. All those years overseas I'd spent shaking my head to the names of people I didn't know—Al Frank? The Nate and Sadie Fessels of Cape Town? Carmen Rabinowitz? The Syd Selitskys of Johannesburg, pronounced "Yohannesburg"?—and now, here I was myself: Do you by any chance know an Indian I know?

"She's an old friend," I explained. "We were friends at school."

In fact, I'd lost Maya at Oxford soon after we'd arrived there. I knew she'd sung in a choir, and had come out with a first. But she'd stayed on to specialise, and I'd come home. Then, she'd come home, and I'd gone to America. We'd both got married. And then it was too late to become friends again.

"She's my cousin," Krishnah said, stretching his arms out and yawning extravagantly. "But Uncle Ravi won't have me in the house."

"Why not?"

He grinned. "Why do you think?"

"Where does Maya live?" I asked.

"At home, with her parents. The husband went back to England, you know. Turned out to be a cad. Uncle Ravi bought him off, good riddance to bad rubbish!"

Maya, with her almond eyes and perfect skin, her hair, her teeth—abandoned by a cad. My heart leapt in my chest.

"Would you like to come over one day?" I asked. "I'm staying at Hugh's, with a woman called Lily Diamond." I wanted to tell him that I too had rich relatives who didn't want me near them. That rich itself was beginning to get on my nerves. It was all over the place out here, everywhere you looked.

He frowned at the empty plate as if my invitation had landed there like a fly. Then he turned away to scan the lunchtime crowd streaming down the steps. "There's Edwina now," he said, "blind as a bat." He stood up and waved her over. "Listen," he said to me, "I'll give you a ring one of these days."

# 16

Lily was right. Catherine's maternity clothes were like flags. I would look like a battleship in them. She suggested Hugh's ensemble of dress-up clothes instead. "Aides-mémoire," she said.

Anyway, it wasn't time yet. I was still thin, slightly sick all day until evening. Catherine advised waiting until I was past the three-month danger point to tell my parents. Kneeling with her in front of the kist of clothes, I wondered whom she was protecting, me or them? Or had she forgotten the father in the sisterly fun of holding up a billowing striped tent against my shoulders?

Since I'd finally written him the truth, Clive had been visiting me in dreams. Sometimes in a crowd, crying. Or looking in through a window, saying things that made no sense, like, "The delineation of life service suggestions." In the dream, the phrase seemed menacing, important to understand, and I'd woken myself up to write it down. But, there it was, scrawled all over a page—nonsense.

"It's not nonsense," Lily assured me. "Things reveal themselves in code. You should read Jung. I knew him, you know, when I lived in Zurich." She added several spoonfuls of sugar to her tea and then stirred importantly. "Actually," she said, looking up, "that's rubbish. I knew him, but he hardly noticed me. I was a twit, never opened my mouth. I've regretted it ever after."

I laughed, and so did she. When she came over, my life made sense. When she returned to the hotel, I prowled around the bungalow like a prisoner. On Tuesday, one of the Stillingtons was coming to take an inventory. Their lawyer was coming with them. Where would I go? What would I do while they were there? When my parents phoned to ask how I was and had I locked the doors, pity for them almost strangled me. Beware of pity, said Catherine, and don't imagine locking the doors will keep anyone out. Nor will a night watchman. They sleep through everything, or get killed off first. I'd be better off with a dog, a black dog, because Africans were terrified of black dogs for some reason. Better still, I should consider Jeffrey's offer to go and stay with them. I'd be left alone. The children were in school every day. And Jeffrey seemed to have come around. He'd been asking how I was doing. He seemed concerned.

"I've been thinking," I said to Lily. "I could have left Clive years ago, or not married him in the first place. All these years, I could have been doing what I wanted."

She reached over for a pig's ear, baked by Grace, and nibbled at the edge. "What did you want?" she asked.

I smiled, I shrugged.

"A vocation is a blessing, my dear," she said. "It is more, much more, than doing what you want."

"I didn't mean a vocation—"

" 'The delineation of life service suggestions!' " she cried suddenly. "Ha! That's it! You wanted Clive to delineate a new life for you! Look at your sister. Isn't that precisely what she's achieved in her own peculiar way? All that so-called service? Life service! More like a life sentence!" She slapped her hands onto her knees and barked in delight. "Don't you see, Ruth? Your good fortune is that the delineation didn't work! You turned down the suggestion!"

. . .

On our last day in Mexico, as I climbed out of the pool, a man narrowed his eyes at me, pursed his lips, and kissed the air. He was Mexican. Tall, dark, very beautiful. In the madness of my sudden conquest, I pursed my lips too. Then, taking fright, I ran over to my chaise, huffed and puffed, and shook the water out of my hair.

"Can't you do that somewhere else?" Clive mumbled, drying the pages of Shogun with the back of his arm.

"Pssst!"

I turned. The man stood in some shade nearby, like a panther. He plucked an hibiscus from a hedge and tipped it towards me.

But Clive had set aside his book and stood poised at the deep end like Christ on the cross. With an enormous splash, he dived in,

125

*making, as he swam, the sort of grunts and cries he made in bed. "Come in," he shouted. "It's great!"*

*At dinner that night, everywhere I looked, there was the man. He lifted his wineglass to toast me. He stood next to us at the dessert table, watched Clive mumble admonishments to himself and pull in his stomach as he heaped four things at once onto his plate. And then turned to me and winked, as if Clive were a stranger to us both.*

*At the discotheque afterwards, he danced behind me or in front of me. If he wasn't to be seen, I heard him. He had a whole repertoire of whistles and sucking noises—the kind used in our world to call dogs.*

*Clive noticed nothing. "Let's go back to the room," he said after a while. "I've had enough."*

*In the room, I hovered at the foot of the bed, wanting two things at once. "I'm not tired," I announced.*

*"Then read."*

*"Don't feel like reading."*

*He turned the page.*

*"Want to go back to the disco?" I asked.*

*"No. You go if you like."*

*I grabbed my purse and plunged back out into the hot air, down to the discotheque.*

*The man was there, laughing, flanked by two friends and some girls. In a minute, he was at my side, leading me away, down one of the paths without a word. When we reached a dark spot, he stopped hard and swung me around.*

*Suddenly, I could only think that Clive would turn the corner looking for me. Or of Clive on the porch of our room, looking at his watch. I couldn't imagine how long I'd been away.*

*"Come gweeth me," he said, "I want djyou!"*

*I pulled away. "I can't," I said. "I have to go back. Sorry."*

*Clive was still reading when I burst back into the room. "That was quick," he said.*

*I froze. Outside was the world, wanting me, begging for me in a foreign accent. And here, absorbed by the battles and escapes and forbidden love of mediaeval Japan, sat the life I lacked the courage to give up.*

*All night, I suffered a sort of homesickness. Early the next morn-*

ing, I ran down to the pool before breakfast. The man was not there. Nor was he in the dining room, nor anywhere else I looked. Suitcases were already lined up at the front of the hotel. A bus throbbed outside the lobby, waiting to take us to the airport. I flew to the front desk and gave the girl a description of the man. I wanted to tell him I would come back, that I was infected by regret, I was on fire with it.

She listened to the silly lie I gave her, and ran a long scarlet fingernail down the guest list, shaking her head. "Gweethout a name," she smiled, "ees impossible."

. . .

Josefina knew how to roast a chicken and boil potatoes. She could also make rissoles out of mincemeat and smother them with a thick, salty gravy. She knew how to boil gem squash, and cut them in half, and then fill each half with tinned peas and a dollop of butter. But, if I bought some fish and told her how to grill it, or how to make a salad dressing, she stood back in silence. And, when I said, "Here, you try now," she stared at the fish as if she'd never seen one before. "Angazi, madam," she said, never looking me in the eye.

I had to tell her to wash her hands before she touched the food. And to wash every day, and to use the deodorant I'd bought her. At first, I suggested these things in a laughing sort of way—the tone I used on taxi drivers in New York when they ran a light. But, when I saw her, once again, hang out the floor rag, untuck her apron and skirt and proceed past the sink towards the mound of thawing mince, I shouted, "No!" and she turned, her lids half shut, her mouth set full, to face me. "Wash first!" I ordered her. I marched to the sink myself and turned on the tap, picked up the wedge of green soap, and washed my own hands vigorously. "See?" I said. "Wash! See?"

In her haste, Regina had left behind some of her things—a scarf on a hook, a pair of slippers behind the kitchen door. These Josefina neither moved nor touched. Maybe she thought Regina would come back to reclaim her job once her husband had been hanged. For all I knew, they could be friends—sisters even. Regina could be living in the bush, watching for signs of welcome. I had no idea.

If Hugh were there, I could confess to him how Josefina got on my nerves, how I followed her around to catch her out, treading lightly, like a cat. He'd explain it to me. He'd evoke history, employ arcane phrases, run a crooked finger along a row of books until he found what he wanted, pull it out, and hand it to me. Then settle back to watch me, as I turned the pages.

I pulled down a history of the Zulus, stared at the sepia photographs of Ceteswayo and Dinizulu, the skins, the spears. On his day off, Nicholas dressed up like that. He sat cross-legged on a tea crate, his black belly hanging over a skirt of skins and furs, dispensing potions of coloured water to African women who wanted babies and couldn't have them.

I heard a shuffling, and turned. Josefina stood in the doorway, waiting for me to notice her. She never knocked.

"Yes?"

"What time the dinner, madam?"

"Seven o'clock," I said.

But she just stood there, waiting.

I closed the book and walked through to the kitchen, pointed to the clock. "Big hand there, see? Little hand there. Seven—o'—clock."

Without Lily or Hugh, time began to warp at the bungalow the way it had when I first arrived in New York. It was only five o'clock, too early yet for a drink. Still, I told Josefina to bring out the drinks tray, and to remember the ice. I settled onto the couch to watch the afternoon storm move in from the sea, tracing around in my head for the seed of irritation that had been there all afternoon.

Quite soon, I found it. It was the word "vocation." More than that, it was the rebuke I'd felt from Lily as she pronounced the word. Lily had said it quietly, with reverence, perhaps for her own lost life as a singer. And yet, the word itself seemed out of fashion, quaint. It seemed to apply to missionaries, or nuns, or nurses on the front. And then, thinking of her lost life, I thought of the thing, the simple nameless thing that had massed in my lungs as a child, given me hope as I swung higher and higher under the avocado tree, singing hymns and dreaming of overseas. My whole future seemed to have been contained in that simple thing without a name. All my hope.

What had happened then? Where had it fled?

Certainly, it had never visited "Jane Austen and the Economics of Middle-class Marriage." Nor did it have anything to do with footnotes, bibliographies, publications edging along the tenure track toward Old Age. That much I'd known a year ago when I walked into the chairman's office to say I was giving up.

He'd looked up, alarmed, in case I cried in front of him, or confessed some personal disaster. And, when I hadn't, he'd asked what I'd do now, what I'd be interested in doing? But I'd always gone dumb in the face of such questions. What do you want to do when you leave school? What kind of books do you like to read? What are your interests, hobbies, sports? I had listened as Americans rolled so easily into their presentations—linking their pasts with their futures, which were, in turn, linked cleverly to some other high good. But I couldn't do it myself. I shrugged.

·  ·  ·

Why not think of it as a year off? the chairman suggested. He spoke slowly, choosing his words with care. His office smelled of books and dust. He had dandruff and a sunken chest, a yellowing nylon shirt. If you publish the Jane Austen piece, if Rosenblum goes on leave, perhaps I could suggest—

Yes, I said, standing up to go. Thank you.

I opened my umbrella and faced out into the wind and rain, through the gates of the university, out onto the street. I picked my way around piles of soggy dog shit and pools of water, bowed away from the man begging for subway fare to Roosevelt Hospital.

Then, suddenly, there it was again, that nameless assurance, that hope. It arrived with the thought of going home for the Christmas holidays, with the diaphragm I'd bought, even with the thought of the antique earrings I'd found in San Francisco at the MLA. Men turned to watch me pass. I smiled, I sang.

"Praise, my soul, the King of heaven; To his feet they tribute bring—"

For once, I would be back for mango season. It would be hot

enough to swim at night. I'd phone Edwina this time, meet some new people for a change. My parents had written to say we'd be going to the mountains for a few days. And did I want to take in the reserve?

I stamped the water off my shoes, closed the umbrella to get through the door. I was thirty years old and I was changing my life. How it would happen, though, I had no idea.

· · ·

Josefina shuffled in with the drinks tray and set it down before me.

"Wait!" I said. "Where's the ice bucket?"

She looked at her feet.

I picked up the bowl of ice, marched off to the kitchen with her behind me. "Here," I said. "See this? *Ice bucket!* For the *ice! Ayisi!*" I tipped the ice into it and slammed the lid down. "Next time," I said, "don't forget."

# 17

"Frankly," my mother said, waving her nose around the lounge, "it looks rather ordinary to me." She sat on the couch, keeping her arm linked through the handle of her bag. "And the girl?" She nodded towards the verandah, where Josefina was laying the table for lunch. "Who pays for her?"

I glanced outside. Contrary to my instructions, Josefina had set the table first, and was now cleaning the surface, between the table mats and glasses, with a dish rag. "Hugh left money," I said.

My mother sniffed. "As well he might have done."

Once—not even once: six months ago—that sniff, the tone of voice, the old familiar phrases of contempt could have turned my stomach, turned me against what I had thought I loved. But now I watched her scratch at the fabric of the couch to test its quality, and I pitied her. "It's linen," I said. "Sanderson linen."

My father had folded himself neatly into Hugh's armchair, arms and legs crossed, one foot tapping the air. "Any word from Clive?" he asked.

I shook my head. Clearly, Clive had had my letter by now, because he wasn't phoning. Nor was he answering the phone. If I phoned the research institute, the secretary said he was out of the office, or out of town, or in a meeting. I wondered whether he might kill himself. Unnatural causes seemed to fascinate him— the necessary dosages, methods of detection.

"Catherine mentioned that you might stay on to the end," my mother said, hanging a cigarette between her lips. "Do you think that wise?"

The smell of the raw cigarette, the click and flash of her lighter, reminded me of Hugh lighting his, the thrust of his chin. His unalterable absence.

My father cleared his throat. "What do you think the chances are of Clive overlooking the paternity situation? In view of the circumstances—his inabilities—I mean?"

"He might even be relieved," my mother chimed in quickly, "a peculiar man like that."

For the second time, I felt the child flitter in my belly. I had felt it the night before, waking out of a dream in which I'd had a litter of puppies, eight or nine of them. People had stood about admiring them, picking them up one by one. And I'd been proud and glad, because I knew that eight or nine meant good luck.

"There are things to be considered if you're going to stay on," my father said. "What about medical insurance?"

They exchanged a glance. The freeze between them was over; my situation had done it.

My mother cocked her head to one side. "If you went back to New York, who would have to know? It would be your word against his."

I had known she'd make this suggestion. It had been hanging in the air above us since I'd told them I was pregnant.

"It happens all the *time*, you know," she said. "Both you and Catherine were late. In fact, I thought *you*'d never arrive." She gave a loud stage laugh. "I was *enormous*! They said you could see me coming around a corner five minutes before I arrived!"

"Josefina!" I leapt up and stormed out to the verandah. "*Not* like that!" I pointed to the table, ran my finger over the surface and held it up.

She stared at it, sullen, silent.

"I tell you—clean *first*, *then* knife and fork!"

She began to clatter the cutlery together, the dirty rag still in her hand. I wanted to snatch it away, throw the mats onto the floor, and tell her to go and wash them. But I just stood there, breathing lightly.

"Can I help?" my mother called, feeling her way over the threshold of the French doors with one foot.

The Bungalow

"Useless," I hissed. "It's useless." I marched to the verandah wall and crossed my arms, staring out to sea.

I heard my mother doing things with the cutlery, asking Josefina her name, how many children she had, where they lived. She used the careful nursing tones she'd used on us when we complained about my father. Or on my father if he refused to have Flo Brasch for another Friday night. Nicholas told me that the servants had Zulu nicknames for my parents. My mother was "Always Shouting," my father "Snake Eyes."

"She's not unwilling, you know, darling," my mother said, coming to stand next to me. "You need to have a little patience." She shaded her eyes to survey the garden. "Good Lord! What a mess! Is there no gardener in this establishment?"

"He ran off when everything happened."

"Darling," she said suddenly, clutching my arm, "you can't close yourself off out here like a hermit. You need to be out among people. Among the living. Why don't you give Myrna Lipinsky a ring? She must know all *sorts* of people."

She brushed off the top of the verandah wall with her hand, and then hoisted one corseted buttock onto it. "Did I ever tell you the story of Rube Morris's daughter? No? Well, she'd had a *terrible* marriage, *awful* man apparently. She was on a ferry, crossing the English channel, weeping her eyes out. She may even have been pregnant—anyway, it was a mess. Then a tall, dark chap, an American dentist, I think—he came up and sat down next to her. His marriage had also just come to an end, apparently. He asked her if there were anything he could do? She shook her head, but he persisted. And, the next thing you know, they fell in love before they reached Dover. And now they're married and living somewhere called Cincinnati. She's had another baby. Rube and Vera are *thrilled* to bits."

. . .

*I felt about becoming an American as I would have felt about becoming a Hindu—very silly. For five years I had been answering Americans' questions: apartheid, the revolution, my family and how they got there in the first place, sharks, shark nets, blacks, whites,*

Jews, apartheid, the blood bath, the Blue Train, surfing, winter in July, the revolution, Christiaan Barnard, did I go back to visit? anti-Semitism, Cry, the Beloved Country, Gary Player, and wasn't I glad that I'd got out?

And now this.

The room was hot and full of Chinese studying "Twenty-five Steps to Citizenship." Children ran about, wild with boredom. Every now and then, a large black woman in a uniform and cap would call out a name she couldn't pronounce, and we'd all look up. "Foo-loo-yoo! Mister Foo-loo-yoo-!?"

I examined the pamphlet I'd been given outside by an antiwar demonstrator. It spelled out how I was to respond to the question of bearing arms for my country. I was to qualify my pledge with certain phrases that were grammatically incorrect. I folded the paper up into a hat and then into a ship, and offered it to a small Chinese boy who stood watching me.

The woman next to me smiled. "Thank you," she said. "What time yo apponmen?"

"Ten o' clock."

"Me too." She looked at her watch and twisted her mouth down to one side. "I miss asawata for this."

"Excuse me?"

" 'As the Word Turn,' " she repeated. "Till today, I never miss one."

"Oh."

"You watch it?"

I shook my head. If I reported this to Clive, he wouldn't believe me.

She cosied closer. "You should watch. Every day something new happen, on and on, it never end." She sat back triumphantly. "I call my daughter Crystal. Two boy and now one girl. My husban, he's a dentis."

"Wong, Vivien! Mrs. Vivien Wong!"

"Ha!" The woman grabbed her boy by the sleeve, and her "Twenty-five Steps." "You nex!" she said to me. "Goo luck!"

· · ·

"You must demonstrate," said the immigration official, "that you can write an English sentence."

134

# The Bungalow

I laughed lightly at this, as if it were a joke we shared. But he stared soberly at me through small pale yellow eyes, the same colour as his hair. He pointed to a blank on the form and then sneezed. "Write, 'The Constitution can be amended,'" he ordered, reaching into a pocket for a handkerchief.

I wrote, wondering how Vivien Wong was coping next door. And whether I'd catch this man's cold.

"Who was the first Chief Justice of the United States?" he asked.

I shook my head. "Sorry," I said, "I haven't a clue."

"It's in the booklet. What is the First Amendment?"

This much I remembered. I recited it word for word, noticing the frightening shape of his head revealed by his crewcut. I wondered whether he would rather be in Vietnam, and if one could fail at becoming an American.

"Please stand," he said, "and raise your right hand. Swear after me—"

The heater hissed and spat. Outside, the sun shone brightly, although the temperature had dropped below zero. In England the sun had seemed to be a shadow, a ghost. But in America I'd learned not to trust it at all. There it was, blazing down directly on people muffled up in furs and boots.

"Answer yes or no to the following questions. Are you now or have you ever been a member of the Communist Party?"

"No."

"Are you now or have you ever been—"

Clive was at home. The blizzard and then the drop in temperature had brought the city to a standstill. He couldn't dig the car out, nor were the trains running. I had thought, perhaps, they'd cancel my citizenship test, but Clive had insisted I take a cab down to find out. Who cared about the cost? He loved the whole idea of my becoming an American. He himself had taken pains to change his accent, flattening out his a's and putting in the r's. He'd adjusted his voice, too, using the sort of monotonic cadence of television newscasters.

Do you abjure homosexuality? Do you swear not to overthrow the state? Will you bear arms for your country?

Yes, yes, yes, I said, watching a small drop of snivel swell at the rim of his nostril.

"Do you abjure polygamy?"

135

*I smiled, determined now, for some reason, to win him over. "With regret," I said.*

*His pupils shrank to pinpoints. He pulled out the handkerchief again and wiped furiously at the nose. "This is not a joke," he said. "I remind you that you are under oath. Measures can be taken. Your application can be closed now if you wish."*

*I flushed. "I'm sorry," I said.*

*"Then, I will ask you again: Do you abjure polygamy?"*

*"I do," I said.*

# 18

"Permission denied."

I stood with the letter in the middle of the lounge, trying to read past the phrase.

The doorbell rang, and then rang again. Josefina looked out of the kitchen. "Madam?" she said.

"Oh, Josefina, please answer it."

There was a date stamped on the letter, and a signature, a scrawl, without a name typed underneath. Department of Internal Affairs. Request for extension of temporary residence permit. Permission denied.

I looked up. Krishnah stood in the doorway, with Josefina hovering behind him. "Sorry not to phone first," he said.

"Oh, Krishnah!" I said. "Krishnah!" I ran to him and stopped, handed him the letter. "Look at this," I said, hoping he'd give one of his laughs, laugh and say, "This? This is 'Masterpiece Theatre!'"

He took the letter and walked over to the French doors, where there was more light.

Josefina was still hovering in the doorway. She flapped her hand at me, cocked her head at Krishnah. "Madam!" she whispered.

"Will you bring us some tea?" I said. I glanced over at him to make sure he hadn't noticed her. Then I smiled at her, nodding vigorously. "It's O.K.," I mouthed.

"Bloody bastards!" He flung the letter onto the table. "The bugger's dead and they're still after him." He looked at me, careful to keep his eyes from my stomach, ran the fingers of one hand through his hair.

I lowered myself into Hugh's armchair. "What will I do?" I asked.

"Where can you go?" he asked, setting his jaw at a peculiar angle, like a child trying not to cry.

"Nowhere."

He covered his eyes with a hand. I thought, perhaps, he was crying. But, when he did speak, his voice was measured, soft. "He put himself out for me, man. He tried—"

I nodded, but I couldn't speak at the thought of being cast out, my child born nowhere. Tears spilled down my cheeks. I wiped them on the sleeve of my jersey. "Sorry," I said.

"What about America?" he asked, sitting down on the couch.

I shook my head.

"You can't go back?"

I shrugged. I felt like a child trying not to tell the truth.

"But you *could* go back, hey? For the baby's sake?" His face, swimming sideways through my tears, looked interested.

"No. I won't."

He leaned forward on his elbows. "You *want* to be homeless, hey?" He laughed softly, as if he'd caught a joke.

The kitchen door opened and Josefina came in with the tray.

"She wants to be homeless," he said, picking up the letter.

I poured the tea and cut the sponge cake Josefina had made. It was stiff and dry. "Krishnah," I said, "I know it's different—I mean, for me, there's a choice, but—"

"Look," he said, "don't compare us. I was a bastard to you, but you got on my nerves, you know? Still, don't compare us."

I nodded.

"Look," he said again, picking up the letter and waving it at me, "the American consul's useless for this, you know that, don't you? They send their small fry out here."

I nodded, although the American consul hadn't even occurred to me. No one had.

"You've got Goldman," he said, stabbing his fork into the sponge. "*Use* him."

"What?"

He looked up then and cocked his head. "Unless you want them to kick you out? You want that?"

I flushed and shook my head.

"Good." He smacked his lips and stood up, leaving his tea untouched. "I thought I was going to be big, you know," he said after a while. "After they let me out, I thought I was a big shot. Started another book." He turned to look at me. "But it was rubbish! Quoting *myself*, you know?" He thrust his hands into his pockets and walked to the French doors, stood there as Hugh had stood there. "*Hugh* was the one," he said. "*He* had my life mapped out here, man. 'Your audience is *here*,' he kept saying. '*Here!*' My life, mind you! Stuck here, in *this* small, pathetic place!" He turned to me, his teeth clamped into the old sardonic grimace. "Actually," he said, "I just dropped in to ask you for lunch on Saturday. I can ask Maya too, if you like. But don't tell Edwina, hey?" He strolled over to the bookshelves, ran one finger along the spines. "I mean, what's the point, hey?" He seemed actually to be asking the question.

I shook my head.

"I've got to get out," he said, dusting off his fingers. "You want to stay, and I want to go. It's a mess, isn't it?"

. . .

The houses started small—shacks, really, of cinder blocks and corrugated iron, at the foot of the hill. But higher up they became suburban boxes with small jutting verandahs, and steep gardens of kikuyu grass, red earth, frangipanis, dogs tied up with rope. People stared at me as I drove past them. They stood about in groups, the women chewing betel, their saris dusty and worn. Two toothless men in bare feet and rolled-up trousers lolled in front of a dry-goods store.

It was hard to imagine Krishnah in this world. Either coming from it or going back into it. Even the houses right at the top, the more solid structures, were painted pink and green and sported sprigs of plastic flowers along the windowsills.

When I saw the Palm Court Hotel, I slowed down. Krishnah had told me not to pass it or I would have gone too far. He had been precise. On the right would be a filling station. He'd meet me there. And there, indeed, he was, saluting from the window of an old Plymouth, starting it up.

It was after noon, and the pumps were closed. Two small Indian boys in shorts and bare feet rolled a steel hoop with a stick. They stopped to stare as I followed Krishnah back onto the street. In my rearview mirror I saw them laugh. One sauntered in front of the other, swinging his hips like a woman.

Krishnah drove past the hotel, onto the other side of the hill, and down into a valley I'd never seen. It was dotted with small painted houses with tin roofs, patches of cultivation, stands of wild bananas and pawpaw trees. Smoke rose here and there. A rooster crowed. It was foreign territory.

We drove down into the valley and up the other side, stopping finally outside some iron gates set into a high, white wall. Krishnah opened them and closed them again behind us. We drove along a rough unpaved track, up to a small, one-storey bungalow with a corrugated iron roof and a pillared verandah all around.

An Indian woman stood smiling at the front door. She came to the top of the steps and held out her hands to me. "Ruth!" she cried.

"Maya?"

It was Maya, beautiful Maya, hopelessly disguised as a matron in a plain white dress with set-in sleeves and a Peter Pan collar, a V-necked, buttoned front, and stockings and sensible shoes. Her hair was pulled back into a bun, unfashionably high, and there were ruby studs in her ears. "Oh, Ruth!" she cried. "I can hardly believe this!"

Krishnah lounged against the railing, playing an imaginary violin at us. It was easy to see that they were cousins. But what was beautiful in Maya—her eyes, her skin, her hands—seemed effeminate in him.

Maya took me by the shoulders. "Let me have a look at you," she said.

"Oh God!" I said, thrusting my hands into the pockets of my skirt. I felt ridiculous with my denim skirt held together with a safety pin, a loose blouse knotted over it to hide the gap. In fact, I looked more fat than pregnant. I couldn't wait to bulge unmistakably in one place.

"Come on, come on," said Krishnah. "The aged ones are waiting."

We followed him into a dim, empty hall that smelled of must
and curry and spices. I was still not free of nausea. It rose to my
throat, like the tide, at the thought of food, or when I hadn't eaten
anything, or for no reason at all. Twice a day now I made the trip
to the Indian supply store down the road, and came back with
foods I couldn't do without—Romany creams, biltong, dried bananas, koeksisters.

Krishnah opened a door and ushered us into a lounge. It was
dark, with a bare wooden floor. Floor to ceiling, the walls were
covered with bookshelves. Piles of newspapers had been pushed
into corners, together with magazines, cardboard folders, boxes of
files. A small, fat woman in a sari looked up from the doily she was
crocheting and smiled and nodded. She glanced at a man, hidden
behind a newspaper at the other end of the couch. "They're here,"
she whispered.

The man lowered his paper and examined me over the tops of
half-moon glasses. "Ah!" he said. "Miss Frank, I presume. You are
staying just over the hill, I believe? In the Stillington house?"

He spoke in a clipped, carefully pronounced, English. It was
formal, and, like Krishnah's, it had an edge of grievance.

I sat down in a chair and Maya perched on the arm beside me.
Her presence there—Maya as she had always been, smelling
sweetly of Knight's Castile and girlish perfume—made me long to
lean back against her and to close my eyes and fall asleep.

"It is not unusual these days to find expatriates returning," Mr.
Chowdree informed us. "Perhaps it is the state of the economy, or
perhaps it is our wonderful way of life—" He expelled a pointed
little laugh. "People seem to find life in the real world out there
not entirely to their liking after all."

"Oh, come on, Uncle," Maya laughed, "Ruth's not one of
those."

"Do you work at home, Mr. Chowdree?" I asked. I had learned,
over the years, that asking questions protected me from having to
answer them. Where do you work? Where do you live? Where do
you come from?

---

141

Mrs. Chowdree began to haul herself out of the couch. "Well, look," she said, "I'm going to see about lunch."

"When I am allowed to work," said Mr. Chowdree, "this is where I work. Right here in this chair, or at that desk in the next room. Unless they put out my eyes, I assure you that I intend to continue this way until I die."

It was to Maya, not me, that he seemed to be delivering this speech. But she just laughed. "Oh, don't be so dramatic, Uncle. Who on earth would want to put out your eyes? You're not Oedipus! They'd just put you in jail. It's so much less trouble."

He eyed us both sharply, and then smiled. "I always liked you, you know, Maya. You're full of cheek, I must say. I don't think Ravi deserves you."

"Come on!" called Mrs. Chowdree. "Lunch is served, everyone."

•  •  •

The small dining-room table had been laid with a cross-stitched cloth, matching serviettes, ornate stainless steel cutlery, and fingerbowls and glasses. Pots and casseroles and been placed on trivets in the middle, and there were baskets of rolls at either end, and dishes of nuts.

"I'll get the drinks," said Krishnah, with a shy smile of pride or shame I hadn't seen before. "Coke? Fanta? Ginger beer?"

"Aunty is a wonderful cook," Maya announced. "I always put on pounds in this house."

"Here," said Mrs. Chowdree. She placed a plate piled high with rice and curry in front of me. She pointed to a tray of sambals—chutneys, dal, hot tomatoes. "Help yourself," she said. "Come on, come on."

Krishnah eyed me carefully as I spooned things onto my plate, and then as I began to eat. Although I was hungry, nausea still slapped around in my throat. I had to concentrate on swallowing each mouthful. And then on taking another. After a while, beads of sweat began to stand out on my forehead. Sweat ran around my eyes, down my neck, between my breasts. "Whew!" I said. "This is delicious."

"Too spicy for you?" Mrs. Chowdree asked. "Too hot?"

I shook my head. But then, suddenly, the table seemed to rise and pitch. I hung on to my chair and pushed it back. "Excuse me," I said, "could you tell me where the bathroom is?"

"The bathroom!" cried Krishnah. "You want to have a bath?"

"I'll show you," Maya said. She took my hand and led me out of the room, down a corridor. "Ruth, are you all right?"

I nodded.

"Here," she said, opening the door to the toilet.

I locked the door and then knelt before the tall, old-fashioned toilet and hung my head over the porcelain rim. Out came everything I'd eaten. I sat back in relief on the bare floor, panting, sweating, my mouth sour and thick.

Someone knocked. "Ruth?"

"I'm fine now, Maya. Thanks."

"I've told them you won't be finishing your curry. Is that all right?"

"Yes, thanks, Maya."

I flushed, washed my hands, rinsed my mouth, and returned, light-headed, to three puddings laid out—a trifle, a fruit salad, and a coffee cream gateau.

. . .

"Hugh Stillington was only a remarkable fellow within the context of his ilk," Mr. Chowdree announced to no one in particular as he sipped his tea. He looked frail and very dark against the light, bending his head like a bird to the cup.

We sat on the front verandah, drinking chai. Mrs. Chowdree had disappeared. Krishnah hooked one leg over the arm of his chair, closed his eyes. Out in the driveway, a mongrel sniffed around my tires.

"There is moral in that whole mess, if one cares to extract it," Mr. Chowdree went on.

"I think that's pretty obvious," I said at last.

He looked up quickly. "Indeed!" he said. "How so?"

"White liberal punished for his presumptions. I'm surprised the papers haven't made more of that aspect of the thing. Visiting enlightenment on the tribal prerogatives of others. It's all been blamed on *dagga* and drink." I sat back, pleased.

143

Krishnah sighed. "Miss America, I think you should stick to Jane Austen."

"Jane Austen?" said Mr. Chowdree. "Are you an authority on Jane Austen?" He fitted his lip precisely to the curve of the cup and watched me over the rim as he drank.

I flushed deeply. Four months, four little months since Hugh had been murdered, and already I was dropping my eyelids, uttering his phrases with authority.

"Uncle," said Maya, "Ruth's not feeling very well."

"Just consider *Northanger Abbey*," Mr. Chowdree persisted. "Consider the power of the word to distort the imagination."

I pretended to consider, but I glanced quickly at my watch. "*Northanger Abbey* is a spoof," I said.

"Precisely so. But the question is, what is being spoofed? Could you consider that?"

"Consider Dostoevski," Krishnah said. "Consider Dickens."

But there was no challenge to his words. He closed his eyes and leaned back in his chair as if he, too, were an old man. I thought of the book he had tried to write, the words that wouldn't come right. And Edwina kept in the dark about the luncheon. If he despised her, as Hugh had said he did, then it was himself he despised as well. I understood. Here, in this diminished place, with the words that refused to come, what hope was left for him?

Maya came to stand behind my chair and laid her hands on my shoulders. "Ruth's tired," she said. "So is Uncle."

Krishnah sat up. "Oh, stop playing nanny, for God's sake, Maya! It's getting on my nerves!"

I laughed. Everything got on Krishnah's nerves. If there was hope for him, it was in his caustic temper, the very thing about him that had first unsettled me. I loved to think of him at the factory gates haranguing Jeffrey's workers. When I had taken the letter to Jeffrey, he had told me that he paid his workers more than other people did, that he had a medical clinic for them, consulted nutritionists about the food they ate, built schools for their children. If he fired them for divorcing their wives, did I blame him? Did I blame him for firing troublemakers? Whole families of men worked for him, he said. He took an interest in them and in what happened to their families. What did they need a union for?

"Well," said Maya, "we must be off, Uncle. I promised to visit Ruth in the beach house, catch up on old times, you know." She slipped an arm through mine. "Is Aunty sleeping? Will you tell her how much we loved the lunch? Krish, want me to prescribe a nerve tonic for you? We've got special *muti* we give to people with your condition at MacHattie's."

# 19

To my surprise, Lily agreed to come with me to lunch at Catherine's. She was curious, she said. And she wanted to meet the Chief. Anyway, her time at the coast was coming to an end. In a few weeks, she was off to Milan for the opera season. Then to a friend on the Mozambique border. She'd be back, she said, in time for the baby.

We parked around the back and made our way through the house to the front garden, where the guests were gathered around the pool. Catherine had taken to dismissing her servants on Sundays after they had cooked the lunch and set it out. Sundays without servants was something new among the rich. A number of people were taking it up, together with gourmet cooking lessons, Magimixes, and dishwashers.

The dogs whined and yelped on the upstairs verandah. "Watch out," Catherine said, bustling up the bank to meet us. "The dogs wee up there and it'll drip down onto your heads!" She shrieked with laughter.

I thought, perhaps, she had drunk some wine. Or that she was delirious with the freedom of having no servants around to get on her nerves.

"Hello," she said to Lily. "Do you want to change? We're just sitting around the pool. I should have told you it's casual."

Lily glanced down at the skirt and blouse she was wearing, then at me. We had laughed about the new fad for casual, and about no servants on a Sunday. But, for once, I didn't glance back. There was an innocence to Catherine's joy that made me want to protect her. She wore the bathing suit Jeffrey had bought for her in Nice.

It swirled with reds and greens and golds, up over one shoulder and down under the other.

"Come," she said, "let me introduce you." She led us towards a table under the avocado tree, where the Chief was sitting in a suit and tie. When he saw us, he leapt to his feet, and his two bodyguards, standing back in the shadow of the tree, came forward slightly. The Chief clasped my hand in both of his. "Welcome! Welcome!" he cried. "What a great pleasure to find out that you are still here with us."

I smiled as he turned to meet Lily, wondering whether Jeffrey had told him about my residence permit and how he'd managed to have it extended. I still didn't know myself, nor did Catherine. Leave well enough alone, she'd said. You're staying on. That's all that matters.

"In a few months," the Chief said, "I am going to America. In fact, your dear brother-in-law has arranged for me to have elocution lessons with your very gracious mother." He chortled lightly. "I believe that the American people will not understand one word that I am saying, unless she teaches me how to say it!"

Lily buttoned up her jersey. The day was overcast and cold.

"Where are you going to in America?" I asked. Suddenly, America seemed very far away, as if I'd hardly been there, had never really breathed its air.

"Oh, many places. New York, Washington, Chicago, Los Angeles." He beamed his public smile at me. "Which do you like best?"

I shrugged. "Oh, I don't know. Other than the museums, I see little virtue in the place."

Lily looked up sharply, and I smiled at her. I wondered whether she too had heard that phrase from Hugh, where else he had applied it. Who knew what places other than this one would have qualified as virtuous for him?

The Chief smiled. "May I quote you on that?" he asked.

"Actually," I said, "the phrase belongs to Hugh Stillington, now deceased."

Immediately, he hung his head, placed his hands together, fingertips to fingertips. "I heard about that," he said. "It is a tragedy, very great tragedy indeed."

Lynn Freed

Lily repositioned a tortoiseshell hairpin in her chignon. "What I'd so much like to know, Chief Sibusi," she said, "is what you envisage for us when your people take over."

He tossed his head back in a silent laugh. She had known just what to ask him, and when.

I glanced over to the pool. "Excuse me," I said, "I'd better go and say hello to my parents."

"Darling," my mother whispered, leaning away from Mrs. Goldman, "where on *earth* did you come up with that dreary outfit?" She grasped the fabric in one hand and peered at it. "Grey?" she said. "Is it *grey*?"

"Yes."

"You look like a schoolteacher! Why don't you let me take you shopping?"

I took her face between my hands and kissed her forehead. "Where's Dad?"

She raised her eyebrows at me. "Inside. Shut up in the study with the blasted television set."

"But TV only comes on at six," I said.

"Ha! You tell *him* that! He's playing with the knobs!"

Jeffrey and Catherine were among the first to buy a television set. Every other night, when the English program was on, Shadrak set out chairs and put out dishes of sweets. Catherine said it was like running a bloody cinema.

"Pimm's, anyone?" Jeffrey arrived with a tray of red and yellow drinks. Mint sprigs and fruit floated festively in tall glasses. He bumped me sideways with a hip. "Oops!" he guffawed. "Sorry! Didn't recognise you!"

Mrs. Goldman laughed too, eyeing me carefully. She and Flo Brasch were friends. They played bowls together, and bridge, and had luxury flats in High Wyckham. Usually, she liked to annoy my mother by mentioning things that her money had bought. But now she just smiled and said, "I had a letter from your mother-in-law, posted in Rio. I expect they'll be landing in Cape Town any minute."

My mother turned on Mrs. Goldman. "Well, they've certainly made a long stay of it this time, haven't they?" she snapped. "Think they got their money's worth, Ettie?"

148

I looked across the pool and waved at Meg Rabinowitz. Despite the chill, she sat there on a chaise, zipped and boned into a strapless bathing suit, and striking the same pose she must have struck twenty-five years before as Rag Queen on top of a float.

"Just look at you!" she said as I came up. "You look *terrific!*"

It was Edwina, in the end, who had saved the day for me. She'd brought me her maternity clothes—simple shifts in adult colours. And, even though I still didn't look quite pregnant yet, I was wearing her long-sleeved, grey Viyella shift, cleverly cut on the bias, with an off-white collar and cuffs, and tiny mother-of-pearl buttons down the yoke.

Peter Rabinowitz came up and hugged me around the shoulders. "Hey, sport!" he said. He was six inches shorter than Meg, and five years younger, compact, ugly, myopic, and a modest failure in business.

Meg held out a hand for him to pull her up. "How *super* to have you home, hon!" she said, coming to stand between us.

Home. I smiled at her. Meg herself had never been quite at home with the world she'd married into. Under her creams and powders and dyes, there was still her colourless Gentile face, a hint of Gentile condescension.

"Come," she said, slipping an arm through mine. "Let's get some lunch. Pete, want me to bring you a tray, darling? Chicken? Cold meats? A potpourri?"

· · ·

The trestle table was laid with platters of roast chicken, cold meats, bowls of salad, tinned asparagus, pickled cucumbers. Meg picked up an asparagus spear, dipped it into the bottled mayonnaise, and sucked it delicately. "I, for one, think you're very brave," she whispered to me. "Flying in the face of all this!"

Meg had always aligned herself with me as an outsider. She took courses at the university for non-degree purposes—philosophy, political science, literature. She was up on the latest books, asked her friends to bring them back from London for her. She had even started a book club.

"Ruth!" Lily arrived, out of breath, across the grass. "Ruth,

Jeffrey has asked me— or 'one of us women,' as he put it—to organise a tray for the Chief—"

"I'll do it!" Meg cried. She grabbed a tray and began to move down the table. Catherine had told me that Peter had been trying to get in with the Chief from the beginning. He wanted to be one of the boys, she said. But the Chief seemed to forget his name every time they were introduced. It was becoming embarrassing.

My mother came up and surveyed the table. "Darling," she said, "be a love and take your father in some lunch. You know what he likes—'a modicum of this and that'!" She snorted, grabbed a tray herself, and moved off along the table, saying, "What's this? Chicken again?" And, "Any of that lovely bread that Catherine makes herself?"

A car crawled up the driveway and the dogs roared into action overhead.

"The Kaplans!" Catherine mumbled.

"Helloo!" Tanya Kaplan cried, spiking across the front lawn. "Helloo, Mrs. Goldman! Helloo Mrs. Frank! Helloo everyone! Sorry we're late. Naty! Do you want a bit of everything, darling?"

"*Ja!*" Nathan stalked off to join Jeffrey at the pool. Like Jeffrey, like so many men out here, he made a point of never helping himself to food. They liked to be able to stare at the plates their women handed them and ask, "What's this? What's that?" And then to send them back to the buffet to remove things they didn't like the look of, or find them something else.

We carried our lunch back to the pool, where we sat under umbrellas like convalescents, our trays fitted cunningly onto the arms of our chairs.

"Seen these new radar systems, sport?" Nathan asked Jeffrey. "Brought one back from the States last month. It's almost paid for itself already."

Jeffrey shook his head and laughed. With his older fortune and his reputation for being aboveboard, he made a point of avoiding illegal contraptions brought back from overseas by people like Nathan. "I use a driver these days," he said. "Can't get him to go over forty K's."

Nathan glanced over to the far side of the pool to check that the

Chief was out of earshot. "Out of your bloody mind!" he said. "Don't you know they get the drivers first?" He himself had a big house and a pool and a television and an alarm system. He liked to consider himself as much of a target as any man.

"What about a gun?" I suggested. "You could always use it to shoot the driver if he turns out to be a terrorist."

Jeffrey frowned at me. "I suppose you think that's funny?"

"If you ask me," said my mother, "guns are dangerous." She shook her head and stabbed unsuccessfully at a gherkin with her fork. "The way things are going in this country these days."

I looked out over the city and the sea, thinking of the parodies I used to write to Clive of scenes like this. The men and their acquisitions, their women, their children. But then, childless year after year, I had begun to feel myself losing ground. I had felt lost myself. At a loss for a future other than the one I faced. Ruth and Clive. Ruth and Clive. Ruth and Clive.

Behind us, an enormous stand of bamboo swayed and creaked and moaned. It was a mournful sound, as mournful as the wind echoing down fifteen stories of drainpipes, or the gasp of the garbage chute when you pulled open the door.

"Can someone let me out of here, please!" My mother grunted and set her teeth and brushed some rice salad from her bosom.

Peter leapt up to remove her tray. He held out a hand to help her up.

"Thank you, thank you very much," she said. She clutched her bag under one arm and swayed slightly on the spot.

"Hey, sport," Peter said to Nathan, "let's have a look at your new toy."

"Toy, shmoy," said Nathan.

Meg laughed. I watched her flutter her fingers through her frothy perm, and the two men, one bald, one tucking in his shirt, walking off across the lawn. How would Meg have done as Nathan's wife, I wondered? Or Bruce Carter's? Or even Clive's? So few spouses seemed specific to each other, here or anywhere else. There was an oddness in the timing of the coupling, especially the young ones, the ones fresh into childbearing. What of Meg fresh off her float as Rag Queen? How did Peter know that he could count on her to make the acquaintance of someone like Catherine, to wangle him an introduction to the Chief?

"Well, I'm off," said my mother. She steadied herself against the trunk of the umbrella, and then launched off across the lawn.

"I *adore* your *maman!*" Meg said, laying a hand on my arm. "Apart from anything, it's wonderful for *them* that you're staying on. Once they've gone, you know, they've gone."

"Not quite," said Lily, coming up, followed by the Chief. "They come back to visit whenever they please, you know. Turn around and there they are under a tree, with something to say about the serpent's tooth."

We all laughed. But I wondered how it would be to come home if they were dead. And about Catherine without them there to bind us. Me anywhere at all, them gone.

I waved at the Chief, who was veering off towards the house. "I hope I will see you soon at your parents' house," he called out. "Heh-heh-heh-!" he chortled.

"Isn't it amazing how things have changed in this country?" Meg said cosily. "I think Jeffrey and Catherine are remarkable, don't you?"

Tennis balls began to plock. Lily looked at her watch. I stood up. "Well, we must be going," I said.

"Do me a favour," Catherine said, scraping the bones and leavings from one plate onto another. "Grab a few things on your way in."

I grabbed some trays, and so did Lily. Meg followed with the glasses.

"Absurd!" my mother thundered, watching the parade. "And the servants reclining back there in all their splendour, if you please!"

·  ·  ·

*Other people we knew were beginning to uncouple. With them, it seemed to happen casually. As if, one day, they stood up from sitting down, and said, "This isn't working out." Perhaps they weren't sealed, as we were, into the neat alliance of foreigners. Like the Cambodians down the hall, who were always smiling when we saw*

them. But, sometimes, passing their apartment, we heard her screaming, things crashing. Once, I'd seen her crying into the pay phone on
the corner and wondered whom she had to call when she was in
trouble. Whom I would call.

. . .

It was our seventh anniversary. Lately, a terror of regret had begun
to infect me. Every man who turned to watch me pass was a lover
passed over, a loss connected quite directly to the five grey hairs that
had begun to sprout, tough and coarse, from the crown of my head.

Clive came home with a dozen roses from the flower kiosk on the
corner. I plunged them into a vase of iced water and put them on the
table, turned up the Vivaldi, lit the candles. For almost a year now,
night after night, we had been making love without passion, without
desire. Clive expected a miracle. "Curse arrived yet?" he'd ask, fid-
dling with the dials of the TV.

"Curse arrive?" he asked, emerging from the toilet.

I nodded. "Remember that first year we were married? Wasn't it
awful?"

He tore off pieces of roll and floated them in his soup. "If you
dwell on it," he said, "then you must want it to be awful." He
cracked open the door behind him and glanced through to the bedroom.

"I've been thinking," I said. "I'd like to consider artificial insem-
ination." I thought, perhaps, I'd go to Planned Parenthood and get
myself a diaphragm. I thought that, somehow, it might bring me the
luck or the courage to find another man, to plan to be a parent.

He laid down his spoon and looked at me. "We've been through
that already. Haven't we been through all that already?"

"But I was thinking—"

"No harm in thinking." He craned around, peering through the
crack.

"Well, what do you propose?" I demanded.

"Propose for what?" asked Clive, pushing his empty plate towards
me.

"For us."

The needle ran off the record and I got up to turn it off. Then I went to the kitchen to take out the soufflé. When I returned, Clive had vanished, his napkin too. The door to the bedroom stood ajar. I tiptoed after him.

At first I didn't see him crouched on the edge of the bed. But then the flicker of the silent TV caught my eye. I saw his napkin stuffed into his pocket like a handkerchief. And him sitting enraptured, his elbows resting on his knees, his chin on his knuckles, watching baseball.

# 20

Since the lunch at Krishnah's, Maya came often to the bungalow. So did Krishnah. Sometimes he came in only for ten minutes,
on his way home from 'varsity. He might just walk through to the
verandah and sit there on the swing seat for a while; then disappear through the garden without a word. He never mentioned
Edwina anymore, although I knew he still saw her, she had told
me. And then, one day, he announced, "I won't be coming anymore."

"Why?"

He set his jaw, flicked and flicked with a finger at his jeans.
"Things are getting bad. Don't you read the papers?"

I blushed. I didn't take the papers, nor did I miss them. I knew
about Soweto, of course, and I listened to the radio. But out here,
with everything just as it had always been, the news seemed to be
happening far away. In another country.

"I just hope your guardian angel knows what's coming to him,"
he said.

"Jeffrey?"

He clamped his teeth into the grin. "Listen," he said, "I gave
you a hard time in the beginning. I'm sorry."

"You're talking as if I'll never see you again."

He looked away, and I said nothing more. We might as well
have been husband and wife, so loose were the silences between
us, so ordinary. The sun had almost set. I shivered, and folded my
arms across my chest.

"You should get a jersey or something," he said. He rolled down
his own sleeves and buttoned the cuffs.

The doorbell rang.

"That must be Maya," I said. "Won't you stay for supper? Please?"

But I knew that he'd say no and dash down the steps and out through the garden. He couldn't bear her presence in the bungalow, or Lily's. He was only just getting used to mine. I knew now that his father had brought him there for the first time when he was eight years old. He'd told me how he'd watched in fascination as his father sat at his ease, talking to a white man with a hand that looked like a claw. And, after that, he'd come with his father almost every week. And then without his father. And it was Hugh who had sent him to Oxford and moved heaven and earth to get him out of prison.

"They watch him like a hawk," Maya explained. "He's doing you a favour not coming here anymore."

We sat in the dim light of the dining room, drinking hot tomato soup. I wore a padded brocade jacket from the dress-up chest. She wore a plain wool skirt and a twin set, pearls in her ears. Every time she came, I planned to ask her things about herself—about her husband, about other men, what she wanted for herself. But, face to face, I didn't know how to bring the subjects up. There was a formality to Maya that seemed to set limits. So, we talked about me instead, and about her job as a pediatrician at MacHatties' Zulu hospital, about Hugh, the jacket I was wearing, Krishnah and Edwina.

"I thought Edwina was quite brainy in school," she said.

Brainy was important to Maya. She herself often found a way to mention the first she'd got at Oxford. And I didn't mind. In her family, a first at Oxford seemed more important than the sort of marriage she had made.

Josefina brought in the steak and chips and took away our dishes. She was used now to having Indians in the house. She even smiled at Maya. "Hello," she said.

I watched Maya cut her steak delicately, eat it in small pieces. Every now and then, she dabbed the corners of her mouth. She wore her hair now in a chignon like Lily's. One afternoon, when we were all at the bungalow together, Maya had admired the intricate plaiting of Lily's bun, the way it nestled at her neck. "Come," Lily had said, making off for the main bedroom. "Ruth, where's the brush and the hand mirror?" She'd sat Maya down on the stool at the dressing table and loosened her hair from its bun, and brushed and brushed. I'd sat cross-legged on the bed, watching as Lily pulled out her own hairpins and held them in her mouth. I'd watched her finger Maya's hair, thick and black, twist it around, tuck in the ends. "There!" she'd said at last. "Isn't she *gorgeous*?" And Maya had tilted her head as commanded, she'd giggled. "Oh my!" she'd said, holding up the hand mirror to see. "Just look at that!"

"After supper," Maya said, "would you show me the other stuff in that chest of Hugh's? I'm really curious, you know."

She knew about Lily and Hugh and the clothes. It was easier to tell her things than to ask. When I'd told her the story, she'd just smiled and said, "Of course." As if she herself had had such a lover, such a friend.

And when I pulled out the sari—burgundy silk, with gold—she gathered it into her arms as if it were alive, stroked it, held it up to the light. I showed her the small oval painting on ivory that I'd found wrapped up in tissue at the bottom of the chest—a round-faced Indian woman wearing that sari, seated on pillows, and playing a lyre.

"You must have the sari," I said, "and I'll keep the painting."

She didn't say no. She laughed as she folded the length of silk between her hands, twisting her wrists expertly this way and that. "Do you know how valuable this is?" she said. "Do you understand that I am getting the treasure, you land up with the cliché?"

• • •

*Myrna Lipinsky and I straddled a high boulder at the edge of the surf, discussing sex, which was new in our lives.*

*"It's such a cliché!" she said. "You lie there thinking away, thinking away, while they're sawing away, sawing away on top of you. I don't see the point, do you?"*

*I laughed. I thought of Hugh running the tip of a finger expertly around my navel, along the insides of my thighs, chanting, "Can you keep a secret, I don't believe you can."*

*"They must suspect it's a bore," she said, "or they wouldn't keep looking down into your face and asking if it was nice!"*

# Lynn Freed

*I raised my arms and face to the sun. Everything seemed right—my degree done, my ticket booked, months of the summer left, and Hugh, the bungalow, my mother's car to go up the coast for an afternoon with Myrna if I wanted to. Now that I was about to leave, I had begun to value what I was leaving behind. And, even as I understood that my euphoria wouldn't last the season, I felt free. I suspected already that in New York I wouldn't matter at all. Hugh had assured me of this many times. And yet there was no question that I wanted to go. All year, letters had been coming from Clive—letters that were spare, like him, with bits of news I didn't want to know, and then, on occasion, some half-admitted wish or hope pertaining to myself that I read over and over, trying to extrude a future for myself, a life.*

*If I were to stay now and marry here like all the others, there'd be no poignancy at all to the moment, no euphoria either. This way, however, I could enjoy the freedom I had to sit on a rock on a beach, or to climb up the hill to the hotel pool and plunge in. To order a shandy, anything I wanted, because I was no longer a child. I even knew, without fully understanding why, that I occupied, that February afternoon, the tiny space of freedom given a young girl between parents and husband.*

# 21

To please my mother, I'd worn one of Catherine's evening tents in red and navy taffeta, and put on stockings, and done my hair in a chignon.

"Here," she said, pulling apart the bow at my neck and then knotting it loosely like a scarf, "that's they way they're wearing things these days." She stood back. "It could be an ordinary evening dress," she said. "You still look as slim as anything."

We were off to the opening night of Jill Stafford's new musical revue. "Probably the usual cheap song-and-dance stuff," my mother said in the car. "Frankly, *I'd* give it a miss, but *he*"—she pointed her nose at my father, who was sitting stiffly behind the wheel in a dinner jacket and too much after-shave lotion—"*he* wouldn't miss one of her shows for the world, would he?"

The foyer was full when we arrived. "The thing is," she said, "hold your head high. Walk on the balls. Make an entrance." She linked her arm through mine and let my father follow us in.

Here and there, people turned to look at us. A few smiled. I pretended to examine the program, but I felt, suddenly, under their observation, wonderfully happy. I wished I'd worn my hair down, and one of Edwina's dresses. I hoped they knew where I was living, and all about Hugh and the baby and the new friends I had made.

My father bowed slightly. "What about something from the wine bar, girls?" He knew he looked his best in a dinner jacket. And, whereas she had taken up creams and tints and cover-ups, following minutely the instructions of the salesladies at Charles of the Ritz, he seemed to understand that age gave him the sort of substance he had lacked as a younger man. That, in fact, people paid attention now to what he had to say. And, even if their eyes wandered when he started to explain the significance of the Rotary International badge he wore in his lapel, they moved no further than his mouth or neck or hands—a long, elegant, immaculately manicured hand handing me a glass of wine and then dabbing its fingertips on a perfectly laundered white linen handkerchief.

The hall had been set up as a bistro. Small, round tables covered in red-and-white checked tablecloths had been arranged around a platform in the semi-round. Behind it hung a scrim, painted to look like Montparnasse. There were candles in Chianti bottles, Indian waiters looking sheepish in red bandanas, red globes in the lights around the walls.

"It looks like a brothel!" my mother snorted, looking around to see who was seated where. She was more at home in a proper theatre, seated one from the aisle, with a box of Black Magic chocolates on her lap. "I can't see the point of dinner jackets in a place like this, can you?" she said. "Roger, you may as well order me a drink."

When everyone was seated, the house lights dimmed down to a pink glow, and some disco music started up in two huge loud-speakers on either side of the stage. Behind the scrim, coloured lights silhouetted a troupe of dancers frozen in a pantomime. Then the scrim went up, the dancers leapt into action, and there, in a rhinestone body suit, fishnet stockings, and cowboy boots was Jill Stafford mouthing, "These boots are made for walking."

I glanced at my father. He smiled his old stage smile, his chin resting on his hand, his face titled to catch the light. Other men smiled too, women swung their shoulders to the beat. Waiters slid between the tables carrying trays of drinks. The song came to an end and another began. Jill's husband, a homosexual fifteen years her junior, came on in ballet tights and shoulder-length hair. They danced, they kissed. The troupe executed elaborate disco routines behind them. When the lights came up for interval, the audience roared into applause. Jill skipped to the front of the stage and blew kisses with both hands, turning in a circle to take in everyone.

My mother cleared her throat loudly. "Frankly," she said, "I think she's a bit long in the tooth for this sort of thing." She reached for her glass. "Ruth, tell your father I'd like another drink."

But my father was still clapping, leaning back in his chair, shouting, "Brava!"

I tapped his arm. "Ma wants another drink."

He turned to me, his face lit up by happiness. "Enjoying the show?" he asked.

I nodded.

She tapped her nails on the glass. "Is he ordering me a drink?"

People were standing up now, still clapping. He stood up too, clapping too.

"What's he standing up for?" my mother demanded.

Jill came to the front of the stage, and down the steps to the floor. She swung her arms as she walked, like a runway model, and made her way to our table, and then around it to my father. She stood before him, baring a set of gleaming white capped teeth and greying gums. "Roger!" she cried, throwing her arms around him. "Roger *darling*!"

For a few seconds, he seemed to stiffen, smiling carefully, his arms at his sides. But then he lifted his arms around her too, he bent his head sideways, kissing her sideways as he had done onstage when they'd played opposite each other in *Brief Encounter* twenty years before.

People turned to look, some smiled. They seemed unsure as to whether this was part of the show. Having actors come down into the audience was becoming the thing. People were coming back from overseas full of *Hair* and *Oh! Calcutta*.

My mother scraped back her chair, grabbing for her handbag and her shawl. "Ruth!" she cried. "Let me have your arm."

She clutched fiercely at me, digging her nails into my flesh to pull herself up.

"We'll just have to phone Catherine," she gasped. "She'll have to come and fetch us."

People stood around the doorway in groups, laughing and talking. I saw Nathan Kaplan there, and a girl in hot pants selling sweets. My mother clung on to me like a child. Her chest heaved, her breath came light and loose. "What's happening?" she asked.

"Hey! Sarah! Sarala! Over here!"

"Ma," I said, "it's Sol Goldman."

She stopped dead, looking up into my face. "Who?" she asked.

161

But Sol Goldman was already at her side, taking her arm, kissing her cheek. "Hey, look what we've got here!" he cried, turning his starched pigeon breast on me. "The littlest Frank. Oh, just take a look!"

I let him take my hands and hold them out sideways. He was losing his marbles, Catherine had told me. He couldn't remember things from one minute to the next, and needed equipment to stop him wetting himself. Ettie, the rotten cow, threatened to put him in Our Old People's Home, and so Jeffrey had engaged nurses, day and night. But the old man was always plunging his hands down their dresses or up their skirts. One after another they gave notice.

"Come!" he cried. "Come and see who we've got here!" He took us each by the hand and led us to his table. "Look!" he announced to the table. "I brought you a surprise!"

My mother pulled her hand away and seemed to shiver back into herself. She hitched the handle of her bag over her shoulder and tossed her head.

"All the in-laws in one place!" Sol laughed. "Ettie, Flo, look who I found!"

Flo Brasch kept her eyes on the Chianti bottle, her hands in her lap. She looked more like Clive than ever. They had the same oblique attitude when giving or taking offense. I saw that Alfred must have given her a rinse, probably that afternoon. Her face was ringed by a line of burnt sienna. Alfred sat next to her in his old brown suit.

"Enjoying the show?" Ettie asked. She winked at Flo.

I turned to Mr. Goldman. "You love this sort of show, don't you, Mr. Goldman?"

He winked, he pinched my cheek. "You little devil," he said. "Sit down, sit down both of you. I'll order drinks."

I felt my mother's hand on my arm, a gentle tug.

"Sorry," I said, glancing around for my father.

The foyer bell was ringing. People moved around us, on their way back to their tables.

"Slut! Tart!" Flo hissed suddenly.

We turned together, my mother and I. Flo had her lips curled back from her teeth like a lynx. Her small eyes danced in the candlelight.

My mother handed me her shawl and stepped closer to the table, as if entering the ring. She lowered her lids, lifted her nose into the old attitude of war. "The Hunchback of High Wyckham, no less!" she boomed. "I'll tell you one thing, Florence Brasch, I thank *God* no grandchild of mine is in danger of inheriting *that* face and *that* figure!"

"WHAT?" Flo screeched. She turned to Ettie, then to Alfred. "Did you hear that, Alf? Did you hear what she just said to me?"

Alfred placed a hand over hers and opened his mouth to speak. But his upper teeth rested neatly on the lower ones and he had to curl down his lips to pull them back into place.

My mother swung back to me, her eyes wild. She grabbed her shawl and flung it over her shoulders. "What a pair!" she cried. "The hunchback and her camel! You're *well* out of *that mésalliance*, my girl! Come along now, let's go home."

· · ·

As soon as my father had gone to golf the next morning, my mother phoned Mavis McClarity. Mavis wrote the scripts for "So Long the Day," a radio soap opera in which my father played a doctor and Jill Stafford his nurse. For four years, my father had been living the part of Dr. Whitehead, quoting lines at dinner, even enjoying the idea of looking down a throat, taking a pulse. But then, when he'd had his heart attack, Mavis had had to write him out for a bit. And only recently had she written him back in.

"Mavis," my mother said, "I'm afraid I have some rather bad news for you." She gave one of her stage laughs and lit a cigarette.

She and Mavis had known each other since the year dot, she always said. Poor old Mavis, who had devoted her life to her aged mother. The only excitement she had was through the characters she cooked up for her rubbishy serials.

"This has to be between you and me, my dear. I'm counting on you, you know—" Twin spirals of smoke rose from her nostrils. She winked at me. "Mavis, my dear, you're going to have to kill Roger off for good."

163

She massaged her eyeballs through the lids as she listened to Mavis's protests. Clearly, she hadn't had much sleep.

"But, my dear," she said, "it's doctor's orders. If you don't do it yourself, he's going to have another attack, and then where does that leave us?"

She winked again. "What about putting Roy in instead? He does a passable American accent.... Yes, now *that's* a possibility, isn't it? *Aren't* you clever? *Jolly* good idea!"

She held out her empty teacup for a refill.

"*Three* weeks? You can't do better than *that?* ... Well, I suppose that'll have to be good enough, won't it? And we'll have to keep our fingers crossed. But, look, Mavis, mum's the word. *Doctor's* orders! You know how Roger is—he loves that part and he's going to miss it—he's going to try to get around you, and find out the reason and so forth. But you won't tell, will you darling, because he doesn't know how bad it is—touch and go, the medical bods are saying. This must be *strictly* between you and me—"

"Ha!" she snorted, replacing the receiver. "*Wouldn't* I like to see his face when he reads through his last script!"

# 22

The winter had come, the rain had stopped. The garden, already overgrown and rotting, had begun to dry out. Monkeys came in boldly from the bush, even up onto the verandah. Sometimes, they snatched food off the table, or stole a cup or a beaded net, or sent a dish crashing to the floor. They romped along the num-num, and sat there chattering loudly. If I went out and waved my hands at them, one or two came forward with yellow teeth bared, screeching.

Josefina was no help. When I said, "What are we going to do about the garden, Josefina?" she just stared down at the floor and said, "It's not my work, madam." In fact, I couldn't imagine what I wanted done. The garden still felt like the bed I slept in, the food I ate. Even the place itself. A temporary arrangement.

On Josefina's day off, I walked around the bungalow naked. I liked to feel the linen of the slipcovers against my skin, or the canvas of the swing seat, the cool wind on my swollen belly and breasts. I liked to catch glimpses of myself, distorted by the curve of a brass bell, or in the mottled mirror of the armoire. If Hugh were there, he'd want the baby delivered at home, that I was sure of. But Stern said it was out of the question. Not only that, he wanted me back in town, and on a stricter diet, taking prenatal classes with other women.

I thought of the house Myrna Lipinsky's father had built for her years before. Before it was even fashionable, she had wanted something out of town, right on the sea. And so her father had bought a tract of bush, hired an Italian architect to design a house along the lines of a Mediterranean villa—right on the beach, all curves and glass and marble, with leather furniture and modern art. Myrna had named it Villa d'Occidente.

As it turned out, however, the place was unlivable. The sea was infested with sharks and the bush around the house with mambas and monkeys. Mambas dropped out of the trees without warning. Troops of monkeys marauded into the garden and ran off with her children's toys. They took over the swings and slide. One of her nannies was bitten and had to have rabies injections. The corporation was no help at all, nor were the monkey police. Villa d'Occidente was beyond the municipal limits, they informed Myrna. And so, finally, she had abandoned the house and moved back into town.

. . .

Lily stalked across the garden and flopped into a verandah chair, fanning herself with her hat like a large and beautiful insect come to rest. When I thought of old age now, I thought of her. She stood between me and images of myself pushing a grocery cart with Clive at my side. Or collecting coupons, considering retirement plans and senior-citizen specials to the Adirondacks. Until now, old age, like poverty, had been a present threat in every choice I'd made. But here, with Lily, with the sea breeze blowing in, the child growing in my belly, old age seemed irrelevant. So did Clive.

She waved her hat out into the garden. "Hugh's hand happened right there, you know. The nanny had the day off, and a monkey got hold of him. His mother, of course, was a notorious opium addict."

I thought of Hugh's finger touching his scars as if they were points on a map. "See here," he'd said, "and there?"

"She came from the Kenya set," Lily went on. "Never quite got used to the local scene. Went through the money first, and then the jewels. By the time Liege offered to pay her off, she was too far gone. Anyway, she had nowhere to go, and Liege didn't have that much left to give. Also, Nigel was mad about her, loyal as a dog. Funny how Hugh resembled Liege, nothing of Nigel in him. I've often wondered, you know, whether Liege didn't father his own grandson. After all, I wouldn't have put it past him. They say she was an *exquisite* thing. Delicate. Bruisable, Liege used to say." She laughed.

"Were you ever jealous?"

"Jealous? Of whom?"

"Of other women."

She sat forward then, looking at me. Even if she hadn't been exquisite herself—just beautiful, as she must have been, still was—it was easy to imagine her capturing a man with her certainties. She slipped out of her shoes and folded one leg underneath her, seasoning the air with camphor and talc.

"He never told you, did he?"

I stared at a cameo pinned to the collar of her blouse, breathing lightly. "Who?" I said.

"When he was sixteen, sixteen or seventeen, and I was living here, and Liege was in London—he came out here for the Christmas holidays—he always loved the place—"

"Hugh?"

She sat back, closed her eyes. "It was sweet, Ruth," she said at last. "*He's* the one who found the clothes locked away in the kist, you know. He brought them out and asked me to try them on for him. That's when the whole thing started—"

The child turned and turned inside me. "And when did it stop?" I asked.

"One day I saw him turn away. I was undressing and he turned away. He couldn't look at me anymore, you see, not without revulsion, or with pity—I don't know which is worse. And then it was over."

I didn't ask again. And, even though the blood was still beating in my ears, I understood with astonishment that it didn't matter to me. In fact, I, too, pitied her. There was an ache across my heart for her, the same ache I suffered for my mother, for things I could do nothing about.

Every day now, I had attacks of hope, as if I too were on opium. They arrived as they had always arrived, without warning, billowing out right there under my ribs. When I'd asked Stern whether this state of mind were an aspect of pregnancy, he'd said, "Possible, possible." As far as I could see, anything was possible. Hugh could have come marching up from the garden right then with a monkey on his shoulder, and I would have asked Josefina to lay another place for lunch.

Lily unhooked the binoculars and went to stand at the edge of the verandah. I wanted to wrap my arms around her, as I wrapped them around my mother, to tell her things Hugh could have said about her, wonderful things. But I didn't dare. She would hear the lie in my voice. She would smart at the presumption.

"After lunch," she said, turning back, "let's have a last walk along the beach. Then I must go back to the hotel to pack. Ah me! Moving on again."

· · ·

*Once, I went with Clive and his parents to California. We went to Disneyland and to Sea World, and then we drove up the coast and stopped at Marine World, Africa USA. There we stood in line and bought expensive tickets and were told which way to go by smiling guides in uniforms standing at the fork of every path.*

*After the dolphins and the killer whale, gorillas, monkeys, and snakes, we filed into the tiger show and sat on tiers under the hot, dry California sun.*

*Presently, eight tigers stalked into a large cage, and, after them, a man with a whip. At his command, the animals turned and faced the audience in a semicircle. They stood up on their hind legs, exposing the gleaming magnificence of their bellies. The man paced before them, flicking at their heads or legs with the coil of his whip. As each was stung, it curled back its lips and snarled. One reached out with a paw. And then, at a word, they all climbed onto small stools and waited, panting lightly.*

*I had never had a stomach for pornography. Something in the staging of it, in the perversion of its victims and its viewers made me want to weep. I wept then, stumbling up the bleachers and out onto the path to wait for the show to finish.*

· · ·

He was there on the lawn when I climbed the last step up from the beach, but it was the car I'd seen first, the white Escort parked on the verge outside the bungalow gate. I stopped dead, plunged my hands into the pockets of the pantaloons I wore.

"What is it?" Lily said. She scrambled up beside me, her shoes in her hand. "Who is it?" she asked.

He stepped out of the shade of the Beaumontia then, just into the sun. He wore bell-bottom jeans, and his skewed, sardonic smile. But it wouldn't hold. I could see his cheek quivering, his nipples rising and falling under the awful mint-green T-shirt.

I waited on the grass, facing the afternoon sun. The muslin, wet from the sea, clung to my legs and stomach. My skin itched. I shivered.

"Yes?" said Lily, slipping on her shoes. "May I help you?"

"Lily—"

But she was striding towards him, bearing down. Long wisps of hair had escaped her bun, her blouse was rolled up to the elbows and her skirt still tucked up into her pants. She stopped in front of him, untucking. "Yes?" she said.

He folded his arms at her and smiled. "I've come to pay a visit to my wife," he said, tossing his head at me. "Are you the nanny?"

"I am." She grabbed one foot and dusted the sand off of it, then the other.

He laughed, comfortable with her old age and bare feet, with what he liked to call spunk. He tapped her on the shoulder and pointed to the house. "Shall we?"

"Tea?" Lily called back to me. "I'll go in and arrange it."

She sailed off, up the steps of the verandah, with him behind her.

By the time I got to the lounge, he was at the bookshelf, taking down a book, frowning into it, putting it back again.

"So!" cried Lily, coming out of the kitchen. "Tell us about your journey. Sit down, sit down."

" 'Us'?" He turned, the smile back in place. "Does the nanny run the household?" he asked.

But she took no notice. Nor did she sit down. I watched with alarm as she slipped on her shoes and looked around for her bag. "Lily, don't go," I said.

"You may as well stay for tea," said Clive. "No need to rush off just because I'm here."

"Can't. Must go back to the hotel and pack." She clicked open her lorgnette and scrutinised her watch, then looked up, her bag in place, as Josefina made an entrance with the tea tray. "Ruth," she said, "fortune favours the brave."

---

# 23

"—eeen weech thee poleeteecl contxt—"

"STOP! Chief Sibusi, let me ask you—is it *essential* that you *read* the speech? Oh. What a pity. Well then, my advice to you is that you mark the pauses I shall give you on the script. Lift your face, find a few marks in the audience, left and right, and deliver it to *them*. All right now, let's start again."

"Thee seetuayshun een weech thee poleeteecl—"

"*Political*, political—can you say *i*? Try it. All those *eeeee's* make the words very difficult to understand, even to me. The Americans won't have a *clue* what you're saying!"

My mother had rallied to the challenge of coaching the Chief. Whenever he was coming to town, Catherine alerted her, so that she'd hold off on her morning martini.

"Thee conseekwens of such a mees-cal-cu-la-shon—"

"Chief!" she cried. "*Surely* you can find a more colourful way of putting all this? An example here and there?"

"He!-he!-he! Mrs. Frank, you are right! Colour is the question all right!"

I crept past the study to the lounge, where Catherine was pouring the tea. It was cold. The electric fire was on. I wore a pair of Catherine's maternity slacks, a large jersey of my own, and socks.

"I don't blame Clive for not wanting to spend time at the bungalow, you know," she said. She was unusually chatty, and her cheeks were flushed. This, I was sure, was connected with Jeffrey, with her having succeeded in placing Clive and me together in their peach spare room.

For two nights now, Clive and I had slept side by side. We dressed and undressed in the bathroom. "Excuse me," we said.

And, "Sorry!" "Want to go first?" When his mother chugged up the driveway in the old white Escort, he said, "You needn't come down. I'll handle her." I'd heard her voice lifting into its familiar shriek, the car start up again. And then he was down on the tennis court, bashing balls up against the wall, or practising his serve.

"What if it's a boy?" Catherine said, handing me the plate of biscuits. "Perhaps it would help to think of things from the child's point of view?"

But I had nothing to say from the child's point of view. Girl or boy, if it failed at school, if it turned into a thief, a blackmailer, a molester of women, I couldn't count on Clive. Even if he assumed the fatherhood he had no right to, I could see my life and the life of my child hanging on his pretension day to day, at every dinner party, till he found another woman more to his liking, perhaps, or began to decide on things I didn't want, for the child's sake. I had seen him stop in the lobby of our building to stare into a baby carriage with his peculiar smile. As if he were staring into a book without words, a world without love.

"Ah!" my mother cried. "There you two are! Cheerio, Chief Sibusi! Friday, then?"

"Really!" she exclaimed, as Catherine and the Chief drove off. "It's completely hopeless, you know. He hasn't a *clue! Nicholas* could do better! And I have the oddest feeling that he thinks *he's* doing *me* a favour! I wonder if he has any idea what my usual fee is?" She went off for the gin.

"Darling," she said, settling back onto the couch, "what am I supposed to say about all this when Clive arrives?"

"Nothing. Just behave as if nothing's happened."

She took a long sip and then pointed her nose at my stomach. "*That*, I mean."

"Pretend it's his," I suggested.

"Ha! With his deficiencies!"

"Ma," I said, "I can't stand the sight of him."

"Nor can I," she said cosily. "He's looking more and more like that mother of his—have you noticed? But they say he's at the top of his field, you know—whatever that is, I could never work it out." She hung a cigarette between her lips and flicked her lighter at the end, closed her eyes, lifted her face, and breathed in deeply.

"Clive's only staying for ten days," I said. "And then he's got to go back."

She observed me carefully through her smoke. "And you?"

I shrugged. One word, a phrase, a nod, and she'd be waving from the upper deck of the airport with everyone else. Clive's deficiencies would only reinforce her claim. Quite soon she'd find it in her to say that Hugh's murder wasn't, perhaps, entirely a bad thing. That I had a lot of my father in me—the sexual side of things, she meant. Was it worth it, she'd want to know? To grow old alone was to live the life of a dog. Was that what I wanted? Was that *really* what I wanted?

She held her magnifier to her watch. "He's not going to let us down, is he? I told Nicholas to open a couple of tins of salmon and some asparagus."

My father looked around the door. "Lunch?" he said. "It's already quarter to."

She looked up, grabbed her empty glass as if she'd throw it at him. "GO TO YOUR WHORE!" she boomed. "Go on! Get OUT, you *whoremonger!*"

"*You* get out, you silly bloody bitch!" he growled.

"You *see?*" She turned to me. "You see how he talks to me these days?"

"Ruth," he said, "may I have a word with you in the study?" He waited for me to follow him, and then closed the door firmly behind me. "Sit down," he said, waving me towards my mother's chair and then lifting his trousers at the knees to settle back into his own. He'd taken to wearing foldup slippers around the house, with no socks, and a cardigan that had been patched at the elbow. "Do you see what I have to put up with?" he demanded. His nostrils flared. His chest rose and fell.

I sat in the desk chair instead, lifted my feet and swivelled from side to side, bang, bang, bang.

"Don't do that please," he said. "It's no good for the chair."

I could hear her out in the hall, her heels clicking across the rugs and boards. "Aren't you going to put on shoes?" I asked.

"I hardly have a chance to talk to you alone anymore," he complained. "If you want me to change my shoes, I shall."

I picked up a red pencil and started colouring in the headlines of the morning paper. SOWETO. A layer of dust covered the glass on the desk. "The desk's dirty," I said.

"The whole house is dirty. You should just see the kitchen. She hasn't a clue what goes on in her kitchen. You'd be doing us a great service if you'd go in there and show Nicholas how to run it."

"*Her* kitchen?"

He chortled. "You and your women's lib! Look, there's something I want to ask you before Clive comes. Between you and me, of course."

I opened the drawer to look for different colours.

"*Ruth!* Will you *please* put those pencils down?" His nostrils quivered, he touched his fingers to his heart. "What I want to know is whether Clive's agreeable to your continuing this marriage?"

"Why?"

He cleared his throat. "I have presumed—perhaps erroneously —that you would wish to give the child a father."

"The child has a father. But he's dead."

"I think you know what I mean."

"You mean money." I heard my voice hard and clear and hoped my mother's ear was at the keyhole, hearing it too.

"Not only money. Although money is important, of course."

"Of course."

"There's the question of status. It might be better for the child. And a lot easier on you."

A car rolled down into the driveway. A car door slammed.

"Dad," I said, "did you ever have an affair with Jill Stafford?"

He raised his eyebrows and pulled his mouth into a thin, wry smile. It was the old stage gesture he'd always used in the face of impertinent questions.

The doorbell rang.

"Between you and me," I said quickly.

"Clive!" my mother cried. "Come in, come in! Nicholas, tell the Master and Ruth we're sitting down for lunch."

Nicholas knocked at the door.

"Once," my father said, pushing himself slowly to his feet. "Quite long ago." He sighed. "Although I don't really see that it's any business of yours."

. . .

"It would be a nice gesture," Clive said to me, nosing out of the driveway.

"Left!" I said. "Look *left*, not right! There's a car coming!"

"Anyway," he said, making it into the traffic, "I came to yours for lunch."

We drove past the Hebrew Nursery School, where women were double-parked, waiting to pick up their children. Nannies hung around in groups, waiting too.

"Don't you understand?" I demanded. "I *hate* gestures! I *detest* the *idea* of a gesture! I detest the *word* itself!"

"O.K., O.K. What do you want me to call it?"

"I don't want you to *call it* anything. It's *it* I object to. Either you want me to have tea with your parents or you don't."

We drove in silence for a while along the ridge.

Then he said, "If I didn't want you to go, why would I ask?"

"You didn't ask. You said it would be a nice gesture. Watch out, there's a stop street just over this hill."

"I'm doing the driving, if you don't mind." He bent his head forward slightly and peered through the windscreen as if it were raining. "I've told them," he said, "that I'd be prepared to pretend that it's mine."

"What?"

We were turning into the driveway of High Wyckham already, and he concentrated on slowing down for the residents, who were out on the bit of front lawn in pairs—women and men, or old women in hair nets, with walking sticks, and their maids beside them.

"There'd be your part of the bargain too," he said, "don't worry." He pulled into a parking slot in the back, next to the servants' quarters. The place smelled of paraffin and rubbish.

I followed him inside. He pressed the button for the lift. "I've never seen those earrings before," he said.

"You've never noticed."

He twisted his mouth into a smirk. "*Ja*, I can just imagine!"

The lift clanged to a stop, the doors jerked open.

"I bought them for *myself*," I insisted. "At the MLA!"

## The Bungalow

He walked out first, held a finger on the button. "With whose money?"

"With money my *parents* sent me for my birthday!" I lied. Tears of real outrage started in my throat.

"Your *parents!*" he sneered. "That'll be the day! O.K., O.K., you've got them now. But, just remember, the gravy train stops here."

. . .

*Clive's lab was quite different from what I had imagined. I'd had in mind a large white room, something like the lecture hall in which I taught, but with oak cabinets, long tables, sinks and faucets, and bottles and bottles of specimens, windows that opened to the outside, and lots of air.*

*But, in fact, his lab had no windows at all, and it smelled of disinfectant. It was small and cramped. His desk was squashed into a corner. Around the walls, on the floor and on shelves was equipment. A stainless-steel operating table, dried lungs, rubber tubing, valves, syringes, bottles of powders, bottles of liquid. In the middle of the room was a large cage, about six feet square and four feet high. Two large mongrels leapt and wagged inside it. They jumped at the wire, mad with joy at the sight of Clive.*

*"There, boy," he said, feeding each dog a biscuit. "Down boy."*

*One dog smiled and rolled onto its back, jumped up against the cage again. So did the other. Again and again, they threw themselves at him, pawing to get out, opening their mouths and snapping at the air, lifting their throats to bark.*

*For years, he'd been telling me of his progress, dog by dog, towards a reputation in the field of stroke. But I hadn't wanted to hear. I had had a life full of dogs. Dogs on the furniture, dogs in bed, mad dogs, unregenerate dogs, dogs that followed me to school, dogs that opened doors, dogs that ate grapes and spat out the pips, dogs glued together under the avocado tree, and then their puppies afterwards. I knew what I didn't want to see.*

*The dogs barked, but no sound came out. Into each dog's throat a tube had been inserted and secured with stitches and surgical tape. It stuck out like a periscope, and made a windy sort of noise.*

*I made for the door, pulled it open.*

175

*"You know what would have happened to them if they weren't here, don't you?" Clive called after me. "Facts are facts! It's all very well to get sentimental when you aren't the one who has to earn a living."*

. . .

They'd heard the lift, and were waiting at the front door in silence. Flo held her hands clasped between her stomach and her shelf of bosom, and Alfred stood behind, one hand on her shoulder, in the sleeveless orange jersey Clive's sister had knitted for him. Flo raised her hands to Clive's face and pulled it down to kiss him on the lips. "Hello, my darling," she said. "Tea's ready. I've got your favourite for you."

They turned in together, leaving Alfred to me.

"Doing well?" he asked. "Good."

The flat smelled of fried onions and varnished teak, mothballs and plastic. Plastic runners crisscrossed over the carpets, wherever people might walk. A plastic bonsai tree rose timelessly from its bowl of rose quartz pebbles on the coffee table. The tea tray was already there—an aluminum teapot with a knitted cosy, thick pink cups and saucers, a plate of cream doughnuts.

"I got them at the Greek's place," Flo said, pouring the men's tea first. "It's the kind you like, Clivey. Milk, Ruth?"

Wind rattled the windows. The sea looked grey. Even though the place was high on the ridge, it was salty and damp, like flats on the beachfront. Clive concentrated on stirring in his sugar. He too wore one of his sister's knitted jerseys.

"Maybe you and Dad want to go for a walk after tea," Flo suggested to Clive.

"Fine with me," said Alfred.

Clive looked at me. "O.K. with you?"

I nodded. I tried to remember that the bungalow was still there for me, that there were ten months left on my residence permit.

"Every evening, they used to take a walk together, from when Clivey was a little thing," Flo said when they had gone. "They've always been so close, you know."

I nodded again, noticing that our wedding photograph was gone from the top of the bookcase.

"My girl's sick," she said, gathering up the cups and saucers. "I'm just hoping she hasn't gone and got herself pregnant again."

She piled them onto the tray and then carried it off to the kitchen. I followed with the doughnut plate.

"She had a baby already," she said, "about a year old, and it died. I think she was quite relieved."

"Why?"

She gave me a satisfied look. "Well, they don't value life the way we do, do they?"

I stood in the corner, resting against the cold, tiled wall. Clive had told me many times that his mother had sat by his bedside when he'd suffered ear infections as a child of one or two. But he couldn't have remembered back that far; she must have told him. She had told me too. Often. And still I didn't believe her. Even if it were true, it was as if all that sitting had been accomplished in order to tell the story to his future wife. Where had she been, though, when Clive had lain feverish with mumps? When his testicles had swollen up like balloons and then shrunk down again, one down to nothing? I had heard nothing of this from her. She only spoke of the ear infections, and of the nights and days she had spent in a chair next to Alfred's hospital bed, when it was touch and go. The way she hung out of the window every afternoon, waiting for him to come home from bowls.

All her life, Flo Brasch had been preparing for widowhood. It was to this end that she had stolen salts and peppers from restaurants, stuffed hotel toilet rolls and light bulbs into her handbag. With the money he made, the money she saved, they opened bank accounts in America and in Israel, they bought gold shares, and blocks of flats. On the first of the month they went door to door, collecting the rents themselves. If the price of petrol went up, they took the bus. If the price of food rose, the servant ate what was left on their plates, or just the bones of the chicken.

Everyone knew that Flo would be inconsolable when Alfred died. At the funeral, her son and daughter would have to hold her up on either side. When she heard the sound of the first clod of earth landing on the coffin, she would faint. She'd sit shivah for the full seven days, pretending not to notice who came and how often. Still, within a year, she'd go to a slimming salon and lose thirty pounds. She'd go to a proper hairdresser, fly to Johannesburg to buy herself a new wardrobe.

When all this was accomplished, she'd go off to Cape Town for the season. There, she'd walk up and down the Parade, she'd meet people she knew. Over tea, she'd let it be known that she had means, that she was lonely. And then someone would introduce her to a man down on his luck, with a string of wives behind him, and in need of a new set of false teeth. She'd smile and simper, place her hand on his thigh in the cinema. After a week or so, she'd let it be known that she was willing to pay for new teeth, perhaps even a suit, in return for some assurances. After a few more trips to Cape Town, she'd bring him home in triumph. She'd phone to tell Ilana and Clive. "No one," she'd say, "could ever replace your father. But life must go on, you know. One can't be forever relying on one's friends and children."

And then she'd go back to stealing salts and peppers. She'd get her new husband to apply the colour rinses to her hair. She'd put on thirty pounds.

Other widows would ask each other how she'd done it. They'd see how she kept the new man on a tight leash, and even taught him to steal salts and peppers himself, and to leave something on his plate for the girl's supper, and they'd wonder what her secret was.

．　．　．

She put the last saucer on the rack and turned to me, drying her hands on a dishcloth. "You've got a good man, Ruth, never forget that—but I'm not allowed to say anything more, so I won't."

I closed my eyes. I felt nauseous.

She came to stand before me, right up close, smelling of tooth decay and cream doughnuts. "Love him, Ruth!" she said, grabbing me by the arms. "Love him with all your heart!"

# 24

With Clive in the house, Jeffrey seemed to relax about me. He liked to ask us questions at the dinner table. What about sport in America, he wanted to know? How did America deal with its troublemakers? And how did Americans expect to lead the world when they let their young people tell the professors what to do?

Clive enjoyed answering, folding his arms and saying, "Well, it isn't quite that simple." Often I made an excuse and went out into the garden, down around the tennis court and back up past the fountain to the courtyard, where I sat on the swing seat until the mosquitoes drove me back inside. Sometimes, I drove off to visit my parents. Or just drove off along the ridge and then came back again.

As the days went on, I became more restless. The garden itself seemed not to be a real garden, but a setting, an idea—a flower bed here, a screen of something there. But there was nowhere in the house I wanted to be either. Despite its furniture, despite its servants and children and visitors coming in and out all day, Catherine's house seemed barely inhabited. Windy. Plain as a motel.

I understood why she had never had much heart for the place, not even for her bedroom. If she ran up there when she heard a car straining up the driveway, if she closed the door, drew the curtains, pretended to be asleep, the house phone could buzz, or the visitors, considering her answerable, could knock lightly at the bedroom door and ask, "Anyone at home?" Trying the handle, finding the door locked, they could go round onto the verandah, where the French doors of her bedroom were fastened back, reach a hand in through the wrought iron gates, and part the curtains. "Catherine?" they'd call softly into the gloom. "Darling, are you all right?"

Jeffrey seemed to like things this way. At his invitation, cousins, friends, friends of friends came in of an evening for a game of tennis, or to watch TV, or for a swim in the pool. If the pool motor broke down, Jeffrey blamed Catherine for not calling in the pool man sooner. If the wind blew tennis balls off course and spoiled a game, he blamed her too. She should have called in the man from the Botanic Gardens when he'd suggested, had the stand of bamboo planted the year before.

I was desperate for my other life, and for the people of my other life. But Lily was gone. Maya worked during the day. And I couldn't phone Krishnah anymore. He had warned me not to. So I phoned Edwina and asked her to meet me for tea at the student union.

She was sitting in the corner when I arrived, paler than usual, not smiling. "I haven't seen him for *weeks*," she whispered, as soon as I'd sat down. "Ruth," she said, "I don't know what to do." She looked at me hard, as if I might have some suggestions.

All around us, students sat at tables, laughing and talking.

"My husband's here," I said lightly. "Can you imagine?"

But she just frowned, as if I'd missed the point. "Dickie thinks Krish is like all the others." She laughed hard and cold. "You understand, though, don't you?"

I nodded, but really, I still didn't have a clue. I watched her carefully—the way she twisted her fingers into her pearls, or fondled the coffee spoon, the curve of her breast. I longed to understand her gift for passion. For her, desire didn't arrive with love, or even with a turn of phrase, a glass of wine. It didn't accost her at unpredictable moments as she drove to the supermarket or stood in front of her wardrobe, wondering what to wear. Passion drove her life. It was there, always there, between her thighs. And, until Krishnah, it hadn't seemed to have specific objects, particular men. She had found them one after the other, or several at once. She had loved them all, she said, she called them all "my darlings." But now there was only Krishnah, with his frightening grimace, his girlish hands, and slim hips, and cold eyes. The way, perhaps, that he despised her. He was all she wanted, she said. The rest had been preliminaries.

"I'm staying with my sister," I said. "I miss the bungalow terribly."

"The consul's fixing him up with something in New York, you know," she said. "All he's waiting for is the exit permit."

Someone touched me on the shoulder. "Ruth Frank? Is that you? Edwina! What ho!"

Bruce Carter and another man stood behind us, with trays of curry and rice, and pots of tea.

"May we join you?" Bruce said, putting down his tray. "This is John Conradie. You know Bunny, don't you, Ruth?"

John nodded vaguely and put his tray down next to mine. He was a craggy man, about fifty or so, with a shiny tie and dandruff.

"How's Bunny?" I asked.

"O.K., O.K." He tucked his napkin into his belt. He seemed sick of the question, or just sick of questions. But I had forgotten her completely since the Carters' party, and now I wanted to know all about her.

"Did she have the baby?" I asked.

He nodded, forking up some curry. "Girl," he said with his mouth full.

"Hey," said Bruce, patting my stomach, "it must be catchy. Heard you joined the club! Listen," he said, "if you ever think of going back to lecturing, we could do with someone in the department. We're losing our best people, one after another."

Edwina started gathering up her things. She'd told me she'd outgrown these rugger-bugger local academic types. Now that she'd found Krishnah, she couldn't imagine what she'd ever seen in them. "Well, I'm off to the airport," she said.

John looked up. "Airport? Where're you going?"

"Nowhere," she said. "I'm fetching Dickie. He's coming back from London."

"We're going to Kingston, Ontario!" John burst out. "We leave in a fortnight." He grabbed the salt and shook it furiously over his curry.

"I thought Kingston was in the Caribbean," I said.

John smiled and lifted his eyebrows and shook his head at me, as if he were about to have the pleasure of failing a troublesome student. "Kingston happens to be right on Lake Ontario," he said. "On the site of Fort Frontenac, in fact."

Edwina stood up. "Bye," she said.

"John's going to be African history prof," Bruce said quickly. "He's going for good, you know."

For good. I looked at John—the fringe of hair growing along his cheekbone, his dirty fingernails, the furious way he scraped his fork around the plate—and I wondered whether Bunny would find other South Africans there to see her through. She was the sort of woman who would need them, their special brand of certitude, of hospitality. This man could never rally to the needs of a young wife crippled by homesickness. She had been right at the Carters' party. She shouldn't go.

"Hey, Ruth," Bruce said, "we're giving them a farewell on the twenty-fourth. Can you come? Cynthia's got the details. Give her a ring."

. . .

*Once, Catherine and Jeffrey had come to New York and stayed with us. It was summer at home, and they were very tanned. Catherine wore her fur coat and hat and boots, orange lipstick and terra-cotta rouge. She looked like an Italian film star. Even Jeffrey looked distinguished in a cashmere coat and scarf. They filled the lobby with luggage and expensive perfume. People stared at them, and then at me in my corduroy jumper, with a shirt and man's tie underneath. They listened to our accents, trying to work things out.*

*When we got up to the apartment, Jeffrey stopped still in front of the Marimekko hanging in the entrance hall. "Hey, Cath," he said, "look at that!"*

*The hanging was only a length of fabric stretched and stapled onto a frame, but he pulled it away from the wall, and looked behind. "That's something!" he exclaimed.*

*When I served tea, he remarked on the cake I'd baked. He commented on the curtains I'd sewn, the bookshelves I'd put up. He wanted to know what courses I was taking at the university, how much money came with my fellowship.*

*"Hey, Cath," he said. "You could learn a thing or two from your sister!"*

# The Bungalow

*One night, we took them to hear Aretha Franklin singing in a club down at the bottom of Tenth Avenue. The place was seedy, and the audience mostly black. Jeffrey looked around him. He shifted in his seat. When Aretha came on, people leapt to their feet. They roared and stamped and shouted and thrust their fists into the air. Jeffrey's lips went white, his ears bright red. He turned to Clive. But Clive was standing up too, shouting, with his fist raised in the black freedom salute.*

*For months, Clive had been enjoying the idea of taking Jeffrey and Catherine to this concert. He loved the idea of being there himself. In scenes like this, he felt himself at the forefront of things. Very far from what he had left behind.*

*Catherine nudged me slightly. I looked up and saw that Jeffrey, too, was on his feet. But he had plunged his hands into his pockets, and his knees were bent as if he were ready to sit or to run. Catherine exploded into a snort. I handed her a tissue and she grabbed it. Tears streamed down her cheeks, streaking her make-up. Jeffrey frowned down at her and kicked her hard with one foot. But she only laughed more, me too.*

*"You two should be ashamed of yourselves," Jeffrey said when we got home. "Catherine, bring me some tea!"*

*But he couldn't retrieve his authority over her so easily. In the kitchen, we just looked at each other and were crippled again with laughter. Every day after that it was the same. And when it was time for them to leave, I cried and so did she.*

*Jeffrey stood back, hopping from foot to foot. "Sisters," he said to Clive. "It's nice to see, isn't it?"*

. . .

When I got back to the peach bedroom, Clive was already there, sitting in the armchair with his head in his hands.

"What's wrong?" I asked.

He shook his head. He'd spent the morning with his father, who volunteered at MacHattie's.

"What?" I insisted.

He looked up then, and I saw that his eyes were red from crying, his lips were swollen. He shook his head.

"Something about us?"

He shook his head. "It's my father," he said. "I have nothing to say to him anymore." His voice was cracked. He began to shudder.

I went to sit at the dressing table and looked at myself in the mirror. "What does he say about us?" I asked.

"We didn't talk about it."

I turned around. "But you *must* have discussed it! You've been home more than a week. How can you not have discussed it?"

"Home!" he sneered. His eyes were muddy, the pupils narrowed down to pinpoints. "I haven't got a home. It took you a long time, but you finally did it, didn't you? You finally managed to wean me away from them!"

I laughed, and pulled open the make-up drawer, took out an eyeliner. I closed one eye and painted a thin line just above my eyelashes. But it came out crooked and I made it thicker. Ha! Ha! I did the other eye, thicker still. And then the first again, right up to the brow line. I sat back to look at myself, pursed my lips and painted a set of whiskers like a cat, then a small goatee, a dot at the end of my nose. I pulled the hairpins out of my hair and parted it down the middle, front to back. Then I twisted each half into a doughnut, one above each ear, and pinned them flat like ears. I stood up and pulled Edwina's shift over my head, unhooked my bra and rolled off my panties, turned sideways to see myself properly in the full-length mirror for the first time in a week. I had grown, there was no doubt. I looked less fat, more pregnant.

"What are you doing?" Clive asked. He stood up, hung his hands by the thumbs from the loops of his belt. I watched him in the mirror. He was looking at my buttocks. He looked into the mirror and saw my face, smiled, and began to walk towards me.

"I had lunch at 'varsity," I said quickly. "Met someone emigrating to Canada."

"Really?"

Outside, a servant was shouting something in Zulu. A car started up in the driveway. "It's almost teatime," I said.

"So what?" He walked to the door and turned the key. Then he went into the bathroom, came out with a facecloth. "You owe me one," he said. He placed the facecloth on the bedside table and began to draw the curtains. "It'll be quite safe, I assure you," he said.

I stood where I was, judging the distance to my clothes, to the door. Then I made a dash. I slipped my feet into my shoes.

"What are you doing?"

I stood quite still.

"Don't play silly buggers with me, girl," he said, crossing towards me. "You're the one who started this."

He took my arm again, and I went with him. I lay down where he told me to and watched him turn away to unbutton his shirt. He slipped out of his shoes, his jeans, everything, and came to lie next to me, already hard, poking at my thigh. The smell of him almost stopped my breathing. When he heaved himself on top of me and parted my thighs, tears began to roll down my cheeks and onto the peach bedspread. I had to gasp for breath.

He buried his face in the pillow next to my ear, arched his back, and knelt between my legs like a dog. "Nearly," he said. "Nearly." I didn't help him. I didn't move. I heard a car door slam, my father's voice, my mother's heels across the tarmac. Afternoon sunlight sliced through a breach in the curtains. It cut across his back, and bounced off the mirror.

I heard them calling for me downstairs, and someone padding up the stairs, down the corridor, a soft knock at the door.

"We're sleeping!" I shouted.

"Nearly," Clive gasped. "Grasp me tight! Tighten yourself around me!"

"No."

He stopped and pushed himself up on his arms, looked down into my face. "Bitch!" he said. "You bloody bitch!"

He rolled off and spat into his hand. Then he curled onto his side, away from me, and grasped himself, and pulled and pulled.

I lay where I was, waiting. The balcony curtains whuffed. After a while, I heard the tea tray rattling through the swing door, down the hall to the study. I watched a large black spider making its way across the ceiling, in and out of shadow. And then, at last, Clive reached for the facecloth. He began his crescendo of yelps and whimpers, bucking and heaving. I slipped my legs sideways off

185

Lynn Freed

the bed and sat staring at the bank of shiny cupboards along the opposite wall. He flopped onto his back behind me, pitched the cloth across the room. He could as easily have stuffed it into my mouth, stuffed my head under a pillow and held it down. He could have done anything he liked, things were so private within the bond of marriage.

# 25

I stopped at the supply store on my way back to the bungalow. Old Moosah himself came out from behind the counter to help me.

"Lovely day, madam. Lovely oranges this week, from the Cape. Apples too. Your girl came in; she bought some milk and bread and so on. Here's the list."

I scanned the invoice. She had bought only the basics, one tomato, two potatoes. I closed my eyes to think of what I needed.

"Madam is quite right to check it up," he said. "You cannot trust them one minute after another minute, you know that. I have to watch them every minute, from the first minute they come into my shop." He shook his head with every phrase, flapping his jowls above the fringe of grey beard. Behind him stood the African woman who helped with his non-European trade. She managed the far counter, argued with black customers in Zulu on Moosah's behalf, refusing credit, holding to the price. The shelves back there were stacked with Jungle Oats and Joko tea, Royal baking powder, cheap blankets, cardboard suitcases, Sunbeam polish, Vim, Jik, Jeyes fluid, Milo, Surf, Omo, Cobra and Sunbeam, skeins of wool, Bic lighters, vinyl shoes.

I asked for things and he picked them out himself—half a pocket of oranges, two bringals, a cauliflower, ladyfinger bananas—handing them to the younger Indian to put into a box.

"We're glad to have you back," he said, running a pencil down the columns, carrying numbers expertly, and then drawing a line under the total. "Are you going to stay?" he asked, not looking up.

I nodded. I was in the mood to buy things. If he'd had shoes for sale, I would have tried on a pair. Or even an African blanket. I scanned the bank of colourful woollen blankets at the far end of the shop.

"A blanket for the girl, madam?" He gestured to the woman to pull some out. "Best quality, madam, pure wool, very warm. Take a look." He held one out to me on both arms. "Very cold at night these days," he said.

I fingered the edge. They would have made wonderful presents to take back to New York. "Yes," I said, "I'll take two, this one and that one. And let me see that teapot." He ducked behind the counter and pulled out a large stainless-steel teapot, the sort they used at the hotel—heavy, very ugly. "Dust this!" he said, giving it to the woman.

"I'll take it too," I said. "I'll take the whole set, including the tray. How much?"

He leaned across the counter. "For you, madam, I'll make a special price, don't worry. Sonny! Wrap up the tea set. Make everything nice. Put it in Madam's boot."

. . .

I stood in the hall, trying to remember whether I'd left the curtains drawn when I left. No, I decided, it had still been light. Josefina must have drawn them so that she could sit on the couch and listen to the radio, do whatever she liked. Nothing had been dusted either, nor had the sheets and towels been changed.

I carried a small stool over to the windows and climbed onto it. The curtains were attached to brass rings, which were threaded onto a brass rod. I shook them. Dust billowed into the air. I jumped down, moved the stool to the end and unhitched the rod, let the curtain fall to the floor. The same on the other side. I held up one dusty heap to the light and examined it carefully. It had faded in patches. Others were in shreds. I found my nail scissors in the bathroom, and then rummaged in the desk drawer for a tape measure I'd seen there. I pulled the heap over to the couch and began cutting off the brass rings, dropping them into the ashtray. When it was done, I went through to the dining room and did the same in there, and in the bedroom, and in the spare room too.

"Josefina!" I called from the hall.

A tap was running in the kitchen, things clattered.

# The Bungalow

"JOSEFINA!"

The door opened and there she stood. She wore a jersey with holes in it that hardly buttoned over her breasts. A vest showed under her uniform. And she wore unmatched socks, and slippers.

"Take these curtains and throw them out. And bring me a bucket of water and some Vim, a sponge, some clean dishcloths."

She stood where she was, staring. Her skin was very dark, quite black in places, and her eyes brownish, the whites mostly yellow. Her hair stood out in a matted hood, quite different from the neat plaited crowns that other African women wore.

"If you want to keep this job, you must wear your doek," I said. "And I want this place cleaned every day, *every day!* Tomorrow I'll give you a list."

I walked off to change my clothes. Nothing had been cleaned properly for years; nothing had been painted either. I'd have to hire a gardener. I'd have to buy some paint, and sandpaper, and go to town for curtaining fabric, and new bedspreads. I knelt down to look at the floor, scraped my nail along the surface. It gathered a half-moon of grimy wax. I'd have to have them stripped, maybe sanded too. And I'd have the Persian rugs cleaned by my parents' man in town. Maybe I'd even buy a new one for the bedroom, to liven things up a bit in there. I'd make a list of everything, so that I knew what belonged to the Stillingtons and what to me. I'd also go through the books and put them in some sort of order. Tomorrow, I'd start Josefina off polishing the brass and silver, cleaning the windows. I'd ask Catherine whether I could borrow her sewing machine.

The sun shone bright and chill. The afternoon wind was up, rattling the windows. If I could find a handyman, I'd have the windows fixed to keep down the draughts, and other things too. I stopped in the spare room for a moment, feeling the blood hammering through my heart. I was happy, terribly happy. If there were a piano in the bungalow, I'd have sat down and played. I heaved my suitcase onto the bed and unsnapped the fasteners, opened the lid. There were my clothes, washed and neatly folded by Catherine's laundry maid.

Josefina knocked.

"Yes?" I said.

---

"The bucket, it's ready, madam."

"Did you put a newspaper underneath?"

She jutted her chin out slightly and rested her eyes sideways on the suitcase. "I'm put it," she said.

· · ·

By suppertime, I'd pulled out all the books and scrubbed the bookcases, right down to the wood, the desk too. Backwards and forwards Josefina had gone with the bucket, throwing out the dirty water, bringing me back fresh. After a while, I didn't have to shout so loudly for her, she came to ask herself. She stood at the foot of the ladder and looked up and said, "Nice and clean." She found some furniture oil and together we oiled the wood until the teak gleamed golden.

After dinner, when she'd gone to her room, I sat on the floor with the books. They were warped and discoloured from the sea air, they smelled of must. Still, there were volumes I'd never noticed. Olive Schreiner's letters—I set those aside. Roy Campbell, Laurens van der Post, Alan Paton, and lots of others I'd never even heard of—many with inscriptions to one Stillington or another.

I made piles around the perimeter of the room, Africana along one wall. Then I stacked them up by author, by genre. I decided to phone the library to find out what to do about the mould and the bookworm. Several times, I got up to admire the shelves. They were lovely, rounded at the edges, beautifully worked. My body ached, I leaned back against the couch with pleasure. And then, when I could not concentrate anymore, I got up and checked the locks, switched off the lights, and walked though to the bathroom to run a bath.

It smelled of Cobra floor polish and plain white soap, smoky towels dried stiff in the sun. After Catherine's potpourri and bathroom spray, I was almost drunk with pleasure. I went through to the bedroom and spread my new blanket over the bed, stood back to look at it, and at the pillows puffed into clean starched pillowcases by Josefina that afternoon.

The phone rang. I leapt to pick it up.

"Darling! You're there!"

"Hello, Ma."

"Darling, I couldn't sleep worrying about you. Are you all right?"

I heard the click and flash of her cigarette lighter and a thud started up in my chest.

"Darling?"

"I'm fine, Ma." I sat down on the bed.

"Have you locked the doors and windows? Is that night watchman awake?"

"Everything's fine, Ma. I'm having a bath."

"Don't sit in a draught."

"Ma, do you want to go shopping? I need some things."

"*Shopping!* You know you don't have to ask me twice! When?"

"Tomorrow. I need all sorts of things."

"Look, darling, if we're going to get anything accomplished, we should leave straight after breakfast. What time can you fetch me?"

I smiled. There were tears in my eyes again. For no reason at all, they came and went these days. "Ma," I said, "I'm so happy."

"Then so am I. What time?"

. . .

"I can't see any point," she said, "in spending fortunes when it's not your place." She fondled some material between her thumb and fingers and then pushed away a bolt. "How much is that one? *You* look! You've got eyes."

"Fourteen a yard."

"Too dear." She moved down the counter, bolt after bolt. "Awfully cheap stuff," she said, "for such high prices."

Already, my head was light from standing around, or from the sweet smell of the fabric. "Let's have tea," I said.

"Well, all right. But we've hardly begun. We haven't even found something for the lounge. You sit on that chair over there, and I'll look."

She looked here and there, pulled out a yard or two and held it to the light.

"That's nice," I said. It was a damask, off-white, and soft. I went over to look at it, and then at the price. "Why don't I take this?" I said.

"I don't know. Maybe because it's a little colourless."

I smiled to have her take my Americanism so literally—why don't you? and why don't I?—asking questions without wanting an answer. "Do you like it?" I tried again.

"As I say, a little colourless. But so is that entire establishment. And the price is certainly right. You know, these days, they're mixing all the colours up together. Pinks and reds and so forth. Catherine's decorator woman even had me bring out all the silver. 'Put it out! Put it out!' she said. So I did. Although, between you and me, it does seem a little silly to have a sugar shaker on display next to a sardine server, don't you think? In *my* day, only Ettie Goldman's sort would put the silver tea service on display. But you never know, do you? Now it's very mod. Would you want lining, darling?"

"I suppose so."

"Where are your measurements. Here, let's find a saleslady to serve us. Miss? Miss? Can you serve us, please? We've found what we want now."

. . .

We sat in Cottam's tearoom eating anchovy toast and drinking tea. It was already half past eleven, but she seemed happy, not missing a drink at all.

"Why don't we pop in and see Gigi?" she suggested.

"We can have lunch in town, if you like," I said. "Would you like to? I want to get something at Gillespie's too."

She pursed her lips and frowned. "That would leave Dad on his own, darling. Shame," she said. "I don't think so."

"Are you talking again, then?"

She snorted and reached for her cigarettes. "What's the use of carrying on? He'll never change. And he's not above the *other* thing either, might I say!" She looked at me with meaning and some pride.

But the thought of my father and his needs, her without her teeth, her hair pinned up in a net, made me anxious to change the subject. I was beginning to realise that if I hadn't been able to ask them questions all these years, it was, perhaps, because I didn't want to hear their answers.

"Darling," she whispered, leaning across the table. "I want you to do me a favour."

"What?"

"One day next week, I want you to drive me down to Eddie Orinsky's office. But you're *not* to tell Dad." She took a long draw on her cigarette and then stubbed it out, half smoked. She had always given drama to a moment with that gesture, and there was still some extravagance in it. "I'm changing the will," she said. "Back the way it was. You're the only one who knows."

"Back to what?"

"Cutting him out. Only this time, I'm *not* telling him. He's a liar, you know. I don't entirely trust him." She looked around her, this way and that way, and then dropped her voice. "If I died, he'd take the lot and spend it on that trollop of his. You'd get umpence."

She was breathing heavily now. The war she was waging had left her exhausted. And, because she was weak and old and furious, she had no allies. No one but me.

"Where do you think we'd have been without my money?" she went on. "I ran the house on my piffling Moss Brothers dividends. And every month, I used to put away, into the building society, what I earned from the theatre, never touched it. I let it build up and build up. How do you think we could afford to come to your wedding? Or all the other trips we took to you? Or even the clothes, the things I bought you, and my own wardrobe. I've always been smart, you know, can't carry off cheap stuff. But, then he was always coming up with some sort of crisis. Taxes, God knows what. If I didn't cooperate, he'd put himself to bed, curtains drawn, the lot. So I'd give in, and in no time he'd be right as rain again!"

She looked around to check that no one was listening. "Well," she said, "*that* little nest egg is no more, of course. And now that Mavis has finally killed him off, he's not bringing in a bean. Spends his time on the phone, selling raffle tickets, if you please! And with my eyes the way they are, *I'm* not getting work, of course. So that's that. I've made up my mind. He'll get the usufruct. The principal goes to you. And if he wants to have another one of his heart attacks—" she tapped the wooden table with her fingers—"*it's just too bad!*"

. . .

That night, I sat at Hugh's desk with the notebook, for which I'd paid a fortune at Gillespie's. It was large and heavy, covered in teal-green cloth. When opened, it stayed open, and the paper didn't blotch ink through to the other side. My nib moved across the page like a paintbrush. "Ruth Frank," I wrote. "1st July, 1976." Even my handwriting looked formed and rounded, with the 'a' closed off, and the uprights not sloping backwards, giving away my bad character.

Josefina had polished the lamps. They gleamed and shone. I'd borrowed a heater from home, and the room was warm. I could get up and move around without bracing against the chill. The woman in the library had told me to put the books in the sun, and to paint them with a special formula to get rid of the bookworm. Nothing, she said, would get rid of the smell. But, after all, that was just the smell of books. For hundreds of years, books had smelled like that out here. It was the salt and the damp in everything. Nothing lasted forever.

# 26

All the way into town, for the Carters' party, I considered paint—bottle green or white for the wicker furniture on the verandah. Green would look more authentic, less predictable. But the wrong shade could ruin the look of the place altogether. And Catherine's pram would go well with white wicker. She'd had Winston, her gardener, pull it out of the storage room for me, and polish it up. And then the factory lorry had brought it out to the bungalow one morning together with a lot of Catherine's other baby equipment. It was a beautiful English pram, cream and grey, with huge spoked wheels that clicked as they turned, and padded leather lining, leather suspension straps, large chrome buckles. It would look lovely in the garden, I thought, parked in the shade, with a mosquito net, and a dog to keep off the monkeys.

In the end, Josefina had come up with a gardener. He spoke no English at all, and so she had to act as go-between. The blades of the mower needed sharpening, she reported. And he needed three-in-one oil for the hinges of the front gate, and a tool for digging up weeds. Did I want him to weed the crazy paving up to the front door? So far, he'd cut the grass, front and back, tamed the num-num hedge, weeded the beds and the lawn. Next, I thought I'd have him start clearing the steps down to the beach. And then, perhaps the beach itself.

Every day, I woke early to the thought of things to do. They hovered in my head as I sat up in bed, writing in the green book. After breakfast, I began to work, room by room, task by task. Sometimes I went into town with a list, filled the boot, and then drove back out. After supper, I switched on the lamps and the heater. I put a record on and lay on the couch to read, the child moving and turning inside me. I understood that my happiness could not last, would not last. But I didn't believe what I understood. And so, even as I inhabited the bungalow as if it would be mine always, I mourned its loss, knowing that I would miss it soon.

. . .

The Carters' front door was open. I climbed down the steps from the street and walked into the hall, staying out of the light. The place looked just the same—furniture, candles, the men on the verandah drinking beer. In the middle of the lounge were piles of presents, and Bunny in an armchair, the baby under her blouse. A few women sat on the floor at her feet, opening boxes and handing her up the contents. A ceramic bowl, a beaded bottle, a book, another book. I had completely forgotten the point of the party, and had brought nothing but a bottle of wine. For one mad moment, I thought of bundling up my alpaca poncho and handing it over. But I didn't. I stood where I was, unnoticed, considering Bruce's offer of a lecturing post.

If I took him up on it, I'd be in danger of sitting there myself one day, handing up presents to someone on her way to Bloomington, Indiana, or Houston, Texas, or Cincinnati, Ohio. I might forget what I knew about the real world. I might develop enormous reverence for the printed page, quote opinions from *The New York Review of Books, Partisan Review, The Times Literary Supplement,* all of them months out of date. Once in a few years, when I took a trip myself, I might make straight for a bookshop, and stand in worship before the shelves, looking for the titles on my list, books to smuggle back in my suitcase. And then I might read them, one after another. I might strain to like what didn't interest me. It would be like losing an eye, or suffering an infection of the middle ear. Oh God!

I backed slowly up against the bookshelves, and then moved along them towards the front door and out. No one seemed to have seen me. I climbed the steps two by two. Someone was lolling at the top, against the gatepost. I kept my head down as I reached for the gate. My blood beat in my ears.

"Ruth!"

"Edwina!"

She stepped more into shadow. But the moon was full, and she wore a white satin blouse. "Was Krish down there?" she asked.

"I didn't see him," I said. "But I didn't look."

She looked down the street, towards Chesterton Road. "May I wait in your car for ten minutes? Where are you going?"

"I'm spending the night at my parents'."

I walked to the car and she followed. We got in and sat there in the darkness, she in the back, me behind the wheel. After a while, the noise of the party drifted up, men's voices, women laughing. A group of Africans approached along the pavement. A car pulled around the corner.

"Do you want me to go back down there?" I asked after a while. She had doused herself in Opium. The car was thick with it.

"Would you? Cynthia said he might come to say goodbye to everyone."

I pulled out the keys and began to get out of the car.

But the car had stopped behind me. Its lights went out. Someone got out. I looked in the rearview mirror.

"I think it's him," I whispered.

"Get out! Get out!" she cried. "Tell him I'm here!"

I got out. But I felt ridiculous. Except for the Africans, who had gathered now under a tree to talk and smoke, the street was deserted. And Krishnah was wearing some sort of a cloak that came down to his knees. He looked like an extra at the opera.

"Krish!" I whispered.

"Ruth!"

"She's in the car. Edwina."

He jerked backwards, twitched his head up and down the street, as if judging which way to run.

"Darling!" She had wound down the back window and was gesturing wildly for him to come over.

"Get away!" he hissed. He turned and made a dash for the steps, flew down them, his cloak swelling out behind him.

"Edwina!" I said. I was angry with her on his account, and on my own. "Tell me where you're parked," I said, getting back into the car. "I'll drive you to your car."

"Wait!" she said, opening the door and getting out. She stood for a moment on the pavement, pushing her hair back, brushing her skirt. Then she wheeled around and took off down the steps after Krishnah.

. . .

*It was Catherine who had phoned me to report that Dad was in Parkview Nursing Home. It was probably nothing, she said, probably just one of his frights. But he was playing it to the hilt, and Ma was in sackcloth and ashes. Could I just picture it?*

*I could just picture it. But still I couldn't bear to think of him even rehearsing the part of death, her the widow. "I'll come home," I said. "I'll leave tomorrow."*

*My suitcase was already packed with the presents I was to take with me two months later, and some clothes for the hot weather, and my diaphragm zipped into the side pocket.*

*"You're going when?" Clive said. He stood in the doorway, back from the Institute, with his parents hovering behind him. "You're going nowhere until my father's found out exactly what's going on."*

*As Alfred located the overseas operator, Parkview Nursing Home, Dr. Slatkin's home phone number, and then, at last, Dr. Slatkin himself, I paced from room to room. I picked things up, put them down again.*

*"I'm going," I said to Clive. "I'm going anyway."*

*Alfred put down the phone. "A suspected—a possible, very mild cardiac infarction," he announced. "No cause for undue alarm."*

*"See?" said Flo. "Now you can unpack your things." She made a lunge for my suitcase.*

*"Leave it!" I shouted. "Get out of my room!"*

*Clive came to stand over me. "How dare you talk to my mother like that?" he shouted. "You apologise!"*

*But I didn't apologise. I locked the suitcase and kept the key in my pocket. The next morning, early, I went to the airline office and bought the ticket. I went to the bank for traveller's checks. Then I went to the consulate for an emergency visa. On my way back to the subway station, I stopped in a phone booth and called the Anti-Vivisection Society. I told them the story of Clive's dogs. I gave them his name and his title, the address of the Research Institute.*

*When I got home, they were all there, even Clive. He'd come home early, he said, to say goodbye. He seemed sorry now, although he didn't say so, and I was too. But his parents were there. I couldn't tell him. And, anyway, what would I have said? Words were useless with Clive, he didn't trust them.*

*He looked at his watch. "Time to go," he said, picking up my suitcase. Flo brought the shopping cart, and instructed Alfred to bring his hat. For a moment, watching Clive flag down a cab, his ears red with cold, the pride he took in landing a Checker, I wanted to throw my arms around him, to kiss him properly for once. But I didn't. I let him hug me, and kiss my forehead, and say, as usual, "Don't stay away too long." Then I climbed into the cab, waved to them all, and drove away.*

. . .

Early the next morning, I went into my parents' room to play with them. They counted on this when I came home. They waited like children for me to wake up, sitting side by side, propped up on pillows, with the newspaper divided between them.

The reversal had come naturally to us, as soon as I was no longer a child myself. When I chased them around the room, or tickled them, or hid their slippers, they would plead with each other for help, beg me for mercy, gloriously happy. It seemed to undermine the furious gloom of their lives.

Sometimes, if the silence was too fresh between them, they wouldn't play. Or, if I went too far, they stopped the game to say so. Once, I'd hidden her false teeth behind the dressing table. "Darling," she'd whistled through her gums, "I feel small without them. Give them back." And I'd given them back, and the game had continued.

"How was the party?" she asked, moving up to let me in.

I jumped in next to her and swiped her pillows.

"Oh *no!*" she cried, making a grab, retrieving one.

My father farted loudly. He flapped the covers.

"Well out!" she cried happily.

I climbed out and made for the door. "It's revolting!" I said. "I'm not staying in here if you fart."

"Roger!" she giggled. "Stop farting!"

"Come back, you!" he growled. "And stop teaching your mother to use vulgar words." He was delighted to be part of the game

---

199

again. I'd been ignoring him lately. I could hardly look him in the eye.

I hovered near the door.

"See!" she said. "You've driven her off with your smelly *farts.*" She broke into a shrieking laugh, laughed and laughed until she rolled into a fit of coughing.

I stood at the door, looking at their reflections in the dressing-table mirror as they looked at me. The air was sour with their breath. The morning sun caught dust on everything—the mirror, the chandelier, the pile of yellowing scripts that had sat for years on her bedside table. To the world, they were remarkable, a remarkable couple. People still turned when they made an entrance. And, for this, they rallied, in dinner jacket and chiffon, ceremoniously taking their places on opening night. From the start, their marriage had been played out in public places. They felt at home with an audience. But here, alone and side by side, they were lost. They seemed to forget who they were.

"How was the party?" she asked again. "What did you wear? Meet anyone nice?"

"It was fine," I said, curling up in the chair and looking into the cups for a clean one.

She reached for the house phone. "Nicholas, bring up another pot of tea—the big one—and another cup for Miss Ruth, please. Who did you meet?" she asked me.

"An Indian. Lovely chap. Gorgeous-looking."

She slapped her hands down on the sheets. "Roger!" she cried. "Do I ever get a straight answer from this one? Never!"

"He's taking me out for dinner next week," I said, examining my toes.

She turned to my father. "What are we going to *do* with this child?" she said, delighted with the turn the game had taken. "She's *impossible!*"

"He said he'd be a father to my child. Only, we'll have to go and live in London. In the hub."

"Don't you dare!"

"I said yes."

"Come on, who did you meet?"

"I ran away."

"What?"

"I met the Indian on the steps and ran off with him."

"Ruth!" my father chortled, "don't tease your mother. She'll only take these things to heart and torment me with them later."

"Ha!" she looked at him with lowered lids. "Don't flatter yourself."

The game was over. She sighed and swung her feet out of bed, reached for her gown and buttoned it up. "Darling," she said, "let me have my chair please. I'll wait there until His Majesty has finished in the bathroom."

# 27

Every week, something had arrived in the post from Lily. Sometimes it was a letter, dated, with a proper salutation. But often it was simply a sentence or two, scrawled on a piece of scrap paper, or on a page of her diary torn out.

"Even with the decline of Europe since the war, the high prices, the diminished standard of living, cold water flats and taxes on everything pleasurable, Europe is where you should go, when you leave that place. Go to Europe to reacquaint yourself with the other of the two worlds in which you will always have to live—to insure, if you like, that you'll be able to go back again and carry on.

"America won't do for this purpose. Fear the eclecticism of America, the pervading motif of money. It is a country in which the thruways seem to have preceded the people. It is also Germanic. That is why the world watches America with the obsessive focus that a frail, exhausted parent trains on the antics of a hyperactive child."

"I'm never warm enough these days. It's ninety in the shade, and I'm never warm. I watch the young women hoeing and tilling with their gleaming plum black skin, and I know they think, 'She's old, that old white woman sitting in the sun without a hat.' I wish I could tell them what it feels like when it's too late. In my day, I too deprived men of their reason. I made my choices as if it would never end. As if it matters."

"When you make the choice to leave home, and you stay away year after year, you find that you belong nowhere anymore. You choose your friends and how to spend your time. When your friends annoy you, you can choose not to see them anymore. This, it seems to me, has its dangers."

"The river is mud brown from the rains, the sky Gentian violet at sundown, sometimes pink and grey. Awful bottle flies. I can't afford another infected bite. But, oh, the cassias are in bloom, the flame trees and leopard trees and liquid amber and Cape chestnuts. It is lovely, lovely."

"Exile is absence; death a final absence."

"In case something happens to me, here are the keys to my little flat in Hampstead (the square one for the front door—pull it closed tightly. Miss Price in flat 3 needs a box of chocolates or some flowers to settle her distrust of strangers.). Instructions are in the desk in the main bedroom, including the estate agents, who manage the place. I've been renting it for years, and always stay myself with the Philpotts in Belgravia. Anyway, I've made the necessary arrangements with my solicitors. It will belong to your son or your daughter—Hugh's son or Hugh's daughter—with you as executor of the trust."

And then, one day, when the weather turned hot, Lily came back. I was sitting on the swing seat with my notebook, hoping to give my bowels a leap. For weeks now they had slept, twisted within my body, solid as lead. Only some fright, or some flight of the spirit seemed able to unsettle them. Sometimes, the notebook was good for this. When I sat rereading a passage, refashioning a phrase, it was as if I were getting ready for a trip, with things to look forward to, places to stop along the way, surprises heaped up at the destination.

"Halloo? Anyone home?"

"*Lily!*" I put the book down and ran to stand at the edge of the verandah, the child crowded itself right up under my heart.

And there she was, climbing the last steps up from the beach, standing still on the lawn to catch her breath, blinking into the afternoon sun. Her skirt was edged with sand where it had caught the surf. She clutched the crocodile bag under one arm, her shoes in the other.

"They told me at the hotel you'd hired a gardener," she said, making for a flower bed and then stooping to have a look. "And that you've been doing up the bungalow. And that you're going to have a boy." She stood up, shading her eyes with one hand. "That much they know at the hotel."

"A boy! What rubbish!" I touched my stomach, and then the wooden backbone of the chair for good luck. Words like "boy" or "girl" gave too casual an existence to what was still unrevealed. Unless checked, the presumption could lead to anything, any sort of punishment. And then there'd be no way that I could know the cause, no way back. Sometimes, when I felt the child turning incessantly, I thought it must be strangling itself on the cord. I'd heard that this could happen. No statistics provided by Dr. Stern gave me any comfort. Nor did his assurances about the pills Catherine had given me after the murder. When the baby was born, I knew things would be worse. It could have missing parts, or have extra parts. Without warning, it could stop breathing. It could be deaf, or mad. It could be anything.

"Green," she said, coming up the steps. "In my day, they were green too." She ran a bony hand along the top of the wicker chair, fingered the material of the new cushion cover.

"I had the walls painted too," I said, pointing inside. "The curtains are new. The carpet's my mother's."

She stopped in the middle of the lounge to look around. I watched her eyes for signs of disapproval, but I couldn't tell. They had turned very black, and her chest heaved slightly.

"You're staying on, then?" she said.

I shrugged. A few days before, a letter had arrived from a New York lawyer. It was full of phrases so mysterious, yet so peculiarly precise, that I had given up trying to understand them beyond Clive's obvious intention of divorcing me and keeping our money and our things for himself. As for the things, they now seemed weightless, arbitrary, foolish. A table scrounged from the Cambodians, a set of chairs from a secondhand shop, everything stripped down to the wood, or covered in course natural fibres, orange and brown and beige. Ceramic dishes, dried flowers, baskets everywhere—we had created a farmhouse in the middle of Manhattan, fifteen stories up.

She settled into a chair and concentrated on putting her shoes back on. "The opera wasn't up to much this year. But I had a lovely time with André," she said.

"André?" She had a habit of mentioning people and places as if I knew them and their history in her life. If I weren't so sure of her, I'd have thought she was trying to make me jealous.

"André de Wet. A very dear friend, quite mad. Lives right up north, in the forests at the edge of the escarpment—a most *beautiful* place, *wonderful* gardens! He plays the organ, too. I think he fancies himself as Schweitzer."

Josefina came out of the kitchen just then with the tea tray. She had made scones without my asking. She wore a doek around her head now, and deodorant, and she kept her uniform spotless. She put the tray down in front of me and then turned shyly to Lily. "Hau, Madam she come back," she said. "I'm bring another cup."

Lily sat back to observe me. "There's something new about you," she said. She twirled a hand, indicating my stomach. "Apart from all this burgeoning, I mean. Since Hugh excused himself from the scene, this place feels like the nest of a tigress."

I shook my head, shrugged, but suddenly my eyes were swimming with tears, my throat ached with happiness. I fished into my pocket for a tissue, pretending to cough.

Josefina brought the extra cup and I poured the tea. Everything made me happy now. The heft of the teapot, its beautiful blue belly, the tea itself arching from the spout. And then Lily's hand laying the teaspoon in the saucer, the way she broke open her scone and buttered it, humming something to herself.

"There's something new about you, Ruth," she said again, observing me over the rim of her cup. "Have you met a man?"

I shook my head. I still couldn't speak, but I smiled at the question. She sounded so much like my mother. Like me, perhaps, in twenty or thirty years.

. . .

I walked back from the hotel along the beach thinking of Lily back in her old room at the hotel, her pots of cream and rouge lined up

Lynn Freed

along the dressing table. The sand was in shadow, with jellyfish strewn along the high-tide line. At the far end of the beach I could see an Indian fisherman sitting on a rock, with a small boy at his side. I'd seen them there before. They must have had to climb over the far cliff, and then wade through the surf at low tide.

I had promised Dr. Stern I'd move back into town within a week, and go to Parkview Nursing Home to have the baby, and stay at Catherine's, and have a baby nurse for the first month. The crib was already set up in Catherine's old nursery, next to the peach guest room. "You have a certain responsibility," Jeffrey had informed me, torturing a small pickle fork. His cheeks and forehead had glowed red. Perhaps, like teenage boys, he still connected babies with sex. "You have a child to think of now," he'd reminded me.

As I walked, my stomach began to turn and growl. My head felt light. Clambering over the rocks between the hotel beach and my own, I sat down for a few minutes. But I had to hang on tight to keep my balance. Things swayed and shifted. The waves crashed high against the rock, soaking me through. I shivered. The sun was sinking fast. In a few hours it would be dark. I swung my legs over the wet rock and eased down onto the beach. The gardener had been working down the steps from the garden, but had only made it halfway to the beach. I wondered, light-headed, whether he were lazy, how one could tell laziness in a gardener when one knew nothing about gardening. I sat down again. But the growling in my stomach had turned into cramps, terrible cramps. I tried resting on one elbow, to one side, but that only made it worse. Every time I took a breath, I wanted to vomit. I did vomit, suddenly, right there onto the sand.

The beach smelled of rotting fish. My head swayed, my stomach twisted and turned. I had to void my bowels. It was a terrible and immediate need. I reached under my dress and pulled down my pants, slipped them off my feet and threw them into the bushes behind me. Then I dug a hole in the sand, and, as I dug, I knew I didn't have time to position myself over it. Nor could I give any thought to the fisherman. I didn't think of anything but waiting for the next surge of pain. And then it happened as I knelt there, right in the grip of pain, the smell of shit. I grabbed for my dress with both arms and pulled it over my head, crawled forward a few feet and laid it out on the sand in front of me.

For a moment, things settled. I saw that the tide was going out, the surf subsiding into swells and foam. Small crabs skittered along the wet sand, disappearing into holes. I was in a clearing among the rubbish on the beach, above the seaweed and detritus. I crouched there, waiting for the pain to come back. And then it did come, fiercer and sharper than before, each seizure longer and more urgent.

A steady wind blew in from the sea. For a while, it seemed to bring moments of sleep. When the pain came back, I tried to say things, I did say things, but my words were nothing with the roar of the wind and the surf. So I crouched there, waiting, groaning, while the surf and the light moved further and further towards the horizon. And then the pain came on, and on, while the sun settled its light into a shimmering silver ribbon between sea and sky.

Hugh was dead. Suddenly I knew that absolutely. He was absolutely dead, as if I'd seen the body lifeless, the wounds congealed from red to black. I lifted my head into the wind. I rose up on my knees. At first, the cry stopped in my throat, then it rumbled in my head, low and hoarse. I gulped in air, sand and air, and, at last, I heard myself over the wind and surf. "HELP!" I screamed. "Help me! HELP ME PLEASE SOMEONE HELP ME PLEASE!"

They came running towards me along the beach, the Indian and his boy, waving their rods like warriors, shouting to each other above the noise of the surf. I could feel the thudding of their feet through the sand, and I didn't care. If they killed me even, I didn't care. I heard my screams subside, felt myself arcing against the pain, grinding sand between my teeth. The man flung down his rod and ran down to the water. He crouched down there and washed his hands.

"I'm coming, madam, coming!" he shouted, running back.

I closed my eyes and held my breath. "Help me!" I said, "Please help me!"

"Madam, please, can you move forward? Here, madam. Like this, madam."

I crawled onto my dress as he told me to. It felt cool and damp under my hands and knees. The light was gone. The sky was grey, darkening to slate. And the wind blew more softly.

He crouched behind me. "Push, madam! Now Madam must push!"

I closed my eyes and clenched my teeth, pushed and pushed.

He shouted something at his boy. "Oh, madam!" he said. "I have done this very many times! You are not to be worrying yourself about it at all!"

I sat back, holding my stomach in my hands. I couldn't help pushing now. I saw the boy down at the water's edge, washing a knife with his hands, heard the man behind me shouting, "Madam! Madam! Here it comes!" And I felt it moving now under my hands, moving with the pain that ran through me like a river. I could feel it slipping, urging itself through me so that I couldn't stop pushing, pushing it out, out into the air.

I hung there panting, my hands resting on my hips. And then I looked down, and there it lay, there on the dress between my thighs, bloodied, white and red, the ribbony cord curling from me to it like an underwater plant. It was over.

"Madam, madam, oh what a lovely girl! What a beautiful daughter you've got!" The man was at my side now. He had the cord in one hand, a knife in the other, and he wore an old felt hat. "I have done this many times, madam, many, many times, don't you worry. Now you must push some more."

I pushed again, watching him working with the knife, tearing a strip from the hem of the dress, tying and knotting and cutting.

"I sent my son running up to the house to fetch the girl. Don't worry, madam, here comes everything at once now, all of a sudden."

And then it was over. I lay down on my side in the sand, curved around the baby. She writhed and twisted, her face bright red, her mouth open. She was crying, I could see that now, but I couldn't hear her over the surf and the wind. She had a head of thick, black hair, two tiny fists, two legs, two feet. I reached down and pulled her up to me. I kissed her forehead, and wrapped her in my arms. And I was crying too, crying, crying.

# 28

Maya sat in the bedroom chair, holding the baby. It was she whom the fisherman's son had found first at the bungalow. She had come there from her uncle's, where she'd gone to say goodbye to Krishnah. Yesterday he'd got his exit permit, she said, and tomorrow he was off to America, just like that. The American consul had managed some sort of position for him at the U.N., working for U.N. radio. One could only hope, she said, that Edwina wouldn't take it into her head to abandon her family and follow him. It was one thing to conduct such a romance out here, where the peculiarities of circumstance lent enchantment and so forth. But, in the cold light of a New York winter, things might look very different, didn't I think?

I lay propped up by pillows, my body quiet and still again. The baby's hair was the same blue-black as Maya's, straight and glossy. It would fall out, Maya said, and other hair would grow in its place. She had held the baby expertly on one arm, while she swabbed her clean with cotton wool. Josefina had been there too, her hand over her mouth, shaking her head with pleasure. Maya had sent her off for the kitchen scale, and then we watched, Josefina and I, while Maya found a level surface on the tallboy, weighed the towel, then laid the baby in the bowl and added the weights, one by one. Six pounds, eight ounces, she announced. No, not exactly premature. She put her ear to the baby's heart and used a straw to suck out her nostrils. She told me how to feed her, and to be patient if it didn't work at first. We decided to call her Hester, after Hugh, and because Hestia was the goddess of the hearth. Hester Lily Frank.

"Hau, madam!" Josefina said. "O! *Muhle!!*"

She brought us supper on a tray. Roast chicken, roast potatoes, tinned peas, and a treacle tart from Moosah's. I told Maya where to find Hugh's special case of Meerlust. And to bring three glasses, one for Josefina. Maya phoned her parents to tell them she was staying with me for the night. But she didn't tell them about the baby. Nor did we phone my parents, nor even Lily. We sat on the bed after supper, with the baby sleeping in my arms, talking far beyond the tacit frontiers of our usual friendship.

As Maya spoke, I watched the fine line of her upper lip, the curve of her eyebrow, her skin in the soft light of the bedside lamps. She was more beautiful than ever, I told her, exquisitely beautiful. No, she said, she was ordinary, Indian-ordinary. Walk down Grey Street and there'd be dozens like her, one after the other. Anyway, even if she were the most beautiful woman in the world, so what? Her cheeks were flushed, she spoke so quickly that she tripped on words. She was frigid, she said at last. Then she said it again, pronouncing carefully. Frig-id.

"It's not a word they use anymore," I said.

She laughed. "Oh, Ruth," she said, "in some ways you're so American!" She hung her head and giggled into her blouse. I felt a fool. So I told her about Clive sawing away, sawing away, time after time after time, and the orders he'd given me, the things he'd wanted me to say. And she told me she could never shut down her mind. If a man touched her, it was like a switch, like fluorescent light, cold and clear. Every happy woman was a mystery to her, a torment. Her husband had read Henry Miller, and once, in London, they'd seen *Last Tango in Paris*. He'd ordered up some ghee from the kitchen, and made her kneel on the floor like a dog. It was horrible, horrible. And, after that, she couldn't sit down for a week.

The baby woke up and cried. "Oh, Ruth," Maya said as I lifted my nightie, "how lucky you are."

She was right. I was lucky. I felt lucky in every way. Lucky, too, to have her with me that night, and no one else. Something in the sight of her as she went back to sit down—her back so straight, her bra straps so very vertical, the neatness of her waist—made me want to set her free. But I didn't have the power, the transforming power that comes with the love of a man. The happiness we took in each other was a different form of love. And I understood that, for the sake of a man, such a pitch of friendship could subside, once more, into little or nothing. That a man's claim could isolate us from each other far more than any other differences between us. At least until we had given up caring about him anymore. Or until he died. Until then.

. . .

The next morning, as soon as we'd phoned my parents with the news, Maya wanted to be gone. Long before the car doors slammed and the doorbell buzzed, I'd felt her waiting for a pause so that she could say, "Well, I must be off." And so I filled the air with talk, watching anxiously as she folded her napkin, and put her cup and saucer back on the verandah table.

"Well," she said, pushing back her chair, "I'll have to be off, my dear." She came up behind me and laid a hand on my shoulder. "I'll come back soon," she said. "I'll ring you later."

It was a balmy morning, with birds out, and the sun, and the roar of the surf far below. The Beautmontia were beginning to bloom again. Their flowers perfumed the air. The num-num flowers were out too. There were grass clippings, and Josefina singing in the kitchen. And then I heard the car doors slam, the doorbell buzz, my mother's voice lifting in the hall.

Maya stood back, smiling her old head girl smile. "Congratulations!" she said when they appeared. "Mrs. Frank, Mr. Frank, everybody!"

They stood quite still in the doorway—Catherine and my parents—staring at the breakfast scene as if it were the site of an accident. My mother blinked a bit. She took the hand that Maya offered her, she even kissed it and whispered, "Maya! Thank you, darling! Thank *God* you were here!" But she kept her eyes on me and the baby, searching for signs of life.

"Look, Ma," I said, tears rolling down my cheeks. "Look."

She came over and peered down into the bundle I held up. She shaded her eyes with both hands, as if she were looking through a nursery window. "Roger!" she said at last. "Just *look* at this face! Look at those black eyes! She's the image of your mother!"

They all came over then, my father reaching down to touch the baby's cheek.

211

"Listen, old girl," said Catherine, "don't you think you should be inside?"

I looked to Maya for help, but she had disappeared.

"*Ochye chornye*," my mother crooned, deep and low, looking at the baby. "Remember when I used to sing that to you?" she asked. " 'Dark Eyes'?" She hummed on in her baritone.

"Sarah!" my father hissed. "You'll frighten the baby."

"Bosh! What do you know? How many babies have you had?" She pulled a chair up next to mine. "Except for the eyes, she doesn't look anything like you!" she said to me. "You were as red as a tomato."

I looked, but it was impossible to tell. I couldn't get used to the idea of the baby, anyway. One glance away, and I forgot what she looked like. I had to look again. And, there she was, looking like no one I'd ever seen, wide-cheeked, high-browed, with pink skin and large, dark eyes.

"I was born with a caul over my head," my mother went on happily. "It's supposed to bring good luck, and it always did, didn't it? Father kept it in a leather box, and gave it to me when I married. And then it got lost somewhere along the way. So much for my good luck. Ha!"

"Madam—" Josefina stood at the door. "That Indian at the kitchen door for Madam, madam."

My heart flew to my throat, my breasts hardened into rocks.

"Indian? What Indian?" my mother demanded.

Josefina looked at the floor.

"Tell him to come round the garden," I said.

"Is this something we can take care of, Ruth?" my father asked.

"Cath," I said, "could you bring me my bag?"

"Halloo? Hello!" Lily appeared in the garden, carrying an enormous bunch of white calla lilies. "Hello, everyone! Oh, look! What a tiny little thing?" She shook the flowers in front of the baby's face.

"Lily!" my mother said, grabbing hold of the flowers. "I'll have those put in water."

"Which bag?" Catherine called out of the bedroom window. "The straw or the leather?"

"Straw!"

My father tapped me on the shoulder. "I'd like to put an announcement in tomorrow's *Witness*," he said. "How would you like me to word it?"

"Madam—" The Indian came to stand at the bottom of the steps, his hat in his hands, smiling toothlessly at me. "How is baby?"

But the sound of his voice again, so soon, deprived me of my own. I held the baby up.

"Here," said Catherine. "Is this the right one?"

"Cath," I whispered, "take out all the money and give it to him."

"Listen, old girl, you'll never get rid—"

"*Please!*"

She found my purse and opened it, pulled out the notes and folded them over twice. I watched him eye the bundle, come up one step and reach to grasp it quickly, like a bird, careful not to touch her fingers. His boy watched too, standing back in a pair of shorts, no shoes, his hair greased down for the occasion.

"What's your name, please," I said.

"Moodley, madam. P. Moodley."

Lily settled herself onto the top step, tucking her skirt around her legs. "They're talking about you all over the hotel, Mr. Moodley," she said.

He grinned at her. "Mr. Stillington knew me, madam, his father knew my father too, and so on."

"What's going on, for God's sake?" My mother flapped the lilies at the Indian. "Why doesn't someone tell him to go away?"

"Dad," I said, "here's the wording: 'To Ruth Frank and the late Hugh Stillington, a daughter, 6 lb; 8 oz., 10/9/76. Thanks to P. Moodley and son.'"

Moodley backed away from the steps.

"Thanks to *whom?*" my mother demanded.

"Listen, old girl," Catherine whispered, "I can take Ma and Dad back for lunch, and then come and fetch you later if you like."

I shook my head. "Mr. Moodley," I said, "please tell the maid where you live."

He grinned, pushing the boy ahead of him. "Mr. Stillington knew our place, madam, down by the river. It's a terrible thing, that thing that happened to Mr. Stillington, madam."

Catherine watched him disappear around the house.

"If he's looking for a job," said my mother, "why don't you tell him to try the factory? My son-in-law," she explained to Lily, "employs literally *thousands* of Indians."

Lily rested her chin on her hand and stared directly into the sun. Her eyes were milky, and her skin was dry and grey. I wished she would notice the baby, stare into its face for signs of Hugh. I wanted badly for her to notice it, to notice it as if it would make a difference in her life.

The baby writhed in the blanket and began to cry.

"May I hold her?" Catherine asked, reaching down to pick her up.

My mother pushed herself up and went to see. "Just look at those black eyes!" she said. "That's *definitely* from our side, isn't it, Roger? Oh!" She clapped her hands happily. "Remember the song I used to sing for you girls?" She lifted her face, held her hands before her as if in an agony of desire. "*Ochye chornye,*" she began deep and low. She struck her old pose—one arm stretched ahead, the other behind, head down. She began to stalk across the verandah. In a flash, Lily was up too, following behind. "*Ochye chornye,*" they sang, moving in a wide circle around Catherine and the baby. "*Ochye srastnye, ochye zhguchye e preyekrasnye, Kak lyublyn yavas! Kale boyusi ya vas! Znati, uvidel vac ya i nyedobryi chas!*"

They both stopped then, and roared with laughter. "Oh, Lily!" my mother cried. "How long is it since one sang *that,* hey?"

Lily, too, looked happy. She went to sit on the wall of the verandah, lifted her face to the sun.

I looked at Catherine. She seemed not to mind the performance. With a baby in her arms, she seemed almost happy. She smiled a normal smile. There was nothing furious about her. She clipped off across the verandah in her high-heeled sandals, clicking her tongue against her palate, singing lightly herself, with her head inclined. In fact, the baby could have been her baby, not mine at all. With all the chaos they'd brought with them, the talk, the noise, the singing, all that was left of the night before was a dull ache in my groin, a terrible fatigue.

"When you children were born," my mother said, lighting a cigarette, "I stayed in bed for two weeks. Never did the exercises they told me to do either. If you want your figure back darling, take my advice, do the exercises."

"Have a heart," said my father. "She's barely had time, has she?"

"You should talk!" she snapped. "You can't pass a mirror without looking in."

He sighed and pursed his lips and tried to catch my eye.

The baby began to cry. Catherine winked at me, heading in through the French doors.

"I'll just go inside for a bit," I said, following. "I'll ask Josefina to bring you out some tea."

Inside, Catherine fetched a pillow and showed me how to rest my arm on it while I was feeding the baby. She also warned me about supporting my back, and not to pick the baby up every time she cried. On the other hand, I should wake her up to feed her, and it was important that she sleep in a different room from me. The peach room was ready, she said, and the nursery, of course. The nurse would only be available on Friday, so, until then, Gladys, her nanny, had agreed to fill in. But I shouldn't tell Ma, because Gladys was Coloured and Ma had a thing about trained white baby nurses.

"The thing is, Cath," I said, "I'm not coming in to town."

I knew it was Jeffrey she'd have to answer to for this, that she'd have to cope, once more, with the nuisance I had become in her life. But I wanted her to understand. I wanted her to know how free I felt now, how wonderfully free of the old tyranny of saying yes while feeling no.

"I'm happy out here," I explained. "I'll be O.K."

# 29

Jeffrey tossed himself from side to side in the study chair. He shot one eyebrow up, frowned at me in silence. I was familiar with this performance. He used it on his children, on his employees, on any uneasy victims of his control.

"Interesting," he mused.

I ignored him and peered over the arm of the couch at the baby, who was sleeping in a carry cot on the floor. This was my first trip to town since she'd been born, and there she lay, mine, proof against the efficacy of separate sleeping quarters, intercoms, baby nurses.

"To think," he said, "of all those university degrees going to produce a nanny." He threw his head back in a guffaw, revealing two rows of newly capped, gleaming white teeth.

"Shhh, darling!" Catherine whispered. "The baby's sleeping." She shrugged at me, and then glanced over at her knitting pattern.

Another time, I would have humoured him, for her sake. But now I was tired of all that. Day to day, I looked after the baby, I wrote in my notebook, I wrote letters to my friend Anna, even to Clive. My parents came to visit, and so did Catherine, and Maya, and, once, Edwina, who had left home and had taken a cottage in the hills, like a hermit. Since Krishnah, who wouldn't have her in America, she wanted no more men, she'd told me. She had a guru now, and incense, and a prayer mat.

"Don't you consider it selfish?" Jeffrey asked.

"Consider what selfish?"

He twitched around, recrossed his legs. "To society, one might say. What one takes away one should give back, isn't that so, Catherine?"

"Don't pull me into this," she said.

"Well?" he insisted.

I shivered. Catherine always turned the air conditioning up full on days like this—hot, damp, heavy days. "I feel no such injunction," I answered. I knew perfectly well that he wouldn't understand "injunction," I intended him not to. "I don't subscribe to marketplace morality," I said.

He flushed. "Aren't you forgetting something?"

I knew what he was after. The residence permit. With one phone call he could have it undone again if he wanted to. "I haven't forgotten the favour you did me," I said.

But he waved me away. That wasn't it. He jutted his chin at Catherine, then nodded toward the pool, where my parents were dozing under an umbrella. Then he frowned at me.

Catherine didn't seem to mind playing these guessing games with Jeffrey. I did. "I have no idea what you're driving at," I said to him.

He shook his head and clicked his tongue. "Really," he said, "I thought you were supposed to be intelligent."

Despite myself, his tone of voice, the same old phrases of envy and blame brought colour to my cheeks and ears. I knew that things were going badly for him at the factory. Catherine had told me the workers had turned nasty, that he was tormented by their disloyalty. He had fired his driver. It wasn't safe to have one anymore, she'd said. Day or night, he drove himself out there. She was worried sick about his safety.

"Don't you think you have a duty to your family, and to your child?" he demanded at last.

"*What* duty?"

But he couldn't say it. He couldn't say go back, get out, leave my wife alone. She glanced at me, smiling quickly.

"When my father came out here from Lithuania, he had to start from scratch. Whatever he made, he spent to bring out the rest of the family."

"So?"

He laughed. "Hey, Cath, who said this one had the brains?" Despite the steady blast of cold air, he was sweating. He pulled out a handkerchief and wiped it across his forehead, under his nose.

217

"Do you mean a *green car*—"

"A *what?* A WHAT?" he shouted. He laughed again, loud and forced.

And then I saw Catherine's frown, and I remembered that Jeffrey had forbidden her to talk of certain things in the house, or even in the garden, where tiny microphones could be buried in the walls, or under bushes, relaying every sound, every whisper, to the government. The servants themselves could be doubling as informers, even Shadrak, who'd been with them from the beginning. One never knew. No one was to be trusted, not ever. Money was never to be discussed, nor was leaving the country. Since the Chief had entered their lives, since the whole country had flared up and Jeffrey had taken on the role of political middleman, his own behaviour had to be above reproach. On both sides of the fence. I understood.

"But what if I stay on?" I asked. "What if I give up being an American?"

He frowned at his watch and stood up. Men were coming for tennis, and he had to change. On his way out, he stopped in front of the carry cot. "Catherine," he said, "I'm surprised at you, allowing your sister to put her baby on the floor, where the dogs can get it. Please," he said, "be a bit more responsible."

. . .

The baby whimpered, tied onto Josefina's back.

"I'll take her now," I said.

She unknotted the blanket, and leaned the baby back into my arms. "About lunch?" she asked.

"My old Madam and Master are coming," I said.

"Fry fish? Salad? Chips?"

I nodded. Her son sat wide-legged at the bookshelf, placing one book carefully on top of another. When I'd come into the kitchen and seen him there one day—a child of about two, with two green streams of snot running from his nostrils, and a deep, loose cough—she'd looked up sideways from the stove, and smiled. "My boy," she'd said.

"Do you think it wise," my mother asked, "to allow that child into the house?" She chewed as she talked, spewing bits of food onto the front of her sundress.

"I haven't considered the wisdom of the matter at all," I said.

"The what?" Her mouth hung open. She reached for the last of her roll and stuffed it in. "Did I tell you Myrna Lipinsky phoned to wish us mazel tov?"

"Yes." She had phoned me too, and asked me to come in for tea, or she'd come out to the bungalow if I preferred. I had said I would phone her, but I knew I wouldn't. "Should I allow Myrna's children into the house, do you think?" I asked.

My father chortled. "Don't tease your mother," he said.

After lunch, however, when she was snoring in the lounge, he dropped his voice and said, "I must say, I don't entirely disagree with your mother about the maid's child, you know. You haven't lived in this country for some time. You've probably forgotten what to look out for."

"Like what?"

"Oh, you'll have to speak to the medical bods about that. I'm not an authority. But these people carry all sorts of germs in from the kraal, I believe. You wouldn't want the baby to catch anything, I'm sure." He wore a medical bracelet now, with "coronary thrombosis" engraved on it. It went nicely with the Rotary International badge on his lapel.

"I suppose that's that for America then," he said. "I must say, I rather regret never having seen Disneyland. You know how fond I am of cartoons."

I looked out at the garden, thinking of the monkey that had loped onto the lawn that morning. Since the gardener had tamed the grass, defined the borders, monkeys kept more to the bush. But this one had been large and male. It had stopped to scratch and look around, and I'd remembered Hugh's hand and tried to shoo it off. But it had just sat up and bared its fangs and chattered and screeched at me.

"You missed nothing," I said. "Disneyland is horrible."

"Still, I wouldn't have minded seeing it." He smiled sadly at me. "You know, we've had our happiest times when we were visiting you."

---

"You're visiting me now."

He sucked his teeth, a new habit. Like Jeffrey, he had given his mouth over to the best man in town—a dentist, who had changed the smile and bite of everyone who could pay the price, and then made off for London.

"Your mother keeps asking me whether you would consider going back to Clive, if he were willing."

"What?"

He linked his hands over one knee and smiled, adult to adult. "She seems to consider it a possibility."

"I have never known Ma to be indirect," I said. If I named things further, he'd bow his head and blink, his eyes would moisten like a scolded child's. I couldn't bear to take part in this anymore. I couldn't bear it.

"The fact is," he said, "she's losing her marbles. She never had much of a brain, you know, but now her memory's going to boot." He chuckled a bit. "The other day she brushed her teeth with my hemorrhoidal cream."

I laughed as he knew I would. But I said, "Shame!" And I thought of the will, and I hoped she'd changed it. "She's cannier than you think," I said.

"Well, be that as it may."

We sat in silence then, waiting for her to wake up, or for the baby to cry, something to deliver us from each other.

"I took Josefina's son to the doctor," I said at last. "He's in perfectly good health."

But he too had dozed off, his head dipped forward almost onto his chest. His jowls were loose. He looked like an old man. I eased myself out of the chair and tiptoed through to the bedroom to fetch my notebook.

# 30

Catherine had brought me the puppy, a plump black Labrador bitch. She'd held it in her arms at the front door, giggling with pleasure. "Here, old girl," she'd said, "look what I brought you."

"OH! CATH!" I'd gathered the puppy up, let her lick my face, kissed her fur, rumpled her ears. I'd carried her out into the garden, where we'd sat, Catherine and I, like two old nannies, passing her between us. Soon I was drunk on the smell of her, the prick of her teeth, her smooth, pink, freckled belly, and then the cheek of her bark. For more than ten years, I'd been without a dog, and now, yes, Catherine was right, it felt normal. It was normal to wake up with her licking my face, normal to scold her for peeing inside or for chewing the furniture, or dragging Hugh's boot across the room. I loved having her underfoot, seeing her spread out flat on the floor, asleep, and then waking up with a bark when the baby cried.

Lily didn't feel the same. "I'm not far enough from the shtetl," she said, pushing the puppy away with a foot. "Jews don't ride horses. Nor do they love dogs."

I smiled at the thought of her, Lily, on a shtetl. "Rubbish!" I said. "I know lots of Jews who love dogs and some who ride." But certainly it was a lack in her, that foot pushing the puppy, the puzzled frown on the puppy's face. If I gave her the baby to hold, it was the same thing. She sat stiff and bony while the baby struggled and whinged. I remembered what she had said the night that Hugh was murdered—"*I am the child, my dear!*" I had wondered at it then, wondered at her, a woman who had loved men, many men. And it had seemed wonderful to me.

"It's all very well to tease that brother-in-law of yours," she said, "but you won't ever abandon your American passport, will you?

Not until you have a proper alternative anyway." She stared hard at me. "Apart from the fact that you're a Jew, Ruth, you've been away from here too long to consider yourself a local."

I nodded. But I was surprised now at her talk of shtetls and Jews. She herself had always seemed quite comfortable as a local. And she hardly seemed Jewish at all. Every week, she dined with Blodwyn Herring-Thomas at the country club. She had friends who played the organ in remote forests. She had been the mistress of Sir Liege Stillington. She had seduced his grandson. I couldn't think of a place on earth where Lily Diamond wouldn't feel at home.

When I had made a fuss about signing the papers to her Hampstead flat, she had narrowed her eyes at me, just like my mother. "Don't be a stupid little *fool!*" she had hissed. And I'd known then, without knowing why, that I would never lose her. Wherever I was, there'd be a phone call out of the blue from her, or a letter. And then there she'd be, sailing out of customs with stories to tell. She'd tell me things about myself too, she'd narrow her eyes at me and notice that something was different. Or that nothing had changed. But, really, it wouldn't be me she was seeing at all. It would be herself.

"I'm straightening out my affairs," she said. "I'm giving everything away, such as it is, before the government can get its hands on it." She stretched out her hand. "Remember I promised you this ring as a wedding present? That night? That terrible night?"

I looked away. "Oh, Lily," I said.

But she was pulling it off, twisting and pulling. "No, no, here, take it! It's yours. You're to wear it as a wedding ring. It will bring you luck."

I accepted it, but I didn't want it on that finger. Anyway, the ring was too big. I slipped it onto my right hand and held it out for her to see.

She pretended not to notice the wrong hand. "There!" she said. "See? From Liege to me to you."

. . .

I waited in the reception area, listening to my mother's voice drumming through the door of Eddie Orinsky's office. When I'd

222

told Catherine about it, she'd said, If you take my advice, you'll stay out of it altogether. But then my mother had phoned to remind me, and I—wondering who but my own child would give me poison when I was too old to get it for myself—had agreed.

Sitting there, however, I was miserable. When my father found out—which he would, because she would find a way to tell him—it would be like a knife drawn across his heart. By me. If he had found moments of happiness with Jill Stafford, who was I to punish him? I didn't even care. I didn't even blame him.

"There she is," she said, standing at the office door with Eddie Orinsky behind her. She had had her hair done for the occasion, and she wore her Magli dress shoes with the three-inch heels, the bag to match. "You know my younger daughter, don't you?" she asked Eddie. "She's quite something, this one, I assure you."

Orinsky patted me on the shoulder. Catherine had told me he had affairs all over town. Any lunchtime, she'd said, curling her lip up into a sneer, you could see his car parked outside some woman's house. What's more, he couldn't keep things to himself. Jeffrey didn't trust him, even though he was a Jew.

I took my mother's arm. She had fallen once already on those heels and had been warned not to wear them by Dr. Slatkin. But what did Slatkin know about fashion, she asked? Look what he looked like, doctor or no doctor, with those Woolworths shirts, and that lock of greasy hair falling across his forehead.

"Mission accomplished!" she said, winking at Orinsky. "Come on, darling, let's go out and celebrate."

I hesitated, uneasy about the baby at the maisonette under Grace's care. But my mother herself was full of childlike excitement.

"What about some crayfish?" she said as we drove down to the beach front. "You've always loved crayfish. They have *lovely* crayfish at the Marine. Gosh, I don't know why we don't go out for lunch every time Dad has Rotary."

"Why are you looking so down today?" she asked, as we sat on the verandah of the Marine Hotel, waiting for our crayfish Thermidor. She took my hand in hers and held it to her cheek. "Oh, how I wish some *marvellous* man would come along and sweep you off your fee— Ah! Steward! This martini is *not* what I ordered! I

223

said *very dry*, and with a dash of bitters." She peered down at my hand. "Where did you get that ring?" she demanded. "Is that real, that diamond?"

"Hugh," I said. If I told her it was from Lily, she would immediately consider her own jewelry, the things she hadn't given me.

"Well," she said, squinting closer, "that's something, anyway."

A warm breeze blew off the sea, bringing with it the smell of the beachfront—salt and beer and popcorn and car exhaust. From the verandah, we could hear the shrieks of the bathers, an ice-cream-cart bell, the bleat of a loudspeaker calling in a paddleboat. She was right, I was down. The beachfront infected me with a sort of homesickness, or timesickness. I felt hopelessly unmarried, frantic to return to my child, close to tears.

"Have your doings come back yet, now that you've weaned the baby?" she asked.

The steward delivered another martini.

"Want the olive, darling? No? You used to love them." She took a sip and then eyed me shrewdly. "If you ask me," she said, "you need something to occupy that mind of yours. Three weeks after you girls were born, I was back in the theatre and I don't think any of you have suffered, do you? It's no good, you know, to have time on one's hands, man or woman. Just look at what's become of your father."

• • •

When we got home, my father was back from Rotary and in a fine mood, walking up and down the lounge with the baby over his shoulder. "Still remember the old routines, what?" he said.

The baby raised her head and crossed her eyes at me. I could see now that she looked a bit like Gramma, except for Hugh's angled jaw, and wide, square smile. In a year or so, they'd be bringing out the plastic tablecloth when I brought her to town, and the miniature tea set, filled with Coca-Cola. There'd be questions raised about the sort of children she was mixing with out at the bungalow, arguments made to put her name down for the Hebrew Nursery School. Even Edwina, who had let her girls play with the local farm children and run around dressed only in Zulu beads, had enrolled them in Rangston when the time had come, driven them into town every day, and then picked them up again.

My mother sank into her corner of the couch and took off her shoes. "How about some coffee, anyone?" she said. "Or some tea?"

"Good idea!" said my father. "Ruth, would you go and do the honours?"

The kitchen was empty. It smelled of yellow soap, and damp dishcloths, and samp and beans. Flypapers curled down like streamers from the ceiling. The tea tray had been set. It stood near the door, covered with a beaded net.

Lily was right. I had been gone too long. The happiness I had at the bungalow was a holiday sort. I'd seen the look on her face as she ran her hand over the green paint, the way she squatted in front of the flower beds, examining the seedlings I'd had the gardener plant there. I'd known this too, almost from the beginning. But now I felt it between my ribs and in my throat.

I panicked, suddenly, at the thought of Josefina letting the kettle boil dry. Sometimes she left the French doors open and went off to have her lunch. Monkeys could come in—anyone could come in. The puppy could run away, be run over by a car. My notebook was on the table next to my bed. What if the house burned up? Or the monkeys got at it? What would happen then to the future I seemed so casually to be constructing for myself?

I ran through to the lounge. "Ma," I said, "can I take my old typewriter out to the bungalow?"

She looked up. "Good! At last! You're taking my advice!"

"What advice?" my father asked.

"None of your business!" She tucked her feet under her. "What's it about?" she asked. "Or shouldn't I ask?"

The kettle began to scream.

"Don't forget to warm the pot!" she called after me. "And Nicholas made some stuffed monkeys. Put them out. And the pig's ears for Dad. They're in the jar in the pantry."

# 31

I remembered the way to Maya's without trouble. And then there it was—the old pink wall topped with shards of coloured glass, the wrought-iron gates, the same Indian gardener—old now, and toothless—grinning and nodding in recognition. He conducted me into the shade of a jacaranda with exaggerated formality, and then leapt at the car door, holding it open while I climbed out, followed me around to the boot, where I lifted out the pram and set it up, and then stood back at a decent distance to watch me bring the baby out and lay her in it.

"Ruth!" Maya kissed me on the cheek, then took over the pram, angling it up the front steps and into the dark front hall.

There they were again—the ancestors in oils, hanging all around us, a woman's laughter somewhere, the smell of curry and sweetmeats.

"They're waiting like mad to see you," she said, heading off towards the sun room.

"Ruth, Ruth, Ruth!" Mr. Chowdree leapt to his feet and came forward. He shook my hand with both of his, the same tidy man in a well-tailored suit. Mrs. Chowdree, fat now, and quite grey, stood over the pram, her hand to her mouth, giggling as her own mother had done the first time I had come.

"You and Maya again!" cried Mr. Chowdree. "Who would have anticipated this? Sit down, sit down."

Maya parked the pram in the corner, sheltered from the draught. It was impossible to think of her father and Krishnah's as brothers, this place related to that.

Mr. Chowdree leaned towards me, his chin on his hands, frowning. "Forgive me for seeming so to stare," he said, "but Maya may not have told you that I'm no good at seeing anymore. I have these darned cataracts, you see. Everything's a blur."

"My mother too," I said. "She has to read with a magnifier."

"Ah! Old age! It is cruel, cruel, cruel! But what can we do? Take up arms against a sea of troubles? Oh no! Oh no! My faith isn't equal to that!" He laughed heartily. So did Mrs. Chowdree.

"Oh, Daddy, do stop showing off!" Maya teased him as she had teased her grandparents years before. But there was something missing in her tone now. The old pleasure, perhaps. Or perhaps I was reading myself into her. And yet there were things I still didn't know, couldn't bring myself to ask her. How the word "divorcée" went down in her world, for instance. Whether they blamed themselves for having come up with such a husband for her in the first place. And whether they were trying to find her another. How, in fact, she could bear to live like this again, here, now, the focus of their old age.

"Where's Yuvassi?" I asked.

"Oh, gone away a long time!" said Mrs. Chowdree.

"At Oxford," Mr. Chowdree cried. "One after the other, like tenpins—isn't that what you call it in America?"

"Ninepins," I said.

"Oh, really, nine is it? How very odd." He settled back into his chair and lifted his face to the ceiling. "I hear you're living out at the Stillington place," he said. "My, my! What a long way back I go with the Stillington family!"

I smiled. I still didn't know what role to adopt in public places. Widow? Mistress? Woman of the world?

"It's a terrible business," he went on, "terrible, quite terrible." He shook his head vigorously and his jowls shook with it. "I take it, you know, as a sign of the times, you know. With all this upheaval and unrest going on, who can be surprised if such things happen?"

"But it wasn't political," I offered. "It was the servant's husband. He was drunk—"

He waved a hand in the air. "I know, I know all that. But it is the *atmosphere* of the times, you see, this violence everywhere we look. When I was younger, I used to think I knew a thing or two. But I knew nothing at all. What answers can we think up when there are such lunatics at both extremes?"

Maya came up behind me. She laid a hand on my shoulder. "Daddy, this isn't the right time for one of your diatribes, if you don't mind. Mummy, will you keep an eye on Ruth's baby? We're going off for a walk before tea."

She took my hand and led me out into the wilderness of their garden. There was hardly a path anymore to follow, but we made our way down it, down past the guava hedge that used to harbour snakes, down to the court. It was a shambles. Tall grasses grew from the cracks. The net hung in shreds. Whole sections of the wire around it had rusted away. In the lean-to, where we used to have juice in the shade, the thatch had thinned to nothing, the table was gone, and the bench was covered with leaves and branches.

Maya brushed them off fiercely. "Do you mind?" she asked, settling herself against one post. "I think the bench is dry."

We sat there, the morning sun full in our faces. Then we took off our shoes and lay out along the benches. I lifted my skirt to tan my legs. A phone rang somewhere. Spitting bugs sang in the trees.

"Maya! Hai!" Her mother's high-pitched squeal rose and fell in an incomprehensible jibber.

"Damn!" Maya said. She struggled to her feet and brushed off her skirt. "It's the hospital. I've *told* them and *told* them *not* to disturb me on a Sunday, but will they listen? No. And Mummy gets so worked up over anything these days. Sorry," she said, holding out a hand for me. "We'd better go back up to the house and see what the fuss is about."

. . .

*Often, after a rain, frogs appeared in the bungalow. One could find them anywhere—in the bath, under the bed, clinging to the hem of a tablecloth or a bedspread, in the toe of a slipper. "Call Regina if I'm not here," Hugh had said. He had no time for the hysteria of white women. And, indeed, Regina didn't seem to mind picking them up with her bare hands, throwing them back out into the garden.*

228

*But I never got used to them. And then, one Sunday, when Hugh was off coping with a faction fight at the Estates, I found a bright green snake curled up in the fruit basket on the dining room table. I backed slowly towards the door, turned there and dashed through to the kitchen, out into the backyard. "Regina!" I shouted. "REGINA!"*

*She appeared at her door with a tin plate in one hand, a spoon in the other. "Madam," she said.*

*"There's a snake in the dining room!" I panted.*

*But she shook her head. "Haikona!" she said. "Master he like the snake. The snake he come in to eat the frog."*

*"Permit me," said Hugh when he came back for lunch. He grasped the snake in two hands and held it up. "Look at these markings, notice the head, see here? The creature's quite harmless."*

*Regina stood in the doorway of the dining room with folded arms. I stood back at a distance too, watching the snake's tongue flicker here and there, its eyes flash yellow in the gloom. The subtleties of difference between life and death were invisible to me. It looked exactly like the deadly mambas I'd seen in the snake park as a child. Or the one that Myrna Lipinsky's gardener had killed at Villa d'Occidente and brought in proudly as we were having tea one afternoon on her verandah.*

*Hugh carried the snake out into the garden and set it free. And then, at lunch, he complained of the consortium that had bought up the Estates. It was their damn-fool, cockeyed, middlebrow ideas, he said—straight out of the classrooms of the business schools—that had led to the trouble that morning. Any fool could see that you don't bring in workers from Mozambique, workers from Swaziland, and put them in charge of Zulus.*

*When I brought the conversation back to snakes, he just laughed and rang the bell for coffee on the verandah. "Ruth," he'd said, "fortune favours the brave."*

• • •

They were all there, when I arrived at Parkview Nursing Home—my mother in the chair next to the bed, Catherine and Jeffrey standing together at the far wall, Dr. Slatkin holding my father's wrist. My father himself lay with his eyes closed, the bed cranked up to a half-sitting position. There were tubes in his nostrils, a tube in his arm, and a machine bleeping next to the bedside table.

Catherine gestured for me to stand next to her, but I went to the bottom of the bed and hung on. He looked like a bird, lying there. His hair had sprung loose and stood out in a grey frizz around his head. Grey stubble covered his cheeks and jaw. His skin was grey too, almost black around the eyes. And his mouth hung open. His breath came slowly, with long intervals between.

A light breeze blew in from the verandah, shifting the filaments of his hair. "Shouldn't we close the doors?" I whispered urgently to Catherine.

She shook her head. Of course she shook her head. She kept everything open—windows, doors—her house seemed to have no roof, no walls. I walked out onto the verandah, unhooked each door, and pulled them shut.

"Ruth!" Jeffrey whispered.

But I ignored him. I went to stand next to my mother, put my arm around her shoulders. Over the awful Dettol smell of the place was the smell of her Joy, her hair spray, her stale cigarette breath. She laid her head against my arm. She covered her eyes with her hand. "How was I to know?" she asked. And then, "Where were you? We tried everywhere. Where did you leave the baby?"

"With Maya."

She sighed, sat up again. Her lower lip hung loose. Her nose seemed enormous. "I need a drink."

I looked at Catherine, but she shook her head.

My father sighed, loud and clear, and I moved to the side of the bed, so did Catherine. Slatkin seated the earpieces of his stethoscope, pulled back the sheet and placed the flat silver circle on my father's chest.

"Someone tell me when," my mother rasped.

But I knew that it had happened already. And that if I stood like that for an hour, looking at his birdlike face, the hair, the strange, coarse pyjamas they had put him into, I would never believe it.

Slatkin straightened up, let the stethoscope drop. "It's over," he said. "He didn't suffer."

"Rubbish!" my mother cried. "What do *you* know?" She

grasped the arms of the chair to pull herself up. "How do *you* know who suffers and who doesn't, *hey?*"

Jeffrey was at her side, offering her a hand. But she shook him off. She swayed to her feet. "What do any of you know?" she demanded. "Ruth!" she said. "I want you to take me home."

And then, taking her arm, stopping while she grasped the foot of the bed and took a grudging look at him, I thought of her without him at her side, her standing at the airport barrier alone, her fingers grasping the rail, and behind her, perhaps, a driver looking sheepish, the long days and years without him to measure her gin, to take her arm at the entrance to the Majestic, oh, and his key in the door, and fastening his own cuff links now that she couldn't see properly anymore, him holding her face to the light as he plucked the hairs from her chin, loving her as he must have loved her, whatever he said, as he must have loved her right from the start, despite the peace she never gave him after Catherine was born, the peace he couldn't have wanted so badly or he would have taken it for himself, he wouldn't have left her like this, like *this*. Oh, Ma!

# 32

My mother had always said Jewish funerals were barbaric. But I had never been to any other kind, so I couldn't imagine how death could be made civilized. I stood beside her at the coffin, looking in. Catherine was next to me, standing stiff and straight.

They had plastered his hair back down, but the parting was too near the centre, and brushed straight down to his ears. He smiled, too, in a way I'd never seen him smile, unselfconsciously, like an old man, full of wisdom. Nor did he look asleep. He looked as if he were playing the part of a dead man, and playing it badly.

My mother stood at my side in her navy suit and new felt hat. She'd asked me to help her with her make-up, and I had. But then she'd had another go at it herself, and her face was a riot of colour. The whole night, she'd been sitting on the couch in her dressing gown, drinking whisky, with a box of tissues at her side. But now she was dry-eyed. So was I. She held my arm in a clawlike grip and lifted her chin. The sight made me turn away, but there, on the other side, was Catherine, her face lifted just the same, the same grim refusal to give a performance of grief to strangers.

Men closed the lid and lifted the coffin. We traipsed after them, down from the bleak prominence where we'd stood, to the freshly dug hole. More than a hundred people followed in the terrible heat and took up ranks around us. Several times, I had to hold my mother's elbow to stop her from falling on the rough ground.

"Quite a turnout," she rasped, as the rabbi cleared his throat. "On a day like this, to boot."

And then it was done. The mumble of prayers, the thud of earth on the coffin, the gasps of the crowd, my mother supported out to the car by Catherine and me, with Jeffrey close behind. I thought once I'd seen Jill Stafford in the crowd, and had looked back to see. But the people were fanning out, and, except for Flo Brasch heaving through the heat with a scarf tied under her chin, the women's faces were obscured by summer hats. They had been observing me from under those hats all through the service. Me and my mother, me and my mother and her daughters—me, standing there dry-eyed at my own father's funeral. I, who had gone to America, and given up, and come back, only to be tied up with the Stillington scandal, and then the birth of an illegitimate child announced in the *Witness*, me standing there, dry-eyed, divorced, for all the world to see.

Catherine put on the lunch, with the Majestic waiters and Majestic food. She had tempered her smile for the occasion, and stood talking at one end of the buffet table to the rabbi and the Chief.

Jeffrey, who was more at home with funerals, launched himself, frowning solemnly, this way and that way into the crowd. "Go and find your mother," he hissed as he passed me talking to Lily in the hall.

But just then, my mother emerged from the cloakroom with her hat in her hands. "I can't cope with the hair when it's been squashed down," she said. "Shall we go? Forgive us, Lily."

Back at the maisonette, I went upstairs to settle the baby in my father's dressing room. I had promised Catherine that I'd stay in town for the week of shivah. I'd stay at the maisonette and help her sort things out. We'd have to discuss Ma, she said—finding her a companion or something, someone who could live in the house, someone white. She'd paused then, and there'd been a question in that silence. But only now, looking around his dressing room, did I think I understood that she meant me.

In the afternoon, with the French doors to the balcony fastened back, his dressing room was the coolest place in the house. A breeze rattled the venetian blinds, traffic hummed outside. I parked Edwina's foldup pram and set the brake and switched on the intercom my father had installed.

There, on his tallboy, was his long-handled bone shoehorn, and the pair of military-style hairbrushes I'd brought him from London a few years before. The electric shoe-polishing machine sat in its box on the divan. He'd fallen in love with it in New York, found it in a shop and bought it, a cunning little machine, he'd said, with a red side and a black side. He'd had them box it up for the plane, and he'd had it rewired for the local voltage, and patiently instructed Nicholas on how to use it. But then, early one morning, he'd come upon Nicholas in the pantry, polishing the shoes by hand, with the polishing machine whirring loudly on the far side of the table.

My mother tiptoed in and stood beside me. She'd changed into her summer gown and slippers, taken off her corset and bra. "Let's have some tea," she whispered. "I want to talk to you."

"Don't think you're staying on here for me," she said, settling into her bedroom chair. "Only last week, I had to cancel that Chief Whatshisname's lessons—I simply don't have the time for that sort of thing anymore. Between you and me, it was a hopeless venture from the start. They seem to think one can perform miracles. Well, one can't! I've got *piles* of scripts to go through, plays to adapt, God knows what."

"What?" I had heard of madness setting in like this after a shock, a whole fantasy world taking over. "Ma," I said, "scripts for what?"

She waved one hand in the air. "Oh, I have plans. Don't you worry about me. One of these days they'll be calling on me to do television work. I have to be prepared."

But I saw her hand shake slightly, some tea slop into the saucer. And I wondered whether she had told me the truth about the heart attack. It had happened, she'd said, because he'd climbed into her bed at three o'clock on Sunday morning. After that, he'd started to feel a bit woozy. She blamed Slatkin, she said, for giving him carte blanche to resume normal activities. As far as she was concerned, however, three o'clock in the morning had never seemed normal, but who was she to say? *She* wasn't the one who'd had the lovers. At least no one could say, this time, that it had anything to do with the will. He'd never even found *out*. He didn't have a *clue!*

"I'll stay on," I said. "Just for a bit."

"Rubbish!" She looked up fiercely. "If you care about me, you'll take my advice and leave this country. I'm not saying America—you've put that behind you, and *gei gesund*, that's that—I mean London, the hub. You'll never have your first audience again, you know, never again. The point is to make a *splash*, make your mark! Once you've done that, you'll have something to live up to, and that's a different matter. I can help you financially. Oh yes, I know, you're Mrs. Rockefeller, but I'm telling you I *can* help, and I *will* help. Oh, look now what you've done! You've made me spill all over the chair! Ring down for Grace and tell her to bring up a wet cloth!"

She picked up the magnifier and looked at her watch. "They'll be coming for prayers in an hour or so," she said. "Why not wear something nice, now that you're getting your figure back. And do your hair up, for a change. You can't imagine the difference it makes when you pull it off your face."

. . .

When I saw him standing at the bungalow gate, I slammed on the brakes, and the baby stopped crying. All the way up the highway, and then down through the cane, she'd been roaring. By the time we'd made the coastal road, a low growl of fury had settled into the back of her throat. But now, suddenly, she was silent. And there he was—the same thatch of hair, the blue eyes, the hands plunged deep into the pockets of his slacks.

"Dr. Frank," he said, coming up to the car door. "Evelyn Stillington. I'm awfully sorry to turn up out of the blue like this, but I've been trying to phone you for a week. And then, of course, I heard about your father. How awful for you. I just came by on the off chance—"

His voice was lighter than Hugh's, the vowels throatier, more English. He stood back from the dust of the car door, careful of his clothes.

"Is there luggage you'd like me to carry? Is this the baby, then?"

Inside, he waited to be asked to sit, invited to stay for tea. When he'd come out for his father's funeral, he told me, his uncle had suggested he come back and join the Estates. He was dreadfully sorry, now, that he hadn't known his father better while he was growing up, hadn't come out more often, and so forth.

235

While he talked, he kept his eyes from wandering around the room. Josefina had cleaned and polished for my return. She had starched her uniform, too, and her doek, and made scones for tea, which she delivered on the brass tray, still smelling of Brasso.

"Madam," she said, lifting Hester from the carry cot, "I'm take care baby now?"

It was the time of day when the sun gleamed blinding white off the sea. Heat rose in a mist from the bush. And the bungalow was beginning to sweat. Rivulets ran down the walls. Lizards moved like shadows. The puppy played and pounced around my feet. I longed to go out and see what had flowered in the garden, what had died. If this gardener ran off like all the others, the place would be thick and wild within a month. Already, I heard the num-num hedge swishing against the house.

"I'll be leaving for England in about a month," I said.

He looked up, then, and replaced his cup and saucer gently on the tray. "There's absolutely no rush."

But there was a rush. I needed to leave before the bungalow became commonplace, and the dahlias began to bloom in rows. I wanted to go down to the beach, and walk along the shore to the hotel to see Lily there again. I wanted Maya to come and stay for the weekend. And to drive out to Edwina's cottage, because she didn't have a phone. Bunny had written her to say she'd run into Krishnah in Times Square, wasn't that amazing? He'd looked so sorry for himself, skulking around in a winter coat and boots. There was talk among the expats that he was an informer. Still, he seemed homesick, heartsick too, maybe, for selling out.

"Shall I telephone you in a day or two?" Hugh's son asked.

I nodded. But already, I was wondering whether Jeffrey would take in my puppy, and what I could get away with—which books, which photographs, which dress-up clothes to keep for Hester. One day she'd come back and ring the doorbell, and explain who she was, her mother and her father. He'd be gone by then, this new Stillington. He'd have sold up in panic and taken his family back to England. But the new people would have heard some of the stories, and they'd be curious to know more. They would have bought the place just before the troubles came, and put in a pool, and reclaimed some of the bush for a court. There'd be proper stairs down to the beach, and shark nets, and an electric fence, and panic buttons, and marble in the front hall, and two huge, life-sized porcelain dogs. They would have old photographs of the place to show her, and the original map from the City Hall. As a child, the man would tell her, he used to come with his family for holidays at the hotel. They'd heard stories about the bungalow, good ones and bad ones. Very often, they would walk along the road to the bungalow gate, stop and look in. But they never saw anyone there except the servants. And never did he imagine that, one day, he—the son of Lebanese immigrants—would own the place himself. He would smile then at the reversals of fortune, surprises of Fate. Over tea, his wife would ask politely about Hester's mother and her mother's books. Her mother would have warned Hester about this sort of politeness. That people who stayed on and thrived, or stayed on and suffered, take a dim view of those who left when the going was good, and then came back with foreign passports, and then went off again to write whatever they bloody well pleased.

# About the Author

Born in Durban, South Africa, Lynn Freed discovered very early her desire to leave the country—or, more precisely, her desire to be away, and to return—to live the life of a middle-class gypsy. Educated at the local equivalent of a British girls' boarding school, she leapt at the first chance to go overseas: as an American Field Service exchange Scholar, in 1963. She started out in Far Rockaway, New York, and then moved to Greenwich, Connecticut. Returning to South Africa, she then completed her B.A. degree at the University of Witwatersrand and, in 1967, flew to New York to marry and to study for an M.A. and a Ph.D. in English Literature at Columbia University. She lived in New York, Boston, Montreal, in San Francisco for twenty years, and now lives in Sonoma, California. She has one daughter.